More praise for *Kinfolks*

"An incredible story about the complexities and frailties of love and relationships and the primacy of family. *Kinfolks* is about recognizing that family is the one certainty that people really count on."
—*Booklist*

"Vibrant, humorous . . . [Lattany] juggles several characters in chapters named exclusively for them, chapters through which each can stretch their thoughts. The voices and movements of these characters are so distinctive that you don't even have to look at the top of the page for clarification."
—*Savannah Herald*

"*Kinfolks* resonates with warmth, humor, and wisdom as it unfolds with the gentle cadence of good friends swapping stories around the kitchen table."
—*Carolina Times*

"Heartwarming."

—*Kirkus Reviews*

KINFOLKS

Kristin Hunter Lattany

ONE WORLD

Ballantine Books • New York

A One World Book
Published by Ballantine Books

Copyright © 1996 by Palmetto Productions, Inc.
Reader's Guide copyright © 1997 by The Ballantine Publishing Group, a division of Random House, Inc.

http://www.randomhouse.com

Library of Congress Catalog Card Number: 97-93720

ISBN: 0-345-41720-8

Cover design by Kristine V. Mills-Noble
Cover illustration by Kreshaun McKinney

Manufactured in the United States of America

First Hardcover Edition: October 1996
First Trade Paperback Edition: October 1997

10 9 8 7 6 5 4 3 2 1

*For all the brave ones who fought for
black folks' freedom.
And for their children.
Because we owe you respect
and remembrance.*

KINFOLKS

Chapter 1

PATRICE

IT JUST DOESN'T FEEL RIGHT. It feels strange. Here we are, stretched out on my living room floor, humming and kicking our sandaled feet to the rhythm of Roberta Flack singing "Killing Me Softly with His Song," and trying to compose a wedding invitation. An engraved if you please formal wedding invitation. Cherry and me. Veterans of Snick, CORE, and God alone knows how many H. Rap Brown Black Power rallies.

"Hey, Patrice, remember the Chant?"

Who could forget it? We sang it, clapped it, stomped it, and kicked it at every rally. The tune of "Land of a Thousand Dancers," by Sam the Sham and the Pharoahs. And by Wilson Pickett: E, DEDE, DEDE DBD BAB AG DEDE. It meant nothing. It meant everything: black unity, energy, the confidence that comes from knowing you are right, and a challenge flung down to the Establishment.

Later for that cool wailing dirge on the radio. These days, we have enough public mourners and freelance pallbearers as it is. More than enough premature eulogies and obituaries. The Death of the Black Family. The Endangered African American Male. The Pathology of the African American Community. The Self-Destruction of Black Youth. At least we'd done, were doing, our part to offset all of that. I turn off Miss Flack and launch into three choruses of the Chant, followed by our cheer:

"Umgawa!"

"Black Power!" Cherry responds.

"Umgawa!"

"Black Power!"

"UMGAWA!"

"BLACK POWER!"

We follow it up with screams and a Black Power handshake: (1) my fingers grasping her thumb; (2) reversed—her fingers, my thumb; (3) fingers grasping fingers, palms up; (4) palms slapping. "There," I say, collapsing happily on the floor. "That always makes me feel better."

Cherry gives me a critical look. "There's a rip in the seam under your right arm. Patrice, do you realize we might soon be grandmothers?"

I check my Saturday caftan, black mud cloth to appease Saturn on his day. I pride myself on having the most fabulous collection of caftans on the East Coast. Just because I'm a big woman doesn't mean I can't be ravishing and gorgeously attired. Sure enough, she's right. A depressing rip under the right armpit, and no seam allowance for repairing it. That's the second time I've regretted buying something from Chic Afrique. Sometimes I think we've overromanticized these Africans. All they do is come over here and rip us off. But then I chide myself for having ungenerous and xenophobic thoughts that are probably not even my own but the result of media manipulation.

Something Cherry just said suddenly gets through to me.

"Cheryl, are you trying to tell me something? Is Aisha—"

"No, no, nothing like that. Just thinking about the probable consequences of all this, a year or two from now."

"Well, that would be wonderful, wouldn't it? Still, I'm glad there's no hurry—"

"No hurry! Patrice, do you realize how boojy you sound? *We* weren't worried about legitimizing our offspring."

We sure weren't. We, Cherry and I and the rest of our circle of fine, brilliant, achieving, liberated sisters, went to great lengths to arrange the opposite. We were determined to go against tradition in every way possible. Premeditated single motherhood was one of the principal ways we chose, because marriage would bring legal and property issues into our personal choices.

"It won't be wonderful," Cherry says in her smallest voice. "We thought we were going to be young forever. Remember?" I look and see two big tears rolling down her copper cheeks.

Cheryl Hopkins is a trip. She has a mouth full of razor blades disguised as pretty teeth, and she'll bare them and cut you up into person julienne in a minute. Downtown she has a reputation for being the meanest loan officer in East Coast banking. But come to her with the right sob story, especially one that features oppression, and she'll give you the entire bank—real estate, deed and all. And when she is hurt, she is all the disappointed little five-year-old girls in the world rolled into one. I give her the hug her sobs call for, but can't help noticing that she has more gray hairs on top than I can count.

"Remind me to introduce you to my friend Miss Clairol," I say when her shoulders have stopped heaving.

We are both a trip, really. One shriveling up, the other ballooning past size 20, and both middle-aged, to put it generously. A pair of grandmotherly ex-revolutionaries. Only we don't feel grandmotherly or ex-anything. Inside, we are still the same young women who dedicated themselves to the Movement, and who didn't want to come near anything bourgeois, legal, formal, or sanctioned by society. Sororities? Tea sipping? No, thank you. Hair straightening? Get outta here. Marriage? Are you outta your mind? We came of age in the sixties. We thought all rules were made to be broken. We wanted nothing to do with churches or ceremonies. Now here we are, trying to compose some la-de-da wedding invitations, and we can't even get the words right.

"How's this sound?" I say, ignoring Cherry's angry expression and her furtive inspection of her cornrows in a compact mirror. "Ms. Patrice Lumumba Barber and Ms. Cheryl Mandela Hopkins invite you—"

"Request the honour of your presence," she corrects me.

"Do you spell 'honor,' O-R or O-U-R?" I ask.

"O-U-R," she replies without hesitation. "And my middle name is Ann."

I write dutifully, trying to refrain from political comment. But it sneaks out. "Honour with a U is British spelling. Do we want to be *that* traditional?"

"It's what Aisha wants," she replies.

Oh, boy. We spent our youth and young adulthood kicking over traces, shaking off shackles, and brandishing our fists in our elders' faces. Sometimes I feel bad about that part, thinking of the pain I brought to the faces of Mama and Daddy and Nana, the extra wrinkles I put there. But retribution is coming, sure as rain follows thunder. Oh, yeah. We are about to be elders ourselves.

Retribution is already being visited on Cheryl, I think—in the form of a prissy, proper daughter who wants everything done by the rule book.

"British tradition is not our tradition," I cannot resist rebuking her.

"It's the only tradition we've got in America. Do you want to invite people to come and watch our kids jump the broom?"

I refrain from asking *Why not?* and read,

"... request the honour of your presence at the wedding of their children—

"MISS AISHA G. HOPKINS
AND
MR. TOUSSAINT D. BARBER—"

My reading is interrupted by a howl of pain from Cherry. "These days my daughter goes by Eliza," she says.

I let that pass because it doesn't deserve my attention. But when I ask Cherry what the G in her daughter's name stands for, something I've always wondered about, she only howls louder. Deep down beneath my navel I feel a funny flutter. I know what that flutter means. Something is deeply wrong.

Chapter 2
CHERRY

It's all very well for Patrice. Her child is a boy. Any old thing will do for boys, even casually jumping an old broom, just like they jump up and down every day on a basketball court.

But I'm the mother of the *bride*. She's sensitive and fastidious and particular, and she wants everything just so.

I don't know how she got to be such a princess.—Don't tell that lie, Cheryl Ann Hopkins. You did it, and you know it.

Physically, my child is the image of me. Maybe that's why I've spoiled her. I sure didn't get much spoiling at home, competing with four brothers for Mommy's attention and a share of Daddy's money—not that there was much to share. All these years, I've looked at Aisha and seen only a darling carbon copy of myself. I've adored every inch of her and tried to give her the perfect childhood I never had.

I knew I was in trouble sometime around her fourth

birthday, after I put her to bed one night and she began crying up a regular typhoon. When I went in to investigate, she said, "How do you expect me to sleep, Mother? These sheets have wrinkles!"

I should have handed her the iron then and there. But what I did was change her sheets from low-count muslin (a bargain set from Marshall's) to high-count percale, and soothe her by agreeing that scratchy sheets were awful. From then on Mommy slept on the scratchies and baby got the smooths.

Little Miss Aisha also got her hair permed from age six on, because she wanted curls. I took far too much lecturing from Patrice and my other politically conscious friends about that.

"Look," I told them, "boys are easy. They're like sheep; all you have to do is get them sheared once a month. *You* try raising a girl sometime—you'll be grateful for the existence of beauty parlors."

'Course, I blew any hope of discipline by always caving in to Aisha. I drew the line at Jack and Jill—I don't think we need an African American Junior League—but I let her have a sweet sixteen party with a long white dress. I wouldn't consider Vassar, but I scrimped and struggled to pay for that year at Spelman.

Actually, I don't think boys are easy. Toni Brookins's Rome is a teenage terror. All he wants to do is cover the earth with graffiti. Can't see a wall without writing "Cool Rome" on it.

And I don't know how Patrice, with no steady man in her life, has done such an outstanding job with Saint. Probably Saint is naturally just one terrific kid. Sometimes

I think half the work is already done for you when they're conceived. A lot of us thought that once, didn't we? Thought we were guaranteeing ourselves super children by giving them super genes—with a capital G.

Well, I'm no superwoman, and my daughter is no supergirl, as I informed her today. I took a long, hard look at her for the first time, and I didn't like what I saw.

I'm not doing much better financially than my parents, which is something Aisha refuses to understand. Actually, I'm doing worse. I make a bigger salary, but they owned a house. Every April I beat up on myself for not having a mortgage interest deduction. But how can I, when I can never manage to save up a down payment? I know I should, but something always comes up—usually some expense for my daughter.

This year, for instance, after I paid for Aisha's gown at Bloomingdale's, I put a down payment on the hall I'm renting for the reception. Even with Patrice helping and both of us cooking, this wedding will have me in debt again for five years—and I just crawled out of the hole.

Last year it was her college expenses. The year before that her senior prom, her class trip, and half a year of business school. The year before *that*, braces.

Until now I haven't minded spending money on my child. Giving her things has seemed like giving them to myself. And I love the results. Her teeth are straight and perfect like I always wanted mine to be. Her hair is soft and shiny, thanks to her father's genes and the cream rinse I buy her by the gallon. Her figure is taut and trim, thanks to the health spa membership I'm still paying for. Her walk is graceful, her carriage erect, thanks to two years of ballet classes.

And, of course, she has perfect, unwrinkled skin. In every other respect my daughter Aisha is the image of me.

She has a small turned-up nose that is cute, unless she's being haughty. Her ears are tiny, and in them she wears a wardrobe of small studs purchased on my charges—gold, silver, pearls, even diamonds. She has long eyelashes and large, misty eyes—misty because she has glasses but won't wear them. Come to think of it, I used to be the same way. But now, with my glasses hanging on a chain around my neck most of the time, except when I need to watch TV or drive, I am only praying to stave off bifocals a little longer— not because I'm vain, but because I can't afford them.

I almost overlooked the most important feature my daughter and I have in common. Both of us are a size twelve: I could use a little toning, but I've stayed the same size since high school.

This year, as usual, taking care of Princess Aisha didn't leave much to spend on myself. I only added one item to my wardrobe, but that was something I'd always wanted. A white suit.

It may not sound practical, but it is, for a professional woman who works in the summertime. I can come to work carrying the jacket, and put it on when the air-conditioning goes on overkill. I can wear the jacket with all of my other summer clothes. Also, I have to give a series of seminars on loan processing at our branches in July, and that suit with two or three different solid-colored shirts will be all the wardrobe I'll need.

My dry cleaning bills will be steep, you may be thinking. Ah, but I know my fabrics, and this is one I can hand-wash.

So, guess what is the first thing I see when I arrive home on Friday? My darling daughter, on her way out, in my new white suit. No blouse—just a pearl choker. I have to admit she looks stunning.

But it's mine—the first new thing I've had in six months—and I *need* it.

"Get back in there and take my suit off," I tell my child.

"Mo-ther," she whines. "Don't be so selfish. This looks better on me than you, anyway."

"I wouldn't know. I haven't had a chance to wear it yet. Don't make me yell at you out here in the street. Get in there and take it off before you funk it up."

Once inside, she twirls in front of the living room mirror, then drifts with maddening slowness toward her bedroom. "This," she remarks as she floats along, "would be perfect for my wedding. I don't like all that billowy satin, anyway."

I can't believe the ingratitude I am hearing. "Good," I say through clenched teeth. "We'll take the gown back. I can use the credit to pay some other bills."

"Mmmm," she hums. "I want to think about it. I haven't made up my mind yet."

Right then is when I lose it. Before I know what's happening, the imprint of my hand is on that coppery cheek.

"Well, let that make up your mind. And let me tell you something else, Miss High and Mighty. I'm sick of your selfishness. I'm already in debt up to my eyebrows, no, *drowning* in debt, paying for you to make up your mind.

Half a year of business school, then you decide you want college. A year of college, then you decide you want to get married. Well, we're both getting too old for so much indecision."

Her eyes are amazed. "You hit me!" she cries. She is boo-hooing by now, the tears tracking down her cheeks. Once, this would have moved me to remorse and indulgence. But not now. I am uptight because I'm so worried about money and about my spoiled child. Spoiled, I realize for the first time, means ruined. Messed up. Useless.

"I should have hit you long ago. Long ago and often. Now take off my suit. And hang it up. And put on something old so you can clean up this house before you go out."

"Mo-ther!" she wails at top volume, rubbing her eyes. "I'm not even sure I want to get married!"

"Fine," I say. "I'm not sure Saint would want to marry you, either, if he could see you now. Let me tell you something, Miss Aisha. You don't have all the options you think you have, do you hear me? You're cute, but you're not gorgeous. You're bright, but you're not exceptional. You're a fairly ordinary little black girl with only one aging, overworked parent. I do not see the boys lining up at our door to marry you any more than the men are lining up to marry me. And they won't, because you look exactly like me—and you have a much less attractive personality."

My anger is spent. I find it interesting, though, that I feel no remorse. I am not sorry, and I am not sorry for my daughter, who continues to sob, in soft, waning gulps.

"So what I think you had better do is find a job to

support yourself, and start paying rent around here. And think about preparing yourself for a line of work, because Saint is liable to get tired of you pretty fast."

She forces a final sputter of sobbing and glances slyly at me for a reaction. My expression is stoic. My mood is relentless.

"Mother?"

"What?"

"If I go back to school in September, will you still pay my way?"

This pretty little monster is all my handiwork, all mine. "I don't think so. If you're a married woman, you won't be my responsibility anymore. If you aren't married, well— we'll see. You'd better get that job and start saving."

"But, Mother!" she wails. "I don't know what to do."

I am suddenly too tired for sentences of more than three words. "Wash your face," I say. "Clean the house. Get a job."

She does clean the house, sort of. She runs the vacuum, swipes at the furniture, and gives the bathroom a lick and a promise.

Then she spends an hour primping in there, comes out glowing and fragrant with my Anne Klein, and puts on a long, lavender, Empire-waisted print dress that I don't recall seeing. At least it isn't mine.

When Saint calls for her, I am over most of my rage. That boy is so sunny and dear, he would bring out the best in Dracula. I wonder for the hundredth time if he knows what he is getting into.

Then, happy to have the house to myself, I lock my new suit in my closet—oh, yes, I have a teenager, and I've learned to install locks in places where most people wouldn't dream of having them—and settle into the bathtub for a long, long soak. I am not about to answer any doorbells or phones. When mine rings, as I knew it would as soon as I eased down into gardenia-scented bubbles, I am sure it is Toni Brookins.

Toni calls up all her friends nightly with her worries about Rome. She cries buckets and wallows in guilt because she hasn't provided her son with a positive male role model. I try to comfort her. Some of those turkeys I used to date weren't such great role models, either. But of course, as she always reminds me, Aisha didn't need them. She didn't need anyone but me.

Until now. And even though I am angry with Aisha, I am sad about her deprivation. I know it's the reason I have overindulged her all these years. What my daughter wants to know, just as I want to know, is—who is going to walk her down the aisle? Who is going to give my little girl away?

Chapter 3

PATRICE

Aᴼᴛᴇʀ I ꜱᴘᴏɴɢᴇ Cʜᴇʀʀʏ ᴜᴘ from my floor and point her toward home, I pop two ginkgo capsules and put on a kettle for Morning Thunder tea. Something is wrong, and I need all my brain cells perking to detect it. I pour hot water in a bowl over some eucalyptus leaves, to inhale so I can clear my sinuses.

After ten minutes of deep breathing, I feel centered and relaxed. But still nothing comes.

So I do what I always do when I'm stressed or confused. I go in my kitchen and start to cook.

I begin, as usual, by surveying the materials on hand. My best meals are never planned, anyway. I rummage in the refrigerator and find three fat green peppers, a bunch of asparagus, two bags of carrots, half a jar of mushroom spaghetti sauce from two nights ago, and half a pot of brown rice. I decide to make stuffed peppers with carrots and asparagus vinaigrette. I throw baking soda in the water with my simmering peppers to keep them nice and green. To me, there's nothing uglier than olive-drab food, unless it's olive-drab clothing. Trust the U.S. Army to come up with a color that uglifies everybody.

As I mix the rice and spaghetti sauce to stuff my peppers I am reminded that this recipe can go in my cookbook, *Cooking with PatRICE*. I make a note as I stuff six pepper halves. Serves six, white folks would say, but I say serves three. I always make enough for at least one extra person. If you're a good cook, word gets around.

Sure enough, Saint brings his fiancée home with him. Née Aisha, now Eliza. My tongue and my memory get twisted trying to keep up with these youngsters' name changes.

Of course my brain goes on TILT anyway every time I see my son.

Toussaint Dessalines Barber. Last year a scrawny beanpole, now filling out into six feet two inches of good-looking tan young man. Glorious teeth, perfectly straight, paid for by a year of weekends I worked at a dental practice, and eyes that crinkle to match the sunrise of his smile. Honesty in those eyes. Compassion, too. Once he cried when I killed a worm that came in with him from outside—it had been a nice worm, he said. Now he puts in eight hours a week fixing meals for the homeless at the Harvest Hospitality House. He's inherited my love of cooking, though as yet it hasn't translated into poundage like mine has, 'cause he lifts weights and shoots hoops. Runs the quarter mile, too. If I weren't his mama, I'd fall in love with him myself.

Saint has a cabinet full of track and field trophies, and, of course, phenomenal intelligence. I almost forgot intelligence, but of course we take that for granted around here. In my house, stupidity is not allowed. His third grade science project was a perpetual motion machine that really worked. In high school he was in the National Honor Society. Now he has a full-genius National Science scholarship, and Phi Beta Kappa is definitely on the horizon. He could have gone anywhere, but preferred to find some brothers and sisters to compensate for his onliness, so chose Morehouse. A science major with medical school or at least medical research ahead. Wants to help people breathe better because he thinks his dad died from emphysema when he was an infant.

That lie will come back to haunt me someday, I often think. I lie awake some nights trying to decide whether to correct it. The fear, of course, is that Saint will hate me for having lied to him.

Now he loves me, though sometimes, I suspect, in the same way he would love a large, dumb pet. For five years he's been able to look down on me from a greater height, and boy, does he take advantage. He actually pats me on the head by way of greeting.

"Smells great in here, Mom. Can Liza stay for dinner?"

"If you mean your fiancée, yes." I'm not ready to call Aisha by her new name. She bothers me tonight. Her hair is braided into extensions, but they are combed out to look like nylon Shirley Temple curls—a combination of natural and weird that I can't categorize. She tosses them, and my political judgment clicks into place. Only white girls toss. The effect is abetted by a long floaty princess-seamed dress in a sprigged lavender print, of the style chosen by English majors who want to look poetic.

I slam some iced raspberry tea down in front of her and Saint.

"That looks delicious. Thank you, Mom," she says.

"I'm not your mom yet," I grumble. Not sure I want to be, either. This girl is about to marry my only child; why does she irritate me so? It is not a good omen. It's a muggy day in May, the oven is on, and the heat in here is getting to me. I flick on the exhaust fan and the window fan, forgetting that this house is only wired for twenty amps.

The power blows.

"Saint! Fuse!" I yell in the ensuing darkness.

"Where's the flashlight?"

"Wherever you put it the last time," I tell him. Getting more than one flashlight for this house, which is actually an apartment, half of a duplex, is one of those things I always mean to do but never get around to doing. My upwardly mobile friends like Toni Brookins keep telling me to move to a modern high-rise where everything is new and safe and maintained, and I know they're right, but I don't like honeycombed shoe boxes for living. I need to grow my own herbs and greens. I need to walk outside my door sometimes and smell the earth after rain. And if a mugger is hanging around out there, shame on him— there's nothing in here to steal. Besides, thieves are scared of Saint. I'll think about high-rises after he moves out.

The lights come back on, and Saint, stripped to the waist, emerges from the cellar door. Aisha holds her breath for so long, I'm afraid she'll suffocate.

"Put your shirt back on, Saint," I tell him. "You're just showing off for Aisha's benefit, and you know I don't like showing off."

"It's hot, Mom," he says, buttoning his oxford shirt, but only to just above the navel.

"All the buttons except the top one," I command.

"Awww," he complains, but he obeys. He's a good boy. Aisha, meanwhile, is so riveted to his gorgeous body she doesn't even notice the plate I put in front of her.

"That's better," I tell him. "What makes you think anyone wants to see those three puny hairs on your chest, anyway?"

"I have more than three," he says, starting to unbutton again. "Lots more."

"Never mind," I tell him. "Say grace, please."

Just to spite me, he launches into one of his Pulpit Perorations in the style of Morehouse Chapel. "O Lord of the Universe," he intones, "look down on your children of the Diaspora, and know that we are all yours wherever we may have been dispersed. All yours, and all one with each other, with You, and with Your Creation. We thank You, Lord, for love, life, light, food, and the energy we derive from it. Bless the hands that prepared this food, O Lord, and bless those who receive it—"

"Saint," I warn him. My food is getting cold.

"—in the names of your sons Jesus, Buddha, Mohammed, and Malcolm, Amen."

"Thank you," I say, and unfold my napkin. Real cloth napkins are my contribution to the recycling effort. They're cheaper than paper, too.

"Do you believe in recycling, Aisha?" I ask her out of politeness, and because the child used to have a brain before she fell in love with my child. I'm sort of checking to see if it's still there.

"Oh yes, ma'am," she says. "Of course there's not much point in recycling paper; we won't be using it much longer, anyway. Saint says the information highway will make paper obsolete."

"Saint says that, does he? What do you say?"

"The same thing he says."

"Always?"

"Always," my son answers for her. "Is there dill in this stuffing?"

"Of course."

"I approve." The second stuffed pepper disappears down his gullet, and I see him looking around for more.

"Have some French bread," I say pointedly, reaching around behind me for the bread-box drawer. "It's fresh-baked—I got it today."

Saint is a good boy, and he understands FHB—Family Hold-Back—at mealtimes with company. But perhaps Aisha is family to him already, because he asks her, "Liza, are you going to eat your other pepper?"

He knows better than to ask *me* that. Family Hold-Back does not mean Mama Hold-Back around here.

"No, Saint," she says sweetly, and lets him take it off her plate.

"It was very good, Mrs. Barber," she says to me. Clearly, the child has not forgotten her good manners. "I'm just not very hungry. Besides, I don't want to gain weight before the wedding. Did Mummy tell you about my gown?"

Mummy? I know Cherry is aging, has a wrinkle here and there, but surely . . . I choke off my laughter into my napkin. "No, she didn't."

"Well, it's a perfect fit, even though it's a size ten and I'm normally a twelve. We had to go to Bloomingdale's Bridal Sale to get it, and I almost died from the crush and the embarrassment, but it really is perfect. It's snug across the bust, though, so I have to watch my weight. It's ivory satin with a cathedral train, pointed waistline and sleeves. It has a scalloped neck and darling little seed pearls embroidered in a fleur-de-lys pattern. It . . ."

Not wanting to have to comment on the darling little seed pearls, let alone the emblem of imperial France and what that stands for, I rummage in the refrigerator for something that might be transformed into dessert. I find two small sponge cakes, a nearly full can of Reddi Wip, and a pint of strawberries. Saint can't eat them, but he's had plenty to eat already. He can watch while Aisha and I top off our dinner.

". . . and Mummy's going to lend me her cultured pearls for the something borrowed. I have a blue bracelet, and lace stockings for the something new, and my grand-mother's garter belt for something old," she prattles. "I think garter belts are gross, Mrs. Barber. How did you ever wear those things, back in the olden days?"

"They're a lot easier to wear than panty hose," I tell her. Back in the golden olden days, I mostly wore nothing under my clothes, but I am not about to shock this child by telling her that. I silently remove her plate and place her strawberry shortcake in front of her.

"Oh, no thank you," she says, and pushes it away.

"Watching your waistline?" I inquire, then correct myself. "Oh, no, that's right, it's your bustline."

"Yes, but that's not the reason. I'm allergic to straw-berries."

I look at her with something like apprehension creeping icily around my heart. "So is Saint."

"I break out in horrible hives if I even bite into one."

"So does he." The cold fingers of fear are creeping from my chest to my abdomen.

My son uses this information as an excuse to hug his girl. "And that's only one of the many things we have in common. Mom, you wouldn't believe how alike we are. I just had to love this woman."

"Uh-huh," I say, ice spreading to the pit of my stomach. "Listen, you all. I hope you'll clean up the kitchen for me. I have a headache. I have to lie down."

"Sure, Mom," says Saint. "Say, you must really feel bad. You didn't touch your dessert. You haven't been binging on pizza cheese again, have you?"

Cheese is *my* allergy, especially mozzarella—that and all other dairy products, though I can have an occasional dab of butter or cream without ill effects.

"No. I just thought of something that worries me."

"She's beautiful, she's talented, she's loved, she has two adorable children . . . what can she possibly have to worry about?"

"What I'm going to tell the cops when they find your bruised and battered body."

"Oops. The mater is in a serious snit. Let us not harass her any further, love. Go rest, Mother. The meal was wonderful. I'll wash, Liza. You dry."

I head for my room. Feeling remorse because I haven't

exactly welcomed Aisha to the family, I ransack my jewelry box. Nana's little garnet earrings are too dainty for me, but they might be charming on my future daughter-in-law, who is nothing if not dainty. I am not dainty, I never have been, and my taste runs to big exotic hoops and clunky dangles, especially silver and semiprecious stones. I have an amber pair that kiss my neck when they swing and make me feel loved. And a pair of silver thunderbirds with turquoise eyes that I put on when I need to feel like Shakes Her Fist, my self-christened Indian name.

I finally find the little studs where they're hiding, and go back to the kitchen to see whether Aisha's ears are pierced. Most girls' are these days, but you never know, and I am not about to put us through any home surgery with frozen needles and dirty thread.

I catch her on a whirl between sink and cupboard, putting away freshly dried plates. " 'Scuse me, Aisha," I say. "Hold still a minute, will you? I just want to see something."

I pick up one of her nylon corkscrews, which feels like a dead caterpillar, and look. What I see sends me flying back to my room to muffle my howls in my pillow.

Chapter 4

SAINT

I HOPE MOM ISN'T TRIPPING OUT on menopause, but it sure looks like it. She assures me that her symptoms are minimal, and that vitamin E and the ginseng-sarsaparilla capsules Brother Bee Smart made up for her at the Wholly Natural shop have them under control. She isn't going to take any synthetic hormones or any horse-piss pills, either, thank you. If she ever gets cancer, she'll deal with it, but she sure isn't going to go chasing after it.

I felt real relieved after that conversation, almost as relieved as I felt after she finally quit smoking. See, I believe they are pushing death in this country—weapons, tobacco, booze, other toxins. Sometimes it seems like the doctors and the pharmaceutical companies are in on the deal.

But after that scene in the kitchen, I am ready to run out and catch drippings from the first pregnant mare I can find. Mom is usually so sane and sensible. Surprises are not her style. That person who looked under Liza's hair and shrieked and ran off like she was demon-possessed was not my mother.

Liza was so startled that she dropped and broke a plate. Not one of the ordinary Fiesta ware plates from K mart, either, but the special ones from JCPenney with Kente borders that Mom had to save up for.

"Yeah," she said when she bought them, "I know, it's a crime that white folks are ripping off our heritage and selling it back to us. But it is our heritage, and I had to have those plates. Besides, I already looked all over the Mau Mau Mall, and they don't have them."

This was shaky logic, coming from the person who lectures me regularly about the difference between needs and wants.

"You don't have to have those designer sneakers, Saint. You just want them. You *need* generic shoes." We used to have that discussion about every six months, when my feet grew to a new size. Depending on the budget, sometimes I won, sometimes I lost—sometimes I got Nikes or Filas, sometimes I got bobos. I learned to save my designer logos and glue them onto the bobos. I did this until I decided for myself that brand-name worship was just another death trap. Too many kids were getting killed for their designer sneaks.

Around that same time, Mom stopped wearing Gloria Vanderbilt jeans because a friend had hers ripped off her on the bus, and if you had to wear your shirttail hanging over your designer logo to hide it, what was the point? Though, frankly, I think it was because she was getting too fat to squeeze into jeans, anyway.

Anyway, I tell Liza the broken plate is unimportant (a lie) and that I don't mind finishing the dishes alone (a bigger lie), and walk her briskly to her bus stop. I am glad when her bus comes quickly. I am anxious to rush back and see about my mom.

Even though I'm grown, Mom is still the anchor of my universe, the force of gravity that keeps it all from breaking up into little pieces. I totally depend on her to remain sane and reliable. Not that I would ever let her know it.

I think of myself as rugged and independent. A Lone Star, like Texas. But even the brightest star needs a center to spin around. Someday, I guess, Liza will be my center.

Liza doesn't feel like a potential center, though. She feels more like a twin star, a heavenly body with a gravitational field identical to mine. Hey—enough astronomy; it isn't even my major. Computer science and biology are.

But knowing my center is off balance, and maybe disintegrating, has a lot to do with the nervousness I feel when I go into Mom's bedroom. It's a cool room—relaxed and different, like Mom herself. The rattan and wicker furniture and the green rug and the curtains in a palm-frond print have the effect of a tropical garden. Tonight it is dark, though, with no lights on and everything barely visible in the grayness.

"Yo, Patricia." I address the form sprawled on the bed. "You feeling better?" Mom hates it when I call her Patricia. Most of her friends don't even know it's her real name. But I figure a little irritation might be just the stimulation she needs.

"Yeah, Saint. Sorry if I embarrassed you." The ghastly whisper is not encouraging. Usually Mom sounds like a cross between a bullhorn and a foghorn.

"What happened in the kitchen, anyway?"

"I was checking to see if Aisha has pierced ears." Mom turns on the Office Warehouse reading light with its tray of pens and paper clips beside her bed, and scoops something into her hand. "These belonged to your great-grandmother. I thought she might like them." A pair of deep red points of light glow on her palm.

"Ooh, neat. Rubies. I'm sure she'd love them."

"Not rubies, Saint. Garnets. We were never rich. Still, they're family heirlooms, and the posts and settings are real rose gold."

"Great, Mom. Thanks. But why'd you freak?"

I don't like the way she turns out the light again, as if she doesn't want me to see her face. "No special reason."

"Come on, Patricia. By the blood of Nat Turner." That is a special code we have between us that means absolutely no lying is allowed. We have sworn, since there are just the two of us, to be honest with each other about crucial matters. Saying "By the blood of Nat Turner" or "Nat Turner died for our sins" is a way of invoking that vow, of saying that the issue under discussion is important and demands truthfulness.

"Oh—all right." Her voice has regained some of its bass resonance, which makes me feel she might be okay, after all. "It probably doesn't mean anything. I was just overreacting."

"To what?"

"The mole Aisha has below her left ear, in the same place as yours."

"Just a coincidence," I say, though I feel uneasy. "Mom, you know how you told me moles are a sign of mixed heritage, and since practically all Americans of African descent are mixed, well—"

"I know," she said, "but your father has one in the exact same spot."

"Has?"

"Excuse me, just a manner of speaking. *Had*."

I sense us getting out into deep, deep waters, past the place where I can get my bearings or touch bottom.

"And did he have another one on his butt, on the left cheek, like mine?" This would be an embarrassing discussion to most sons and mothers, I know, but Mom and I don't embarrass easily.

"Uh-huh. Does Aisha?"

Now it *is* getting embarrassing. No matter which way I answer, I will be trapped into admitting that Aisha and I are intimate. No way am I going to admit a thing like that to my mother.

I kiss Mom a gentle good-night on her forehead and back out of the room.

Her Klaxon scream follows me down the hall.

"Well, does she? *Does she?*"

Chapter 5

AISHA

THIS HAS TO BE the worst day of my entire life. First, my mother practically disowns me because I put on an outfit of hers. It seems I now have to work for minimum wage at some smelly hamburger joint, just because she saw me wearing her suit. It must be menopause. I've been borrowing her clothes all my life, and she never minded until now.

And then Saint takes me over to his house, and his mom flips out on me.

It would be funny if it weren't so tragic. The swinging Sixties Sisters, once so liberated and glamorous, going through the change together. Toasting each other with prune juice and Geritol while Alzheimer's sets in. Well, they had their fun in their day—to hear them tell it, they had a ball—so what can they expect? They're ancient now.

But, in Patrice's case, it has to be something worse than menopause.

That scene in Saint's kitchen was enough to make me

cancel the wedding plans then and there. The way his mother came at me like a big yellow mountain lioness and *attacked* me—grabbing my hair, drooling on my cheek—then ran screaming off to her room like a howling monkey . . . well, it was like something out of a Stephen King movie. *Supper with a Psycho.* I've never been so upset in all my life.

The woman seemed possessed by something evil. She must have picked up a vicious voodoo spirit on that one trip to Haiti she's always raving about. Probably stabs pins into dolls when there's nobody around. And the way she has let herself go is a shame. She doesn't wear a bra under those corny caftans she thinks are so exotic. The way she bounces around is pathetic. If I had honeydews like hers, I'd sure wear some support for them. It's disgusting in a woman her age. So is that big fire-red Afro she wears. You'd think she'd have enough pride to invest in a good cut and a little Lustrasilk. But, no, she lets it stay long and nappy, and she sees nothing wrong with bouncing and jouncing all over the place, even in front of her grown son.

They're so close, sometimes I wonder if—

Now that, Eliza Hopkins soon-to-be Barber, is a vile thought. You had better cancel it right away.

But maybe you'd better cancel the wedding, too. Saint is wonderful. The very thought of him makes me go all weak. He's so tall, so fine. Then there are his magical eyes, his sensitive hands, his deep voice, his marvelous mind . . . but his mama looms over him—over us—like an evil shadow.

That image of the yellow mountain lioness attacking me

won't go away. I thought she was going to kill me—I'm sure she wanted to—and there was nowhere to escape to in that cramped little kitchen of hers. This big oval pedestal table is wedged in between the refrigerator and the sink, and next to the sink, taking up all the rest of one wall, is this huge steel stove. An eight-burner stove, because, you see, Patrice imagines that she's this great international world-class cook and that people are just lining up for her recipes. She has copper skillets and wire whisks and spoons and strainers, more things than she can possibly use, hung all over this tiny wall above the sink. She has more utensils hanging from the ceiling, and, on the counter, she keeps her collection of big, vicious-looking knives. She asks her guests to do the dishes because there's no room to squeeze in a dishwasher.

Maybe she thought she was treating me like one of the family instead of like a guest. But I resented it because I could tell she didn't really want me in her family. I practically grew up in her house, but after Saint and I got together, she stopped liking me.

Actually, dinner wasn't bad. I liked the stuffed peppers, though I can't deal with strawberries. And I'm sorry I broke her tacky Kente-border plate. Forgive me for being politically incorrect, but I don't want anything ethnic in my house. I prefer roses on my china.

The way Saint hustled me out of there, practically *put* me out, you'd think I'd broken a piece of Lenox. One thing was made clear by that little incident: his mother comes first with him, while I am somewhere near the bottom of his list. Well, I've got news for Mr. Toussaint D. Barber. It won't be that way after we get married. *If* we get married, that is.

The more I think about it, the bigger that IF becomes. His mother is definitely the most overbearing, obnoxious woman I have ever met. I can't bear it if she's going to be a large part of our life. And I can't see Saint, her only child, abandoning her. He's such a conscientious guy.

I think she was snarling, too, when she attacked me, or at least frothing at the mouth. The lioness doesn't want to share her cub.

Well, she just should have had a couple more while she was at it. The welfare checks are bigger when you do, aren't they? And once you've had one out-of-wedlock baby, it must be easy to have more.

I know she and Mother and their girlfriends all chose to do it, but I will never understand them. I couldn't bear it. I would just die.

Of course, I'm sure Patrice had no other choice. After all, who would propose to her?

It's a shame, with my wedding gown bought and the reception hall booked and the invitations at the printers and everything. But I might as well face it—my fiancé's mother and I hate each other. This could be a big, big problem. The only way around it is to move somewhere far, far away from here.

But even then we'd have to see her at least once a year. Twice—Christmas and Mother's Day. Oh, *darn!*

Chapter 6

PATRICE

J UST BEFORE SAINT COMES IN, I am lying there in the dark, thinking about the trip I took to Haiti twenty-two years ago with his daddy. The scratchy Haitian cotton pillow under my cheek probably stirs up those memories. It is tearing up my face, but I am too depressed to move off of it.

The Haitians are amazing people. They create gorgeous objects—fabrics, paintings, musical instruments—out of next to nothing. They keep old cars running with bobby pins and prayers. And they overthrew the French invaders in a few years—which is probably why the American government is so cruel to them. They don't want any proud, independent black people coming here and inspiring uppity attitudes among the ex-slave population.

When I see how Haiti is being punished for its pride, I want to cry

But back in 1974, when I went down there with good old Eugene Dessalines Green, it was magical. The

Dunham Dancers were still performing voodoo ceremonies in the garden of LeClerc's old mansion. There was
an outdoor nightclub, Chez Bob, where we merengued all
night long under the stars.

The Haitians are such polite people. They invented the
merengue, their elegant dance in which you drag one foot,
because their hero, Dessalines, had a bad leg caused by
French torture.

And all the men stood when I came into a room. Stood
up, and remained standing until I took a seat! Imagine
that happening here, among these louts who think rudeness equals manliness.

What's more, the men followed me everywhere I went
because I was big. The Haitians adore big women. In a
country where everybody is a little hungry, skinny women
are not the ideal. Someone like me, who hasn't missed
many meals, is. That memory helps a lot these days, when
I am busting the seams on even my biggest caftans.

To make it all absolutely superdelicious, as lush and
sweet and juicy as the mangoes that grow all over the
place, Haitian men are not interested in white women.
There are no white Haitians, anyway. Haitians come in
every shade from ivory to ebony, but they all have a touch
of African ancestry, and that's the way the Haitians like it.
If the tar brush hasn't touched you somewhere, they want
nothing to do with you.

I was in love with Gene at the time, so I didn't respond
to all the attention, but I sure enjoyed it.

Of course there was poverty in Haiti—but our staying
home wouldn't have helped it. I figured that our presence
guaranteed meals for about five Haitians apiece during

our stay. I know it, in fact, because we were the only guests in the hotel, and I went to the kitchen once to ask the name of an especially fabulous fruit, and saw at least a dozen people back there eating.

Back in that time, there was a sensational movie, *The Comedians*, based on a novel by Graham Greene, that made most Americans scared to go to Haiti. After my trip I saw how ridiculous the movie was. First of all, like all Hollywood productions, the movie was all about white folks, which was absurd because, as I said, there are no white Haitians. A *blanc* or a *blanche* is a yellow person— or a foreigner. Secondly, the movie showed the police and the army brutalizing these silly white folks, when they don't want anything to do with them.

But white folks are like children—they have to be the center of attention. They have one hotel they live in down there, the Oloffson, which they think is the center of the Haitian universe. It was featured in the movie. Gene and I made a point of avoiding it. We stayed at a bare-bones hotel in town, the Excelsior, for our first week, then moved up the hill to a gorgeous place called Sous Le Manguier—Under the Mango Tree—for that last magical night, when Saint was conceived.

When we got back, there was a cops-and-robbers shootout in progress on my block. Gene and I made the taxi wait and hunkered down in the back seat until it was over. Yet, all that year, people who'd seen and believed that silly movie said, "Haiti? How did you stand the violence?"

I told them more violence is done to me and my self-esteem every day here than I experienced in my whole two weeks in Haiti.

Oh, I tell you truly, I didn't want to leave.

I was treated like a queen—hand-kissing, chair-holding, all that. I ate rare fruits and dishes I have never seen since—pigeon, turtle, prawns. The whole place was an art festival—sculpture, paintings, music, food. And I was with the man I had picked to be the father of my child, the princely Eugene D. Green.

I hear that he has fallen on hard times lately, but in those days Gene Green was divine. He was like Edgar Lee Masters's Richard Cory, "clean-favored, and imperially slim," with a regal bearing that commanded deference. Sort of a combination Montel Williams, Avery Brooks, and Yul Brynner, with those high cheekbones and magnetic, slanted eyes.

One night when the barriers were down between us, he told me he had an inferiority complex for years because he was his mama's first child, and her only bastard. So, for a whole year, he worked on his self-esteem. He stared in his mirror every morning and told his image, "You are a king." Well, practice had made perfect. He was kingly, and I felt like a queen on his arm. So did a lot of other women, I found out later.

What, exactly, I often wonder now, was so wonderful about old Eugene? He had published a few articles and poems, none of which have been reprinted, as far as I can tell, so no one can reread them to see if they have held up. I suspect that they haven't. He had strong opinions on art and politics, and loved to hold forth on them for hours. He always had a willing audience for his rapid-fire monologues. But I can't remember a single brilliant thing he said.

And, of course, he spoke French fluently, which made doors open like magic in Haiti, while my plodding French sounded like a kid's in high school—which was where I learned it. Eugene was Haitian on his mother's side, so fluency was his birthright.

The Haitians were so nice, though, applauding and encouraging my stuttering efforts, that I think I would have become fluent, too, if I'd stayed another couple of weeks. But of course Eugene was there to talk for me.

When I told him my plan for us to make a baby, his response was, "You understand that I am an artist, and an artist cannot be tied down by a family."

I assured him that all I wanted was for him to plant his superior seed in my womb. I, and I alone, would provide for our glorious issue. I don't know where I got such brass-balled confidence, but we all had it then.

He shrugged and said, "Whatever you wish, Patricia. I will not be responsible."

He held up his end of the bargain, all right.

He was the only man I ever allowed to call me "Patricia"—except my father, and now, of course, Saint.

When we came back to the Gunfight at the O.K. Corral that was my block, Saint was already under way.

I never saw Eugene again.

There is a painting opposite my bed, of festive people eating in a grove of mango trees. It is green and mysterious, darkly bright, and is the only thing I brought back from that trip to Haiti.

That and Saint, of course.

And the credit card receipts for the plane tickets and the rooms I paid for.

Saint was worth it.

I turn on my other bedside lamp, the one with the bamboo base and the wicker shade that I usually reserve for intimate occasions, and take a long, thoughtful look around my room. I have always enjoyed its tropical-summertime effect. Green and white curtains and bedspread, the Sous Le Manguier painting, another of parrots in a lush tree, an emerald rug, a wicker chaise with green cushions. And plants—a window full of plants. If I had to describe my room in one word, that word would be "Green."

Whoa, Patrice.

What exactly has my subconscious been up to here?

I pick up the phone and dial Cherry. My best friend is not dumb; just not deep. To put it another way, it isn't that her elevator doesn't go all the way to the top story, it's that it doesn't know there's a basement underneath the building. Oh, let's face it, she's smart enough to crunch numbers with a snap! crackle! pop!, but otherwise she's a dipstick. Still, I've never known her to lie to me.

Instead of the expected familiar voice, after four rings I get Cherry's machine. I listen through four verses of Helen Reddy's "I Am Woman," then say, "Yo, Cherry. Patrice calling. This is really important. Call me as soon as you come in."

Then I hang up and start thinking. Though Cherry and I are solid-bedrock, tight-forever friends, there are big gaps in my knowledge about her. She disappeared for about a year after Saint's first birthday, and I have never learned where she went. "I went somewhere to find myself," was all she would say when she returned. My best guess was some kind of rehab, because Cherry and liquor definitely do not mix, and after she came back, she touched nothing stronger than ginger beer. But I don't really know.

Once she began a sentence with "When I was in Chicago . . ." but when I asked her, "When was that?" she clammed up tighter than a virgin's knees. She's also been very close-mouthed about her love life, and I've always respected her wish for privacy in that area. Sure, I'd love to know, but it really is none of my business, and I know that my big-mouth tell-all style is not comfortable for everybody.

I think some more. Toni Brookins is one of the only other two women I know who had a Gene Green baby. The other one, Esther Easton, is somewhere in California, I've heard. But Toni stayed right here, working for Brad Hall's public relations outfit. Her Rome, Romare, is sixteen. Saint is twenty-one.

Aisha is nineteen.

Both of them, I tell myself as I dial, are way too young to be getting married.

"Yo, Toni," I say when she answers. "Patrice Barber."

"Oh, Patrice." She sounds guilty. "I meant to bring that Africare brochure over to you on Friday, but I got tied up. Hope you aren't starved for work. I'll run by with it tomorrow."

"I wasn't even thinking about it, girl. How are you? How's Rome?"

"Driving me crazy," she admits, sounding suddenly tired. "That's why I couldn't come Friday, I had to spend the day in court. He spray-painted his name all over the Hall of Justice."

"Living up to his namesake, I guess," I say, though somehow I doubt that was how Romare Bearden got started.

"Well, they released him into my custody, but he's on probation. The judges really like their new building. Patrice, tell me this is just a phase. Tell me he'll grow out of it. Did Saint give you this much trouble?"

"Sure," I lie. "They all do." Actually, Saint's teens weren't bad. There was his period of cutting school, which I short-circuited by saying that if he didn't go to school, he'd have to get a job—the boring, minimum-wage sort of job that he would be stuck with for the rest of his life. Saint was sensible enough to see my point right away. Then there was that episode when he sneaked a floozy into the house. I threw them both out, saying, "If you're big enough to play house, you're big enough to keep house." Aside from those times, Saint had an easy adolescence. But I can't let Toni know that.

"That makes me feel a little better," she says. "Listen, maybe I can bring you a speech to do, too."

There are as many kinds of whores as there are women, I always say. I am glad I made her feel better. I can use the extra work. "Listen, Toni, I wanted to ask you something. Have you been in touch with Eugene?"

She pauses. I can hear her suck in her breath, then release it with a sigh. "Not lately. Why?"

"I was trying to figure out something. I was wondering,

really, who he was involved with after me. Was there someone before you?"

"Patrice, really, that's not the sort of information I keep in my memory bank. It draws no interest, if you follow me. But if I happened to know something like that, would I share it? I don't think so."

Her voice is frosty. I can see my next freelance check from Brad Hall disappearing.

"Sorry if I offended you, Toni. Didn't mean to open old wounds or anything like that. Please forgive me. I really hope you can come by tomorrow."

"I'll try to fit you in," she says, with the chill of a lemon sherbet. Right away I begin thinking of making some. Lemons, sugar, a little whipped cream to fold in when half frozen . . .

I pull myself up short. This is perverse. This is sick. Just what the hell do I think I am doing? Planning a midnight snack while I am committing economic suicide, that's what. Besides the possible loss of my juiciest freelance account, the one that pays for Saint's designer sneaks and my gourmet groceries, what have I accomplished?

I really hope Toni will get over her resentment. I am planning to try a new stir-fry recipe tomorrow, one that calls for water chestnuts, snow pea pods, and Portabella mushrooms, all items that are not on my bare-bones budget. I say a silent prayer and dial Cherry again.

Once again Helen Reddy belts out four choruses in my ear. I remind myself to suggest some Sade for Cherry's machine, then leave a more specific message.

"Cherry, I need to talk to you. This may sound trivial, but it isn't. I need to know Aisha's middle name."

"Hi, Patrice," says the small, familiar voice. Cherry is the only black woman I know with a wimpy voice. A lot of white women have soft, wispy voices because they are afraid to be understood. I remind myself to find out what Cherry is afraid of, deep down—if she ever becomes brave enough to look in there.

"What a cheap trick!" I yell into the phone.

Her voice gets even softer. "I was monitoring my calls."

"Yeah, but why'd you make me go all through with leaving a message before you spoke up?"

"I wanted to know what you wanted."

"Of all the dumb shit!" I let loose with a few more expletives, then say, "Well?"

"Well, what?"

"What's Aisha's middle name?"

"My daughter calls herself Eliza now."

"Yeah, right. That'll last about two weeks."

"She will be dropping that middle initial after the wedding, anyway. She's picked out her towels and her silver pattern, and the monogram will be EHB."

"It should be TDB," I inform her. "The bride takes her husband's initials. I'm asking about the name you gave her, the name she has now, the one on her birth certificate. I want to know what the G stands for."

There is a long hesitation. Then Cherry says, "Green."

My own voice becomes strangely subdued. "I can't afford to buy silver. But I may get her a big towel to cry in."

"What does that mean?"

"It means get your skinny ass over here, girl. We got trouble."

Chapter 7

PATRICE

My GRANDMOTHER, who used to be a midwife and a root doctor down in Georgia, had a big raggedy book she called her Blood Book. In it she had recorded the births and bloodlines of all the babies she'd delivered, the names of their parents, and those of their parents' parents. In some cases the father's name was not the same as the husband's name. Sometimes the father was someone else's husband. Sometimes the races were secretly mixed. She had written it all down—in some places, where there were damaging secrets about white people, in code.

That book was almost as big as an urban phone book, but she carried it with her everywhere she went. It was the most precious thing she owned, she said—even more precious than her Bible, because that could be replaced.

When we went on trips, we couldn't persuade Nana to leave that book at home. She didn't want any eyes but hers to see it, she said.

"Some of the information in here is mighty delicate,"

she said. "People aren't always what they seem, dear heart. Oh, sometimes they are. But other times . . . well, the facts in here are so hot they could scald somebody. That's why I keep my mouth shut. But I keep my records in my Blood Book."

Her job had been not just to deliver babies, but to keep the bloodlines of some mighty closely related southern families, black and white, from getting hopelessly tangled. She took that part of it very seriously, and never really retired from it.

I remember her getting long distance calls late at night. I was about ten years old when I eavesdropped on those calls. She would get out that book, look something up and say, "Yes, that would be all right." Only once did I hear her say, very sternly and sharply, "No, that cannot be allowed. They are too close." She listened patiently for another minute, then said, "I told you, they are too close. Closer even than second cousins, and I don't recommend that. I have seen what comes of it, and it isn't pretty. Can't you send her away? . . . All right. I'll keep you in my prayers."

She stayed awake almost all of that night, humming and praying. In the morning she got another call, and when she put the phone down, she smiled and went to sleep.

I used to laugh at Nana. But now I wish I'd had the good sense to appreciate her wisdom. It could have spared a lot of people a lot of pain, pain like Saint and Aisha will soon be feeling. Pain like Cherry and I are feeling as we sit in my kitchen, drinking kava kava and comparing notes.

She is surprisingly easy to convince. Knowing Cherry,

I'd expected a lot of denial. But she accepts it and takes it calmly—at first.

"They both have prominent canine teeth that came in before they lost their baby teeth," I say.

"Mmmm," she responds.

"Saint used to get so many ear infections, I made him stop going to the public pool."

"So did Aisha, and she didn't even go swimming. She still can't swim, because . . ."

"Because of her hair," I finish for her. Even if we hadn't been such close friends, I would have known that was the reason. From the age of about five on, we black females are obsessed with our hair. We pull it, tease it, scorch it, twist it, braid it, pick it, color it, roll it, augment it, and douse it in chemicals, all to make it conform to the great white ideal of tossable straightness. We never reach the ideal, but the effort consumes about half of our time and energy. If we didn't have to deal with our hair, we would probably rule the world.

Water nullifies most attempts to acquire Good Hair, that is to say, Caucasian hair, so we avoid bringing our heads in contact with the stuff except when absolutely necessary. Hence, few of us can swim.

"Saint's eyes aren't really brown," I say next. "They're hazel, with little green and gold flecks."

"Have you looked, really looked, at my daughter? Really studied her features?"

"Hazel eyes, huh?"

She nods, then bursts into tears. I pat her shoulder until she recovers. When she does, all she says is, "Well, this is my year to face reality, it seems. Patrice, how could we have been so *dumb*?"

"We were caught up in the excitement. The freedom, the anti-establishment mood. Remember?"

"Yes, I remember." She sighs. "Freedom. Do your own thing. So I decided to have a baby by the first glamorous phony that walked into my life."

"We both did," I remind her. "Did Gene ever recite 'Cynara' to you?"

" 'I have been faithful to thee, Cynara, in my fashion.' Ernest Dowson." She shudders.

"That always used to give me the shivers, too."

"It was just an elegant excuse for doggishness."

I ignore her and go on dreamily, "And the way he had of breathing on my neck, and that cologne he wore. What was it called?"

"Patchouli," Cherry says. Her face is grim. She looks old. Hell, she is old. We both are. "I suppose you were turned on by his paisley smoking jacket, too."

"Yeah." I am remembering. "And the tweed jacket with the leather elbow patches, and the briar pipe. Remember that pipe? He *was* fine, wasn't he?"

"No," she says, pulling her lips into a tight little bow. "He just knew how to accessorize. God. I could have had a dentist or a doctor."

"A dentist? A doctor?" I can't believe I am hearing this from Cherry, who once wanted to burn down a hospital because they'd botched her mother's operation. "Why not go ahead and make it a mortician?"

"Why not?" she says, shocking me. "Death pays well.

I'd have a house of my own instead of an apartment. A real car instead of a joke that only runs on odd-numbered days. Charges at all the good stores, none of them maxed out. And my children would have someone's name."

I see her slipping into a fantasy of two-car garages, walk-in closets, and Cuisinarts. "It's too late for that, Cherry," I tell her. "Besides, embalming fluid stinks."

She blinks and comes back to the present moment. "Yes, it's too late. Personally, I blame Nikki. She was the one who started this I-can-have-a-child-all-by-myself shit. We all worshiped her and followed in her footsteps."

"I didn't worship her," I say. "And later, when she came out in print asking, 'Who is going to teach my son to pee?' I wanted to kill her. But I don't think we should blame Nikki. The ideas were in the air. We just picked up on them. We're children of our time."

"Children having children." She sighs deeply. "Aisha will be heartbroken. She already thinks we were crazy. This will just confirm it."

"Cherry," I ask, very sincerely, "do you think we were crazy?"

She begins ticking off the elements of her situation on her fingers. "I don't own the roof over my head. I probably never will. I can only afford one new outfit a year, and Aisha borrowed it yesterday, which is why we are not on the best of terms. I haven't been to the dentist in two years, and something is very wrong on the upper left side here."

I can see her tongue probing the area. When it strikes pay dirt, she winces. "My car is about to die," she continues. "I keep giving it expensive CPR, but the way it rattles and wheezes, I should let the poor thing expire. I have no savings or life insurance. I'm a loan officer, and my credit is so bad, I wouldn't give myself a loan. Thank God I have good health." She closes her eyes and is silent for a minute.

"No," she finally says, "I don't think we were crazy."

I want to shout hooray, but for once I have the sense to keep quiet.

"It was a wonderful time," she goes on, "a time that will never come again, and we were lucky to live in it and take part in it. I wouldn't trade it for all the dentists in New Jersey. But my child is from *this* time, and it's a grim, scary time, and she wants different things. She wants safety, I think, and Saint offered her that. How am I going to help her pick up the pieces?"

"You'll find a way," I tell her. "Maybe she'll find it herself. She's not really a child anymore, you know."

"But this is so *terrible*!" Cherry is sobbing. Not as terrible, I think, as it would be when the first grandchild got here with one eye in the center of its forehead. But I don't say that. I hand her a towel—this isn't a mere shower, this is a typhoon no mere Kleenex can absorb. And I just sit there and let her cry.

"Sometimes," I say gently, "we just have to sit back and take our hands off situations, and let God take over. You do believe in God, don't you?"

Head bowed and dripping, Cherry nods. When she finishes snorting and yowling, and is down to a few gentle sniffs, she says, "I feel better. What do we do now, Patrice?"

"Well," I tell her, "it has occurred to me that there are probably some more women who were suckers for poetry and patchouli. That means there may be more of these children out there. I think we should to try to find them. After we tell our children, of course."

Her face as she leaves is ghastly. But brave.

Chapter 8

CHERRY

Of course I believe in God. What a question for my best friend to ask, after our being so close for so many years. And I'm not saying I'm a believer because I got back in the A.M.E. church—I did that mainly for Aisha's sake. But because this crazy and yet exquisitely orderly creation we inhabit just has to have a divine intelligence, one with a sense of humor, behind it. His wisdom is infinite. He knows just how much we can bear.

For instance, suppose he had given us the power to see the future. I would not have the strength to face the rest of my week, or even the next hour.

I drive home, praying that my twelve-year-old blue Dodge, Sapphire, will make it to the next payday without a major crisis.

I hear music coming from the back of the apartment, what I call whack-whack music. You know what I mean—those merciless electronic beats over which rappers lay down tracks of scratches and words. Usually

Aisha has less irritating taste. She listens to any one of a dozen interchangeable female vocalists who sing love songs as if they are being strangled.

I knock.

"Come in."

Stretched out on her bed, my daughter is wearing pajamas and a gray mud mask and watching MTV. She is surrounded by her collection of teddy bears. I feel as if I am about to snatch them away from her.

"We have to talk, Aisha," I tell her.

She hugs one of the bears close and puts on an impatient frown. "Yes?"

"There's no easy way of telling you this," I say. "Saint's mom and I had a talk tonight. We decided that you and Saint should postpone the wedding."

"Oh? You old hens had a talk, and decided that I should postpone my life? Well, I'm sorry, Mother, but I can't oblige you. Just because you don't have lives anymore is no reason why we should put ours on hold to keep you company—"

"Aisha," I say, as gently as possible, "that's not the reason. We were comparing notes. We realized that she and I were involved with the same man in the years before you and Saint were born."

"Mother," she says, "I don't want to hear about your sordid past. It wouldn't shock me to hear that all three of you shared the same bed. I'm a decent girl, and I'm planning to have a decent life, not a life like yours."

I am trying hard to keep my emotions under control, but an edge creeps into my voice. "My sordid past, as you put it, is not the point. We weren't involved with your father simultaneously. Patrice broke up with him a year before I met him. Remember, you and Saint are two years apart."

"I don't see what—" The glaze over her eyes melts. "Mother, what are you saying?"

I try to be gentle. I lift one of her braids. "Patrice noticed some things, like the birthmarks on your necks, and the allergy you both have to strawberries, and she began to put two and two together. Then she called me. Now we're almost certain."

She looks at me blank-faced, willfully uncomprehending. She is going to make me say it.

I take a deep breath and let it out. "We're almost certain that you and Saint had the same father." Using the past tense bothers me, because it is time for total honesty, but I have promised not to blow Patrice's game.

My daughter rolls over on her stomach, pounds her pillows, and howls, "No! No! I won't believe it! I won't! Do you hear me, Mother? It can't be true!"

When she turns her hopeless, streaming face to me, I get out of there. I can't stand it.

Chapter 9

SAINT

I THOUGHT I'D NEVER GET TO SLEEP for thinking about the mysterious storm that had blown up from nowhere, causing Mom to go bananas in the kitchen and upset Aisha. But when you're a young, active guy, your body takes over and tells your brain in this deep, commanding voice, "REST!" And before you know it, you're out.

When I wake up, I've slept ten hours. It's Saturday morning. I remember that I promised to defend my court against some new characters from out of town who think they can play basketball.

I take a good hard shower. I don't want to disturb Mom, so I tiptoe into the kitchen in sock feet, chug some juice, grab a fistful of corn bread, and head out for the court.

The court is on the old school playground, which the city has turned into a community recreation area now that the school is closed. Nobody is there but my old buddies Ed and Tug practicing lay-ups, and a bunch of little kids watching them. I feel sorry for little kids these days, dealing with dangerous streets and lousy schools without anybody to set them straight. I try to do my part.

One of them kind of sidles up to me, advancing while seeming to move sideways, and asks, "Are you the Saint?"

"That's what they call me," I admit. "What's your name?"

He is about eight, skinny and on his way to being tall. Somebody cares about him, but in the wrong way. They have braided his hair in a couple dozen spiky plaits and stuck an earring in his little left ear. Not that I'm stuffy about jewelry and hairstyles. I just think people should be old enough to understand what styles mean before they make those decisions.

"Lamar Harris," he says. "Say, are you really the king of this court?"

"That's right," I tell him. "You just watch me prove it."

Ed and Tug approach us. "What's up, homes?" I ask.

"Company didn't come," Ed informs me.

"The big mouths from Brooklyn didn't show?"

"Nah," Tug says.

"Well, let's not waste a good morning," I say, and start to dribble.

The three of us used to be tight as good booty, but now we only see each other in the summers. Ed is the one they call my twin—tall, mustard-colored, lanky and knobbly-kneed. He has bad eyes, wears Coke-bottle lenses, but has a good mind. His head is on straight, too. He got a scholarship to Brown but decided to do pre-law at Howard.

Tug is built low and wide, like a tugboat. He wants to be a podiatrist—don't ask me why. He says it's because he's so close to the ground he's made a lifelong study of feet. Guess that's as good a reason as any.

It's one on one on one. I shoot one from the field, then start plotting one of my famous zigzag courses toward the basket. Ed tries to block me. I have to laugh because he's so predictable. See, his mind works just like mine, so I always know what he's going to do. I am faking him out, swinging the ball from side to side, when Tug comes up behind me and knocks it loose. That's his specialty. He's short, swift, and sneaky. Also strong. I trick him easy, get in close, and score with a jump shot. Blam! The backboard reverbs. Tug scoops the ball away from me, scores once, and then I get it back. Just those little kids cheering in my ears are enough to get my adrenaline pumping. I swing the ball, left to right, behind my back, like a gorilla, while Tug jumps up and down. Then I let it fly from my fingertips and it homes straight in, like a homing pigeon. Ed gets it and rams it in. We're almost even. Next try, he rams it too hard and it rebounds off the rim. I'm at eighteen and he's at sixteen when I snatch it back and those other two guys start closing ranks to keep me from making twenty-one. They are on me like white on rice but I am flying. Invincible. I pivot, fake, and throw from about ten feet. Right on the money. Tug grabs it, fumbles, and drops it. His loss is my gain.

Naturally, I have to make the last one with a spectacular throw over my shoulder. Blam! Supersaint rules.

The little kids go wild.

"It's still my court," I tell my boys. "Pay me rent."

"You really are the king!" Lamar crows.

I give my fan a careful once-over. He has on a clean

white T-shirt, patched jeans, and some old, scuffed bobos. "Why'd your mom braid your hair?"

He shrugs. "I couldn't comb it. Teacher sent me home 'cause it was so messy."

I nod, knowing that is only part of the story. "Yeah, I bet you needed a power pick for them nubby naps." I touch his head. "Ow! Them snakes bite! You must have needed a Roto-Rake!"

The kid and I laugh, but there is pain in it. Shared pain. Teachers, especially the white ones we mostly got since integration (translation: we gone integrate you right out of your jobs) don't understand about black hair. When it's long and natural, it's hard to comb. But haircuts cost money.

"Tell you what, Lamar. I think I got a job for you later on today. Then maybe you can afford a haircut."

"A job? What kind of job?"

Tug interrupted us. "Yo, Saint, your lady's here. Lookin' fine, too. Ow! You better hurry before somebody beats you to it."

Out of the corner of my eye I can see Aisha, wearing a short dress in the shade of red that makes bulls run amok and causes traffic accidents. "Hey, Lamar! You know where the Harvest House is?"

He nods. "I think I ate there one time."

I thought the kid looked familiar. I know him from the soup kitchen, that's it. And he's been there lots more than once. "Well, meet me there at three. We'll see if chopping onions makes you cry. If it doesn't, maybe I'll teach you how to make potato salad. Deal?"

He slaps my outstretched palm. "Deal."

I turn briefly to Tug. "I gotta talk to my lady, then get to my gig at the Harvest House. Maybe we'll catch you guys later." See, at this point, Aisha and I are still a "we."

"Party at the Doghouse tonight," Tug informs me. "You coming?"

The Dogs, the Q-Dogs that is, are the members of Omega Psi Phi Fraternity. They have a rough style of partying, and I wouldn't take Aisha within ten miles of them, but I learned down South never to shut a door. "Maybe I'll drop by. Catch you later."

I stroll over to the bench where Aisha is sitting all by her fine self. When I get close, I see that she has been crying.

"What's wrong, sweetheart?" I put my arm around her shoulders.

"Everything," she says in a sniffly voice, and picks up my hand and sort of throws it back at me.

"Hey, what'd I do?"

"Nothing. I just don't want you to touch me."

Her dress is low-cut, and I am peering down it at all that fine brown territory that is mine, or so I think. "What you mean, girl? It's too late for that. I already touched you." I squeeze one of her nipples gently, just to remind her.

She slaps my hand away. "I told you, don't touch me. Not anymore."

"What's wrong?"

She sighs. "Didn't your mother tell you?"

"I didn't talk to her this morning. I got dressed and left as soon as I woke up."

"What about last night?"

"She was still raving, so I left her alone to sleep off her insanity."

"What was she raving about?"

"Something about you having a mole in the same place as mine. That's why she went off when she looked at your ear."

"Well, don't you get it?" Aisha is impatient. That is what is different about her today. Usually, she sits patiently and waits to hear whatever I have to say. She isn't batting her eyelashes and turning soulful looks on me anymore, either.

"Get what?"

She sighs. "You're making this awfully difficult. For a smart guy, you sure can be dumb. Saint, we might as well face it. Our mothers are sluts."

I feel the redness I hate rise into my cheeks and ears. I always turn red when I'm embarrassed or angry. I wish I weren't light enough for it to show.

"Don't you say a thing like that about *my* mother, Aisha. You can say what you want about yours. I think she's a nice lady, though."

"She's not nice, she's a slut," Aisha says calmly. "And our father is a dog."

That singular pronoun hits me like a jolt of electricity somewhere close to my heart.

She speaks, not to me, but to the graffiti-covered wall across the street. "Yes, Saint, we had the same father. Your mother just figured it out. To give her credit, she's not dumb. It's *my* mother who's the *dumb* slut." She twists the engagement ring on her left hand. To her embarrassment, it seems to be stuck.

Of all the stupid things to do in an awkward moment, I try to help her. But then, there's no chapter in the Miss Manners Handbook on what to do when you find out your fiancée is your sister.

She holds up her other hand in a "stop" gesture. "Wait." In her enormous purse she finds a miniature bottle of lotion, applies it, and works the ring loose. "Here you are. The wedding is off, of course."

"Of course," I say. "I mean, I guess it is—if they're sure."

"They're sure. They weren't *that* slutty. Of course there are blood tests we can take, if you want."

"Yes, I think I do want," I say. "This is just so incredible." Some foolproof data, some objective computer printouts, some graphs and slides and other scientific mojo are what I need to help me accept this news. But at the same time, I think I already know. Some scattered pieces of knowledge come together inside me, grow solid and make the dreadful revelation almost satisfying, because it explains so much. Our similarity that borders on twinness is no longer such a deep mystery.

Also, I'm ashamed to admit it, but part of me is relieved at being let off the marriage hook. All year I've been feeling too young and unready to take this step. But Aisha wanted it, and when she wants something, there is no putting her off.

She knows what I'm thinking and feeling. Not for nothing is she my soul mate; my sister. "You dog," she says, with a sidewise glance and a flash of cold smile. "Okay, we can take the tests. I can't think about it now. I have too much pain."

"Well, what do you think I'm feeling? Ecstasy?" My insides are seared, as if someone has set a charcoal grill blazing in my guts. My brain is barbecued, too. "Now what do we do?"

Maybe we can help each other, I am going to suggest next.

But this is a new Aisha, hard and angry, not the sweet, soft, giving girl I thought I knew and loved.

"I don't know about you, Saint, but I have to look for a job." She stands up. The dress is really scarlet, blinding scarlet, and clinging to her in all the right—or wrong— places.

"In that? What kind of job are you looking for in that dress?"

"None of your business, Saint. You're not my protector anymore."

"Oh, no?" I yell. "According to what you say, I'm your big brother. And that makes me still your protector. And I say you shouldn't be out alone in that outfit."

Ed, my so-called twin, has been hanging around eavesdropping, the low snake. "I heard that," he says. No way he could help but hear it, I guess—I was yelling so loud.

"I'll keep the young lady company," he offers, looking like a fat man salivating over a platter of pork chops. I know what he is thinking. Like I say, his mind works exactly like mine.

My fist connects with the side of his face with an extremely satisfying thunk. He sits down suddenly, holding his jaw. He won't be talking trash to Aisha or to any other woman for a while.

Actually, Ed is a decent guy; I might approve of him for

Aisha someday, if he just holds his horses. But right now things are happening too fast. I need time to sort them all out.

"Sorry to do that to you, Ed. Things were just getting too confusing for me and moving too fast. Can I help you up?"

He merely glares at me. Maybe I broke his jaw; maybe he can't talk. It occurs to me, since Ed and I are so much alike, that maybe Dear Old Dad got around even more than we know. I laugh out loud at the idea. In a perverse way, it makes me proud.

"I might have just done you a favor, Ed," I tell him. "It's a wise child that knows its own father. Do you know yours?"

"Son of a bitch," he mutters, and spits out some blood. No teeth, though. The Saint's luck still holds.

"Well, Ed, you said that, not me. And what I learned today is, you got to check out the bloodlines before you mount a filly and ride. Check 'em out real carefully, Ed, or you might be in for a nasty surprise." I am mostly talking to myself, and I do not entirely recognize this rude, lewd guy who is speaking.

I turn to Aisha. "Hey, our dad must have been some kind of ladies' man, huh? Kind of impressive, don't you think?" I begin to sing softly, "My father was a jockey, and he taught me how to ride . . ."

"I think he was a low, disgusting dog. And I don't like being called a horse. So long, Saint."

I look around for Tug. He has split. Aisha is already headed down the block on her high heels, stopping traffic as efficiently as a light the color of her dress. There is such defiance in that walk, such brittle, vulnerable pride, that it breaks my heart.

I have an hour to go before my volunteer gig, so I head down to the riverfront to catch a breeze and think.

I guess, at one level, I have always known. The bond between us was so much deeper than the usual girl-boy magnetism, I took it for granted that it meant that Aisha was The One. But nothing could explain the many ways in which we were alike, even down to both of us whistling with our mouths slightly open, and both of us breaking our arms when we were eleven—she, skating; me, falling out of a tree—and each of us owning and treasuring a rock collection. I had looked forward to amalgamating those collections.

Well, zap me with some Raid. Destroy me with some d-Con. Spray some Black Flag around and it will all be over for this miserable, dejected black boy, sitting here weakly waving his antennae.

Like I say, the Q-Dogs' rough parties are not my usual type of scene. But hey, they beat sitting around singing the lonesome insect blues.

Chapter 10

CHERRY

IN THE MORNING, Aisha is gone. It is Saturday and the bank where I work is closed, but I have at least six hours of work to do there, getting ready for the auditors, as well as my shopping and my regular household chores. I wash some dishes, make a grocery list, throw some laundry into the trunk of the car and take off. I think about how I would have a dishwasher and a laundry room and maybe a maid if I'd married that dentist. He had bad breath, though—how successful could he be?

I have to work later than I planned. I've been training two new girls—one white, one Pakistani—and both of these minimum-wage marvels, who are being groomed to take over my job, have messed up royally. I have to redo all of their work before I get to my own. Of course, knowing the master plan, having seen it operate at my friends' workplaces, I am not training them very thoroughly. At the first opportunity I will complain that one is stupid and the other uncooperative.

It is almost ten o'clock at night when I get home, after doing laundry and shopping at the all-night market. I open the door rehearsing comforting phrases to say to my child, praying for her recovery, our reconciliation.

The apartment is empty. There are no notes on the magnetic message board on our refrigerator.

I gave up all drugs, including liquor, when they began to compound my problems. I won't go into the gory details—the car wrecks, the embarrassments, the black-outs. I'll just say that it wasn't easy—I needed a *twenty-four*-step program—but I made it. And having seen several of my friends die painfully from the grisly effects of substance abuse, I am deeply grateful.

But tonight, if the Devil had stashed any tranquilizers, pot, or vodka in my house, I would use some. Probably I would use all three. Going out to cop is out of the question, however.

Instead I resort to chamomile tea and three capsules of valerian combined with other sedative herbs, a truly lethal compound created by Sister Fatima at the Wholly Natural Herb Shop.

That and my tape of waves and seagulls finally set me adrift and then send me down to the depths. I go so far under that when the phone rings, I don't know if it is day or night; and while the man is talking to me, I can't under-stand him; and when I try to respond, I can't make sense.

This man who is saying something terrible to me is a soul brother, I can tell that. A fine, mellow brother, judg-ing by his deep voice.

I can feel myself going weak for that voice until I grab the main thread of his remarks and hold on.

They are holding my child at the police station on a charge of—what?

Did he really say "shoplifting"?

Suddenly I am wide-awake, and the man on the phone does not seem so mellow and fine. He is not a brother, but the Man who has put the collar on my child.

The words I use as I splash my face and put a pot of coffee on and brush my teeth and dress in my most respectable summer outfit—a navy A-line dress with a white jabot—and drink two cups of black coffee and fill an emergency thermos with the rest of the pot, are not nice. They include the F-word and the S-word and all of the B-words, interspersed with unkind references to oinking pigs and spoiled brats.

Our police station seems unchanged from my demonstrating days. The same depressing olive-green paint, the same hard benches, the same bored desk sergeant, even the same flies buzzing around the light. Only yesterday, it seems, we were hauled in there after picketing the home of a judge who had sentenced our comrades. But it seemed noble then. Heroic. Even fun. While now . . .

Aisha, it seems, has attempted to boost a small fortune in merchandise from a department store.

The arresting officer shows it to me. He turns out to be a cute young brother with a round baby face he has just begun to shave. Cops turn me off anyway, but these days, all the men with enough authority to be sexy are young enough to be my children, it seems.

In the pile are a diamond tennis bracelet, a gold Swiss watch, a Chanel scarf, a pale leather clutch purse, and a white linen suit. I cover my face with my hands so that strangers will not see my agony. What have I left out of my daughter's raising that makes her crave all these yuppie baubles?

"Bail won't be set until Monday," he says, "but you can see your daughter now."

"You mean she has to spend two nights in this place?"

He nods. "I'm sorry, ma'am. But there will be no judges available to set bail until Monday."

I think, Well, I spent my share of nights in jail; it probably won't hurt Aisha any. Maybe it will even teach her something, though I have always doubted that any useful lessons are learned from incarceration in cold, cramped cells.

When she is brought up from the holding cell by a tough-looking matron who is gripping her elbow, Aisha looks pathetic but defiant. She has on a crinkled rayon dress with a lettuce hem that I've never seen before, in a shade of red that makes me blink. Since she has the bad taste to wear this item, perhaps she stole it, too. I am learning that I hardly know my child.

She gives me a hard stare. "What took you so long, Mother?"

I stifle the urge to slap her again, and give her the hug she needs instead. I feel her shoulders heave, and go pat, pat, pat.

"I just heard," I say. "What are you doing here?"

"I don't know. These people claim I stole some things," she says, her chin uplifted defiantly.

"Well, did you?"

She mumbles something into her sleeve while wiping her eyes, then says, "I don't know why everybody's so upset. I have a job. I can make restitution out of my salary."

My daughter is exactly like me in most respects, including eyes that gush like faucets. My hugging her again really makes the tears pour.

Then I step back. "What job?"

"I haven't had a chance to tell you, Mother. I knew you wouldn't understand, so I thought I'd wait a while and see how it worked out before I told you about it. It's not what you think, it's—"

"How can I think anything if you haven't told me anything?"

"It's a class act, no nudity or anything. I'm dressed, and I'm protected by this glass booth, so nobody can touch me."

"What are you doing while nobody can touch you?"

"Dancing. I'm an exotic dancer at a place called Tequila's."

I am silent, so she throws down a challenge. "At least I'm not sleeping around and trying to get pregnant. I'll never understand how you could do that, Mother. It's disgusting. I'm just earning an honest living—and the pay is a lot better than McDonald's."

I think I hear a snicker from the bulldog-faced police matron who still has a grip on my daughter's elbow. I ask her, "Will you excuse us for a minute, please? We need to have a private conversation."

With about a dozen cops between Aisha and the door, the matron probably figures my daughter isn't going anywhere, so she relents and steps back.

"How much is your salary?" I want to know.

"Ten dollars an hour," she says. "Twelve on weekends."

"Now, Aisha, you and I both know you are not that great a dancer."

"I'm good enough to fool white folks," she counters.

"Granted," I concede. "But how long do you think they will pay you that just to dance?"

"For as long as I show up," she answers. "It's not what you think, Mother, it's a decent place." She glances at the wristwatch I bought her, a pretty little Timex with a lavender face. "I have to be there in two hours."

"Listen, Aisha. Listen good. Even if there were a way for me to bail you out tonight, and there isn't, I wouldn't do it so you could go to a job like that. I'm going to let you sit in here all weekend and cool your heels and think about the direction you want your life to take. And you'd better think of a way to turn it around, because right now it's going straight downhill."

"Fine," she says coldly. "Everything I was living for has been taken away from me, and it's your fault, and you tell me to turn my life around."

"Yes, and I'm sorry, baby, I know it hurts, but it really isn't anybody's fault, and you have to go on. I know you took those things because you were angry, but you haven't hurt anyone but yourself."

"Okay," she says. "If that's how it is, okay. Fine. Will you bring me some clean underwear?" Her false bravado is so heart-piercing, I want to run to the Man and tell him to let her go and lock me up in her place.

"Sure. You want some clothes, too?"

"No. They've got a cute outfit for me downstairs in the newest shade of Day-Glo orange."

I don't get it, so she explains, "A prison uniform." She

hands me a greasy card with a number and the name Joe Vespe scrawled on it. "Will you call this guy and tell him I can't come to work tonight? Mother, please make up some good excuse like a high fever."

I don't want to do what she asks, but the bulldog is heading our way, so I whisper, "Okay. I'll bring your things tomorrow."

After I leave, I don't call Tequila's—I go there.

Chapter 11

PATRICE

I T's A BIT LATE, as I told Cherry, for either of us to be wishing for security. What we don't have, we are not likely to get.

Still, her depressing review of her financial situation forced me to consider mine.

All my worldly goods are spread out around me on my bed. Assets: a $10,000 life insurance policy (Saint's has lapsed; forced to choose last spring, I was logical for once and kept my own); a deed to an acre of land in Buck Swamp, Georgia; another deed to a duplex cemetery lot (sell it? plan on cremation?) and $350 in a savings account.

I can't believe that this is all I have to show for a life-time of work and struggle. Plus Saint, of course, but he can't be assigned a monetary value.

Liabilities, long-term: personal bank loan, balance $8,200; revolving Sears charge (my kitchen), balance $3,500; Computerland account (my computer), balance $1,400;

JCPenney (linens, dishes, etc.), $400; and a Master Charge balance of $3,200. Whoever called it Massa Charge was sho nuff right.

Also current liabilities: rent, $650; Power and Light, $180; dentist, $100 a month on a balance of $800; distilled water deliveries, $112; chiropractor, $50 a week; telephone, $40; cable TV, $65.

How am I ever going to get out from under these debts, let alone begin to save something for my old age? Cut your expenses, the experts say. But there is nothing left to cut. I have not had a beauty appointment in a year.

I look it.

I have not seen the podiatrist since March, and all new shoes purchased around here are for Saint.

My feet hurt.

All right, cut out the chiropractor, too. Maybe my back pain will make me forget my foot pain.

Cut the cable TV, too, though it's cheaper than going out for entertainment. Thank God I'm a member of the last generation that reads for pleasure, and books are free at the library.

Circulate a letter to see whether someone in the family wants to buy my Georgia land? No, they all have their own, which some of them, poor fools, have tried to sell to me. Besides, I can always throw a trailer up on it and move in when this city becomes unlivable or the rent goes up again.

Can you imagine? Me??? In the country??? No way.

Tenants' insurance, grace period almost elapsed, $240; on-line computer connection, three months, $63; Dr. Moody, gynecologist, $75.

I am not willing to give up the Internet now that I have

just figured out how to get onto it. I may have to let the insurance go. I reach for the phone, then put it down. I have a persuasive voice I call my "sweet" voice, but there is no point in calling creditors and making promises unless I have some means of keeping them.

Moody can wait. I am suspicious of the free hormones he gives me, and the mammogram which I would need if I took them is something I can't pay for.

I have not heard from Toni Brookins since our conversation. Now, that might be a more productive line of inquiry. That brochure she mentioned, plus a release or two for Brad Hall, with a check or two to follow . . .

Nah. My nosiness about Gene really pushed her buttons. She's going to need at least a week to get over her mad.

Without knowing how I have gotten here, I am standing in front of my refrigerator, mentally assembling the ingredients for pasta primavera: red peppers, scallions, spinach . . .

I check my olive oil supply: good. And there is a box of rotini on the second cupboard shelf.

My Parental Voice asks, "Patrice, how is cooking going to improve your situation?"

My Inner Child answers: "It will make me feel good, It will make me feel that I am abundantly provided for and that I have wealth to share with others."

My Parental Voice says, "Patrice, somewhere between the little girl and your fantasy of being Everybody's Earth Mother is an adult woman. I want you to fake being her until you make it. Proceed directly to the computer and work on your cookbook."

Oh, all right. My cookbook, tentatively called *Cooking with PatRICE*, has been overdue at the publishers for about a year. I spent the initial advance as soon as I got it. I won't get another chunk—well, crumb—until I turn in the completed manuscript. The amount I will get then is so insulting I won't reproduce it here.

My Parental Voice, which is sounding more and more like my father's, says, "Never be insulted by money."

Oh, all right.

But I hate the limitation imposed by the title. It once seemed cute, but now I am bored with rice in all its combinations and permutations. I want to deal with pasta, potatoes, salads . . .

Yes, I know. I signed a contract.

I scroll through the thirty pages I've done so far, past rice puddings, rice cakes, pilafs, and the chapter on "Wild Rice and Other Exotica." Maybe I can sneak in couscous, kasha, and other grains there. I make a note.

It's time to do the boring chapter on "Basic Rice," the technique for which eludes so many people. I advise eschewing the Instant and Quick varieties, which are for lazy dolts, and tell my readers to roll up their sleeves and go for the real thing. The trick is cracking the lid about a quarter of an inch while simmering the rice, to let the steam escape.

I then decide to crank out a page or two on Uses for Leftover Rice. Fried Rice: ransack your refrigerator and cut whatever you find into small cubes. Pork (especially ham), a scrambled or hard-boiled egg, chicken, carrots, bits of bell pepper in as many colors as you can find, onions or scallions, pineapple, and peaches are all good.

Heat a tablespoonful of oil in a skillet, then stir-fry rice and leftovers, adding teriyaki sauce to taste.

I think most of my recipes are obvious, but then, it's surprising what most people don't know. I reflect for a minute, then add after "skillet": "(Oil is hot when a drop of water flicked into it sizzles)" because what is obvious to me may not be obvious to others.

I am painfully reminded of my first advertising job, for which one of my duties was to write a weekly recipe column for Miss Mary Mayfield's Mayonnaise. I had to invent these rancid little horrors and let them fly without a test run, because there was never enough time to take the recipes home and test them, and the ad agency where I worked had no kitchen.

When I protested, my boss said, "Look, mayonnaise has no taste. You can put mayonnaise in anything and it won't hurt. Just take your favorite recipes and add some mayonnaise. No one will know the difference."

My integrity and my sense of culinary aesthetics were both offended, but I followed orders. All I could do was pray that no one would try my recipes, and add a coda to my prayers hoping that if they did, they would not get sick.

I still have nightmares about going to the funerals of people who ate my concoctions and died.

I think that the Four M principle might work for my cookbook, though. Write out all of my favorite recipes—cassoulet, fish-head stew, Brunswick stew, whatever—and then say "Add rice" or "Serve over rice." I'd do it if I were lazier or more desperate. Maybe I'll just change the title instead.

Well, at least I've written two pages on rice today. I stretch, and my Sunday caftan, bright gold with embroidered sunflowers, rips under both arms.

I am suddenly disgusted with myself. All this concentration on food has a down side. I resolve to go on a diet—though dieting, when you think about it, is just another way of focusing on food. And writing about food is not the same as eating it, of course. Writing adds no calories. Burns none, either, which is another reason why I'm so big.

I give myself permission to open a new file and begin playing around with another project.

I write, in 18-point Helvetica type:

WANTED

I add three bang marks:

WANTED!!!

That should command attention.

WANTED!!!
Information on the Whereabouts of
Eugene Dessalines Green
Writer · College Teacher
· Black male, age 55, about 6 feet tall.
· Last known residence: Atlanta, Ga.
· Wears elegant, eccentric clothing and patchouli
 cologne. Smokes a briar pipe.
· Frequents little theaters, college campuses, other arty
 venues.
· A cultivated speaker. Quotes poetry.

· Fluent in French. Visits Haiti often.

REWARD!!!

Especially interested in contacting women who knew
Green between 1960 and 1980.

GENEOLOGICAL RESEARCH

I debate whether to say "knew Green" or "were intimate
with Green," and finally settle for "knew Green intimately."

I don't have any money for a reward, but then, I did not
specify what the reward would be. It might just be a
feeling of relief.

I figure that people who notice the odd spelling of
"geneological" might get my meaning and purpose—
while those who don't, won't.

I put my address and phone and fax numbers at the
bottom of my flyer. This should get some results. All I
need is for just one of the right people to read it—just one.
Word of mouth will do the rest.

Chapter 12

SAINT

At the soup kitchen, I keep waiting for my little friend Lamar to show up. But he doesn't. It's Saturday night, the second of the month, right after check day, so probably not many people are hungry. There are no children at all to benefit from my fine culinary skills. No ladies, either. Only a couple dozen very old people with about five teeth among them, hawking and spitting in their bowls of my heavenly five-bean soup. They look terrible and smell worse. Most of them eat, then go immediately to sleep.

One old guy who is wearing corduroy pants and using a cane hobbles through the chow line. His glasses are thick and almost opaque with dirty smears.

As I hand him his soup, he wipes his runny nose on his sleeve. I'm not sure, but it looks to me like some of his snot flies off and lands in his soup, which is a delicate blend of leeks, dill, and pinto, kidney, lima, black, and white navy beans. This sets me off. I can't help it.

"That was the most disgusting thing I've ever seen," I tell him. "Spitting and coughing, eating and excreting—that's all that's left of your life. Why do people like you want to go on living?"

"Son," he replies in a surprisingly cultivated voice, "you don't know what my life is like. You can't possibly know."

We're supposed to be polite and respectful to the people we serve at all times, and usually I take pride in setting an example. I can't believe that those horrible words came out of my mouth.

Immediately I am all over the old guy with apologies and helpfulness, carrying his tray to his table, bringing him extra juice and napkins, but it is too late. The other volunteers, including this little white high school girl named Mary who always hangs around me like a worshiper at my altar, have heard.

I turn on Mary, who is standing there with her mouth open, her eyes like twin blue lakes.

"What are you staring at? You waiting for me to do you? Well, come on, then, come on." And I make an obscene gesture with my index finger against my palm.

Poor little Mary, who is barely sixteen, lets out a wail and runs screaming toward the ladies' room, dabbing her eyes with her apron. I guess I just proved what whites believe, that we're all dangerous rapists.

I take off my own apron and slam it down on the freezer behind the counter. It's time to make tracks.

As I head for the door I pass the well-spoken old guy, who says, "If it's a woman who has upset you so, forget her, son. There are as many available women out there as there are pigeons in Venice."

"How would you know? None of them would want you," I tell him, though I can't help being impressed by his cultivated manner of speaking. He looks like a bum, but he sounds like one of my professors.

"Ah," he says, "but there you are wrong. All I need is a little more attention to grooming. Would you have any spare change on you for some soap and a razor?"

I give the old dude some change to help him clean up his act, and leave. I need some exercise to work off my anger, so I head for the court, but no one's there. Ed and Tug must be home getting clean for the party. I settle for a run to the river, ten blocks, and another run along the length of the waterfront promenade, about a mile.

By the end of this workout I'm pretty steamy. I could definitely use a shower and a change. Normally I'm quite fastidious about my hygiene, especially when I plan to be around some ladies. But tonight I don't care. I don't want to go home yet. I think about my destination, and figure a little funk is appropriate.

The Q's, the members of Omega Psi Phi Fraternity, call themselves Dogs, meaning all that the word implies. They will bark at the slightest encouragement. They profess to believe in exploiting women, not respecting them.

Quite naturally, the women who hang out with the Q-Dogs are referred to by the term that denotes female canines. They do their best to live up to the designation, too.

I am in a mood to get down and dirty tonight. Being already dirty, I am halfway there.

If I were blind, I could still find the Doghouse. I can hear the party from two blocks away. Their neighbors have taken them to court about the noise more than once, but the judge is usually a frat brother who lets them off.

Somebody's bass is laying down the jungle rhythm, a heavy thump. A saxophone is giving the call, and live girls are producing high-pitched wails in response. Just let me in there.

I drop five dollars in an upturned black and gold hat—how do you think the Q's maintain their clubhouse, white corporate sponsorship?—and push past the gorillas at the door who are there to discourage freeloaders. The funk inside is so thick you could cut it up and serve it like cheesecake. In heat so intense it feels like a blast furnace, a hundred gyrating spandex-skinned rumps are doing the Butt, the Bump, and variations thereof. I hang back. I stay cool. Then I spot her over in a corner.

She looks like Bat Woman or Cat Woman or one of those death-dealing fantasy women from the seventies blaxploitation flicks: Pam Grier, Tamara Dobson, Coffy. At college we kick back and watch them on Black Culture nights. They're all great, but my favorite was the one who snatched helicopters out of the air one-handed in an otherwise dreadful Gary Coleman movie, *On the Right Track*.

Well, this woman is definitely of that supermama genre, approaching but not quite reaching the awesomeness of Grace Jones. She is at least six feet tall. About four feet of that consists of fabulous crossed legs, fully displayed by a slit and parted skirt. Her dress, which is black satin, is also slit down to the waist to reveal less than awesome cleavage, but what the hell? I'm a leg man, basically, and besides, this woman is a stone freak. Her teeth are bared like fangs—can you believe it? As I approach, she snarls.

Just what I need. A black panther, lowercase. Instead of asking her to dance, I grab her hand, a claw with purple talons, and pull her to her feet. She rises lightly—on heels, she's as tall as I am—and there I am, with a panther in my arms. She is wearing some kind of heavy musk oil that I find intoxicating tonight, though I am sure that at another time it would nauseate me. The way she sucks on my neck as we slide around the floor drives me mad.

This witch is not really interested in dancing, and something tells me she is not much on conversation, either. Neither am I, tonight. What is there to talk about? In less than ten minutes we are out of there.

Chapter 13

PATRICE

I DECIDE THAT I NEED some photos of Gene to complete my flyer. Even though he must have aged, his features haven't changed, and someone might recognize him.

My old photo and clip art files are in the front room. As I pass my son's door, I notice that it is closed, and remember that I didn't hear him come in last night. I guess he's still asleep. Young people require a lot of rest. In my chest there's a little flutter of anxiety because I haven't officially broken the news. It's my guess that Aisha already told him, though. Those two haven't spent a Saturday night apart in a year, except when he was away at school.

On top of the pile in the file box labeled PHOTOS: 1965–1975 is a full-length portrait of Gene. He is straddling a chair, his arms folded on its back, and manages to look as if he is about to leap onto the back of a horse. He is wearing riding breeches and a dark turtleneck; a riding crop dangles from one hand. I doubt if Gene ever came within three feet of a horse. Everything about this photo screams "Posed! Phony!" and yet it has enormous power. His eyebrows are crooked and expressive; his slanted eyes, looking up toward his brows or the cameraperson, are magnetic, compelling, lit from within. He looks like a hypnotist. Perhaps he was one. I have come for something else, but it is several minutes before this picture will let me go. Finally I turn it over and find the two mug shots I need, one full face and one profile, to put under the

WANTED!!!

If I had the money, I would run my creation as an ad in *Ebony*, *Essence*, the Atlanta *Constitution*, and the black paper down there, the Atlanta *Daily World*. But I don't have the money, so I will have to settle for a flyer we will post here ourselves and send to some friends in Atlanta to distribute.

On my way back from the living room, old snapshots in hand, I have a close encounter of whatever kind it is when you find an alien in your house.

This alien is about six feet tall and is wearing leopard-print bikini panties, a matching bra, and very little else. She is attempting, I figure out later, to sneak from my son's room to the bathroom.

At the moment, though, I don't have time to think. I merely scream.

So does she. Everything about her is long—her legs, her face, her hair, her scream. Her teeth, I notice, are huge. So are her bare feet. She is an Amazon. Or a Tutsi woman, but they're not ugly, and she is. She whirls, tossing a two-foot hair weave in my face, and attempts to run back into Saint's room.

I bar the way and yell my son's name several times.

Finally, his head pokes around the doorjamb. His features have changed overnight from a youth's to a faun's—his ears are pointed, his eyebrows arched, his sleepy eyes slanted. Something secretive and mean has subverted his usual bland, benign look.

He knows.

"Now, Ma, don't go getting hysterical. There's a perfectly reasonable—"

"Saint, how many times have I told you that the landlord doesn't allow pets in here? I put up with your turtle and your snake, but this one is much too big to hide, and besides, it doesn't look housebroken. Oops—I was right. It isn't."

The dripping Amazon is jumping up and down and wailing. "Are you just going to stand there and let this woman call me an animal?" she demands.

"I could call you worse things," I say, almost amiably. "I could call you what you are, for instance. My, what a lot of fur you have down there. Is that a weave, too?"

The creature hisses and spits.

My son pulls her inside his room and closes the door.

"Five minutes!" I yell. "You have five minutes to clear out of my house."

I stomp back to my bedroom, hearing a high voice screeching and a low one rising in volume and drowning it out.

I flop on my bed and push my face into my pillow to muffle the noises I am making. I am not crying this time, though. I am laughing.

Five minutes later I hear doors slam.

I laugh out loud. Then I call Cherry.

Chapter 14

CHERRY

Casinos were always my idea of perfect Hell—all that noise and flash, all those poor addicted people gambling away their savings—but Tequila's will do. It is dark and stinks of beer. A lighted Plexiglas cylinder sits on a platform above and to the right of the bar. Some other mother's poor child is caged up there, gyrating lewdly to loud music.

When my eyes adjust to the darkness, I can see clumps of men sitting around the bar, smoking and laughing. They are all white. Mostly mean-looking. But they don't scare me as much as the solitary ones scattered at tables here and there, their eyes glued desperately on the dancer. Her pelvic thrusts are a bit too graphic. So, too, are the memories triggered by the liquor smells assailing my nostrils. They flood me with terror. Maybe that's Joe behind the bar, pouring gin from a Seagram's bottle, maybe not. I don't hang around to find out. I race home.

I have to call a bail bondsman. The bondsman says that I can expect Aisha's bail to run from ten to thirty thousand dollars. That means one to three G's in cash to ransom my child. Somehow I have to lay my hands on it over the weekend.

Sometimes I am very grateful to have Patrice for a best friend. For someone who leads a crazy life—no husband, no steady job—she can be very sensible. Her approach to life is "Don't cry over spilt milk—just mop it up and forget it." That's so practical, it's better than sympathy.

When I'm telling her on the phone about Aisha's latest escapades, that is her reaction. I'd rather have sympathy, though.

"Don't worry," she says. "We got through colic, teething, and the week the snow was so bad the diaper service stopped. We'll get through this."

"How?"

"Look, we have to expect both our kids to let off steam. Last night Saint brought an ugly she-bear here and kept her overnight. I understand why he did it, and I'm almost glad. But he knows that is something I won't put up with, so he didn't complain when I put her out this morning. He also understands that if he does it again, he'll be out on the street."

Patrice seems like one of her chocolate brownies, all soft and sweet and nourishing—but underneath is hard, cold rock. "You wouldn't," I say, but I know she would.

"Oh, yes, I would," she says. "And it wouldn't be a game to teach Saint a lesson, like I played six or seven years ago. It would be serious, because my son's a man, and Mama's got to be about her own survival now. Come on over here, girl. Let me give you some lessons on survival for parents of adult children."

It sounds like a new twelve-step support group: Parents of Adult Children. If there's anything I'm enthusiastic about, it's support groups. But one of our mottoes in the program is First Things First, and I have to raise at least a thousand dollars by Monday.

"I don't have time," I say. "I have to get the bail money together." Even I can hear the edge in my voice, so I'm not surprised by Patrice's response.

"You have to get yourself together, too, Cherry. We'll work on the bail money. I can let you have three hundred and fifty for starters. Bring your phone book. We'll call people."

I say a prayer, crank up Sapphire, and thank my Higher Power for letting her start one more time.

When I get to Patrice's, she is spreading out some beautiful Indian and African yard goods on her futon sofa. "This blue stripe and this green design would both look good on you—you have lots of copper in your skin. Which do you like best?"

"Oh, I don't care," I say.

"Pick one," she insists.

"Either one," I say. "Patrice, we have more important things to talk about."

She is maddeningly dense. "Like what?"

"Like, how am I going to get Aisha out of jail?"

"I already called my dentist. He'll let us have two hundred. So will my gynecologist, even though I owe him.

With my three fifty, we've already raised seven fifty. Did you bring your phone book?"

Humbled and grateful, I take it out of my giant Guatemalan sack.

"Look up your dentist and your doctor, and anybody else you know who might hold a wad of cash. We'll call them in a minute." Humming, she drapes the green cloth around me. "I like this one best on you. I'm sick of green, anyway. Interpret that any way you want. It's yours. Let me put some henna on your hair. That gray is really dragging me, girl."

Impatiently, I wave the phone book under her nose.

Three more calls, to my dentist, to my doctor, and to a lawyer I know who used to work for the Movement and is now a judge, and we have fifteen hundred. The tension drains out of me as if somebody has pulled a plug.

Getting my hair washed feels kind of good, even though it is in Patrice's kitchen sink, and even though she tends to be rough, shoving and punching the head she's working on to put it in a convenient position.

When she shows me the results in the mirror, I see reddish glints where the gray was. I am pleased, but puzzled. "What's this for, anyway?"

"To make you feel better. Feeling good attracts good things into your life, including men."

"I haven't thought about men in ages."

"Then it's time you did. You're not exactly a senior citizen, you know. Besides, the seniors I know all have active love lives."

All this is a totally strange way of thinking for me. I

haven't thought of myself as a woman for years. I am a mother and a wage-earner, period; a worrier and a drudge. I am not ready to be anything else. I wouldn't even know how to have a life of my own. "Did I tell you that Aisha is working as a go-go dancer?"

"Yes," she says. "What will you do with the green print? There's enough there for a dress or some pants, but not enough for a pantsuit."

"After I saw her last night, I went to the club where she works. Patrice, it's awful—a sort of an underground cave, like Hades. The tobacco and beer stench just hangs around in a cloud. The patrons all look like Kluxers."

"Actually," she murmurs, "I think you could get a pantsuit out of this, you're so disgustingly tiny. Still a size 12?"

"Patrice, I have other things on my mind besides clothes. Saint's sleeping with floozies, Aisha's sitting in jail, and you want me to pick out a dress pattern."

"They're not kids, Cherry," she says.

"Patrice!" I yell. "My daughter's in terrible trouble, and you act like you aren't even interested."

"Cherry," she says softly, "you've got to let her go."

I manage a smile. "Even let her go-go?"

She smiles, too. "Yes."

I think about it. "I don't think I know how to do that, Patrice," I say slowly. "How can you be so indifferent?"

"What do you expect me to do?" she asks.

"React, dammit! Act like you care."

"I care. But I can't change anything. They're grown." She does look helpless. And, suddenly, old, with sagging shoulders and serious nose-to-mouth lines.

An impish impulse seizes me. I want to see Patrice

laugh. "The girl Saint brought home, was she really ugly?"

"Girl," she says, rolling her eyes a full circle. "That child was *ruint*! Looked like Eddie Murphy in his Buckwheat wig. To give my son credit, he met her in the dark. I know he wouldn't have brought that bow-wow home if he'd had a good look at her in the light. I just know I raised him to have better taste."

I am coughing with laughter. "Girl. Stop it before I choke. I still want to know, what are we going to do about our kids?"

"Wrong question," she informs me. "It's 'What are we going to do about ourselves?' "

My silence and, probably, my face reflect my bewilderment.

"Look," she says, "our kids are raised. A lot of folks might not agree with me, but I think the cut-off age is fourteen. If you haven't built values into them by then, it's too late to start."

"But they're screwing up because we screwed up!" I am shouting.

"Cherry, Cherry. So what? If we died tonight, if we went for a ride in that bomb of yours and it finally blew up, do you think our kids would recover and go on to lead good lives?"

I give this some consideration. "Probably," I finally admit.

"Then we didn't screw up," she concludes smugly.

"I said 'probably.' I can't be sure. Aisha is pretty fragile right now, and I've always thought Saint was too good to be true."

"Me, too," she says, surprising me. "I'm kind of glad to see him sowing some oats."

I am angry. "There's the double standard. Boys sow oats. Girls ruin their lives."

"Sure, there's a double standard. We can't change that, either. I still think we've raised some pretty good kids. They're hurting right now, but they'll recover. The question is, are we going to be a pair of obnoxious, interfering old biddies, hovering around where we're not wanted or needed, or are we going to find something else to do?"

I know she is right, but what she's saying is so terrible I want to cry. The truth is, I don't know how to live without making my daughter the center of my life. She's been that for as long as I can remember. "What else is there?" I ask.

"I may have just the thing right here," she murmurs. She turns on her computer and prints a page.

I look at it. A face from the past stares up at me from the middle of a "Wanted" poster. I forget my depression and burst out laughing.

"So ol' Gene has finally landed where he belongs. In the rogues' gallery."

"You like it?" Patrice asks.

"I love it," I tell her. "You always were the most creative one in the crowd. But what's it for?" I look at the picture, imagine a row of numbers under the face, and smile again. I feel my tension easing up, a lovely loose feeling replacing it. Maybe it's the laughter, or the henna in my hair, or the good smell of the cream rinse conditioner Patrice uses. Maybe it's the fragrance of the chamomile tea we're sipping, or its effect, but I feel a sudden lightness and ease.

Patrice is reclining on her red futon in a sky-blue striped caftan, arms behind her head, looking like a Matisse odalisque. Maybe she's feeling the same way I am.

"I have some ganja," she says suddenly. "Want some?"

"No, but feel free to indulge." Patrice turns on the seventies station and gets something mellow. She comes back with a joint, which she lights. She says, in that high, squeezed voice that comes from holding in smoke, "I think we ought to try to find them."

"Who?"

"Saint's and Aisha's brothers and sisters."

She has said this once before, but then she referred to the objects of her quest as Gene Green's other children, not our children's brothers and sisters. Somehow, that idea never sank in. I am upset.

"I thought we were going to become selfish in our old age. I just had about thirty minutes of selfishness, and I was beginning to enjoy it. Why do we have to track down some more kids?"

"To be responsible, not like white folks with all that crazy sperm banking and blind adopting and surrogacy." She continues counting off her reasons on fingers which, I note, are newly tipped with gold nails. "To keep more romantic accidents from happening. To develop a data bank of names, addresses, medical histories, and blood types. To give our kids a family to lean on, even after we're gone. *And* to give ourselves a project to absorb us and stop us from worrying."

She has really given this a lot of thought. Her arguments are well-organized and persuasive. And just when I
was getting lazy and self-indulgent, and thinking about
doing my nails for the first time in months. "Uh-huh. You
talk a tough game, girl, but inside you're nothing but
melted marshmallow, and you're still being Mommy. Got
any more of that gold enamel?"

"Sure."

It's gorgeous stuff, looks like real gold leaf. It won't do
at the bank, though. Regretfully, I put it aside. "Nope. I'm
a working woman. Got any clear?"

She goes into her room for some transparent polish and
comes back with it, saying, "Only thing is, this could cost
googobs of money. I figured out an ad budget just using
local papers in towns where he's been. We'd need at least
four thousand bucks for decent-size ads."

"Don't look at me. You know I don't have any
money." I wave my hand in the air to dry it. It doesn't
look like an old-lady hand. "Groovin'" by the Rascals
comes over the radio. I think of fried chicken, deviled
eggs, red Kool-Aid, vivid clothes. That green stuff she's
giving me in a short set, with a head wrap thrown in. With
it, white sandals and a pair of big white hoops in my ears.

"Remember the fund-raisers we used to throw for Snick
bail money?" I ask.

"Yeah," Patrice says dreamily, working on her roach
with the help of a safety pin. "We had some fine musicians. Al Handy and his Handymen. Lord, that man got to
me. I wanted to be his bass, the way he wrapped his arms
around it."

Someone is singing "Midnight Blue": "And I think we can make it one more time . . ." I am inspired.

"We worked our buns off, Patrice, but we used to rake in the receipts, remember? Listen, they won't return my deposit on the hall for the wedding reception, so why don't we use it to hold a fund-raiser?"

Now, what did I want to go and say that for? Suddenly, it seems, I have nothing but time. I can't pick up my loans till late tomorrow, after the good folks who have restored my faith in community get home from church. There is no one at home, and I don't want to think about why that is so. So I might as well stay at Patrice's.

We are up all night, working hard, making plans.

Chapter 15

GENE

Something, I don't know what, has possessed me. Call it a demon. Call it pride. But, finding myself for the first time in many days with enough coins to purchase a supply of shooting sherry, I find myself stopping instead at the neighborhood Rite Aid for shaving gear and deodorant. This is most unlike me.

What is it about that young man at the feeding site that gives him the power to move and shame me? *Je ne sais quoi.* He seems a bit brighter than my students at Gloaming Junior College; a bit quicker, perhaps. The greater stimulus afforded by urban living might account for that; there is, as I have long noted, very little to stimulate the intellect in Gloaming or in the surrounding hills of West Virginia. Church services, ham and oyster suppers, patriotic parades, Bingo games, and a very low median IQ, not helped by inbreeding, are the basic features of life in our little valley. I amuse myself by observing the local cretins, and by readying a volume of verse about them, to be called *Gargoyles*.

When the fog that sometimes clouds my vision lifts, I observe that this boy is taller and better looking than average. There is something impressive about the way he carries himself, too—a regal quality—the bearing of the unrecognized prince, or at least the kingly common. But none of that explains why his rebuke could sting me so and send me scurrying into this overly bright place whose fluorescence hurts my eyes, instead of the dim, welcoming cave of Buddy's Bar & Grill.

Rite Aid: a most curious name for a chain of stores offering pharmaceuticals and personal care items. It communicates absolutely nothing. What could the founders have been thinking of? They should have hired a poet to create a suitable name. Well-Way? Health-Ease? Fit-Aid? Those are not ideal, but they are improvements.

I despair, however, of this so-called civilization's ever appreciating the utilitarian value of poetry.

If poets were seen as useful, not only would stores have apposite names, streets would have sonorous appellations, and odes would be available for every state occasion. We have a Poet Laureate, but does she compose elegies for presidential funerals? No. Instead, when a President dies tragically, half the streets, schools, and hospitals in America are named for him, creating mass confusion. There are three John F. Kennedy hospitals in the quadrant of the city in which I live, as well as two Kennedy Avenues and one Kennedy Boulevard. This makes the giving of directions well-nigh impossible, and could have dire consequences when summoning a rescue wagon, which I sometimes feel I might need, especially late at night. The only thing sillier, which I noticed while teaching at Morehouse, was Atlanta's proliferation of Peachtrees in a city where none grow. Folks are so silly down there. . . . Alas, Morehouse. A disaster, simply because I was not used to bourbon.

Yes, useful work for poets abounds, but no one is hiring. I am in my usual summer slump, my savings gone, my last royalty check for *Drumfires*, received in June, a mere fourteen dollars and twenty-two cents. I almost tore it up and sent it back to my cretinous publishers, but common sense prevailed. Fourteen dollars bought a lot of fried chicken and several sips of sherry at my convivial neighborhood café. Now my tab there is so high they won't serve me. I should have arranged to have good old GJC pay me twelve months a year.

I will do so in the fall without fail, if my annual contract is renewed. I have enemies—Marsha Glick, who thinks every course should have a female component; Joe Suarez, who thinks Hispanics should be in charge of the multicultural curriculum; and of course that pompous little Oreo, Fred Purdy, who wants to be the driver on our little plantation, and therefore in charge of me, the only other black member of the faculty.

I am not worried. Though the pathetic little egos of my colleagues need their silly little power games, my student evaluations are superb, and I have two respectable volumes of verse. What, after all, have Glick, Suarez, and Purdy published? They are just jealous because they never dreamed up a course like my "Literature of Depression," which is a natural for Gloaming, where the sun never shines. Céline, Kafka, Poe, Nathanael West, Dostoevsky—the students adore it. This time I think I'll team-teach it with someone from Psychology.

Perhaps I will augment my course in "Writing About Depression" with that literary magazine for which the students keep clamoring. I will call it *Nadir*. A clever move. Students at Gloaming are too depressed to produce more than one issue a year. If the new chairperson, who is unfortunately rumored to be Glick, will allow me to drop one or two of my other courses in order to edit *Nadir*, I may at last have time for my own work.

In the meantime, maybe I can drum up some book reviews, and sell some of my review copies. With one of those new lighted magnifiers, I should be able to speed-read again.

Then, too, I have received word that one of my angels is strategically placed in a bank. A loan to tide me over the summer would be just the thing.

Memories of my angels help me to survive the long, bleak winters at Gloaming. Toni, Cheryl, Patrice, Esther—at odd moments I imagine this one's lips, that one's breasts, the other's smooth thighs. Nightly I sleep with a woman who is a composite of all of them.

In the days, I permit myself a bit of voyeurism, an occasional surreptitious glance at the dimpled knees and bountifully filled sweaters on the front row in my Harlem Renaissance class. There is a teaching assistant in Romance Languages who wears tight sweaters and a knowing, provocative smile. There is a goddess in the Music Department who strides along with her violin case, tossing her curls, her bosoms sliding around in the V neck of her shirt. Like all goddesses, she is haughty and unapproachable. One of the English Department secretaries has eyelashes that sweep her cheeks. From beneath them she gives me sly looks, but she is married. The campus is, of course, full of delectably rounded bottoms in jeans and, on our few warm days, magnificent legs in cutoffs. But to dare more than a glance at them is risky. A biology professor has been suspended for dating an older student—a woman in her twenties. I spend my nights alone with my fantasies.

All of my angels wanted to have my child, as I recall. Sometimes I wonder whether any of them actually did. Ah, those sixties. Mad, bold, marvelous years. Rowena, Wanda, Alberta, Jean—I have been faithful to all of thee in my fashion.

I do not know my way around this store. Seeking guidance, I address a looming, genderless hulk.

"My friend, can you direct me to the personal hygiene products?"

My request is met by stony silence. Not long ago, I recall to my embarrassment, I questioned a mannequin, but surely there are none in drugstores. No, the case here is clearly that Gloaming has no monopoly on imbecility. Rephrase, Eugene. "Razors, shaving cream?"

"Yer lookin' right at 'em."

I close my fingers around an object and ask craftily, "Would you recommend this one?"

"Fer broads, maybe. That's a Lady Shaver."

The object, before I drop it, does appear to be pink. "Oops. I was looking for a men's Gillette."

"Disposable or regular?"

"Regular, I think."

It is thrust into my hand. "Here y'are. Blades included. I think Wilkinson's are better, though."

"These will do just fine. And shaving cream?"

"On your left. Top shelf."

I pat and paw my way along the shelves until a can is handed to me. "Here. Don't they give out white canes to people like you?"

I resist the urge to tell him what his mother does for anyone and how little she charges. "My friend, if you can tell me where they are giving out anything to anyone, I will gladly go there. Where do I pay?"

An iron grip on my elbow turns me and shoves me toward the cashier.

Six taps to the corner, a right turn, two blocks, and I am home, with only one cacophony of screeching brakes and curses.

My arrival at my boardinghouse is well-timed. My landlady, who waylays me almost daily in the hope of extracting back rent, is setting out to walk her dog, Nemo. I hear it yipping down the block until its cries grow faint in the distance. This ridiculous animal, a sort of bull terrier, has neither beauty nor ferocity to recommend it. It has by turns attempted to befriend me and to attack me. As she turns the far corner with her ugly beast, I round the near corner and nip up the stairs. Safe.

First, a bath, ignoring the disgusting detritus left by the other roomers who share this facility. Taking a shower is no easy feat. I try to hold onto the towel bar at all times, if only by curling a pinky around it, but it is hard to accomplish all of my ablutions with one hand. Soaping and rinsing my back, for instance, requires two. I do that with first one side and then the other leaning against the tiles to brace me. The biggest danger is dropping the soap, which I do, of course. I imagine that this happens to everyone now and then when their eyes are full of shampoo, but mine are full of—what? The mist of regret? The fog of failure? Whatever it is, it grows daily more opaque, like milk.

I peer in the mirror, pushing my face close to view my cloudy image. Not bad; in fact, almost presentable. My hair is gray and unkempt, but at least I have hair, and a tight stocking cap will compress it and conceal my need for a haircut. My mustache merely needs trimming; my cheeks, shaving. Watch that unsteady hand, Prince Eugene. If only I had a tot of sherry to steady it. But I have unaccountably spent my money on hygiene.

I continue my personal inventory. My legs often refuse to support me, hence the cane which ages my appearance. If it were ebony and ivory, or carved teak, it would seem an elegant affectation, not a necessity. Tomorrow I will scour the local antique shops and flea markets.

By some miracle my teeth remain. I scrub them. The pouches under my eyes might benefit from a good night's sleep. A little effort, and I will roll back the ravages of more than half a century.

Next, clean garments. The outlook gets brighter and brighter. My khaki Dockers are clean, and so is my white cotton band-collar shirt. I will toss these old K mart cords—pungent, unpleasant reminders of lost self-control. I do regret the disappearance of my panama straw on that recent unfortunate evening when Buddy went temporarily insane and had me forcibly removed from his premises. Ah, well, two more months and I can resume wearing my beret. I have forgiven Buddy, but I think I will find a more civilized place to drink hereafter, and restrict myself to two sherries a night, after six P.M. Then early to bed, and early to rise and write.

Half an ounce of patchouli remains—more good fortune.

I have tarried in the hinterland for so long that my courting skills may be rusty. It might be a good idea to practice on my landlady first, before approaching my angel. The poor dear appears to be lonely except for that miserable hound. If I am successful, he will spend the rest of the summer in her yard, while I remain here rent-free.

How good it is to be clean and sober, and to be making plans!

I am still confounded, though, by why I care what that youth thinks, and why his words had such a powerful reformative effect on me.

Chapter 16

AISHA

I AM SO EMBARRASSED IN COURT, I want to die. I am wearing Mother's boring navy dress that I asked her to bring me so I could look demure, and she shows up looking like she is going to a party, not a hearing. She has on a fluorescent lime-green thing with a short skirt, harlequin sunglasses with purple frames, and a pair of bright parrot earrings. Her hair is hennaed, and her bright gold toenails are sticking out of a pair of white sandals. When the judge gives me a lecture about adulthood and responsibility, she nods so vigorously the parrots are flying.

When he sets my bail at ten thousand dollars, she smiles broadly. When he says I will have to do a hundred hours of community service, she throws back her head and throws up her arms like someone getting happy in church, and gives a little laugh.

But when the judge says my court costs and fees will add up to one thousand dollars, her smile disappears. She whispers to the greasy-looking lawyer she has hired, grabs his arm, talks so vigorously the parrots dance up and down. He stays serene. He shrugs. It's not his problem. She tries to beat him up, banging her fists on his shoulder. He grabs her wrists and she calms down.

"You better keep that dress, Aisha," she hisses to me as she hustles me out of the courtroom. "You'll need it to get a decent job, because you are definitely going to pay back every dime of that thousand I borrowed for you. I thought we would get it back, but they kept it all. Our lawyer says they always do."

"What were you so happy about back there?" I ask her.

"Isn't it obvious? I had enough cash to put up your bail. You got community service instead of jail time. You're a lucky, lucky girl."

"I don't feel lucky," I tell her. "I hate being forced to do community service."

"Aisha, I can't believe you're really that selfish."

"I'm not. I'm all for helping others, but I want to choose where and when I do it." I say this, half believing it, half knowing it is an excuse to put off volunteering.

"You've forfeited that right, Aisha. You're going to do every hour of your community service, and you're going to do it gladly, because otherwise you'd be sitting in that stinking jail. And when you're not working or doing your service, I want you home where I can see you."

I am utterly, utterly shocked. "Why?"

"If you run away, I have to pay the rest of your bail, and there's no way I can get my hands on nine thousand more dollars."

"Mother!" I cry. "I'm an adult. What about freedom? What about trust?"

"You've forfeited those, too," she tells me. "Look, the judge released you into my custody. That means I have to be responsible for you and know where you are at all times. I could have refused custody. Then he would have sent you someplace where they would lock you up every night. Would you like that?"

"No," I say, but I'm thinking that it wouldn't make any difference. I have simply traded jailers.

And then my mother says an incredible thing. "I don't like this any more than you do. I was looking forward to finally having a little freedom of my own."

"Is that why you're wearing that—that harlequin outfit?"

"Yes," she replies. "It pleases me. I had to take the day off for you. On my days off, I can wear what I want."

"But did you have to wear those sunglasses?"

We are sitting in the car. My mother turns to me and slowly removes the purple-framed harlequins. Her eyes are as red as ripe tomatoes. "Any more questions?"

As she replaces the sunglasses, I ask, "Do I still have my job? Did you talk to Joe, the manager at Tequila's?"

She is very quiet. Finally she says, "Aisha, I went to that place. I couldn't stand to be there long enough to talk to anybody. I guess I can't tell you what kind of job to take. But I'll tell you this: I'd rather see you make a career out of days' work."

My mother drives me home in silence. Once we are inside our apartment, though, I notice little things she has done for me: clean pajamas and a new robe laid out in the bedroom, new bath salts in my favorite lily of the valley scent in the bathroom, new slippers under my bed, a Kid

'N Play movie all set to pop into the VCR. I appreciate every one of these things. I hug her my thanks. She cries.

I cry, too.

Because I went to Catholic high school, and, I suppose, because I stole clothes, I am sent to do community service at the Good Samaritan Gift Shop. It's not really a shop. It's a place where things are given away free to the needy. That, I guess, is the reason for the "Gift" in the name. Cute, huh?

I don't know which smell worse—the donated clothes or the people who come in to get them.

My first assignment is to go through the bundles of donations and sort them. I have to decide which of them need to be washed or dry-cleaned and which can go directly onto the racks and tables in the front room. Those that are ready to be given away have to be sorted according to gender, style, color, and size. Those that have to be dry-cleaned go back out to the loading platform for pickup. And if clothes have to be laundered, guess who washes them?

I think I am in an Early American museum when I'm shown the laundry room. It is equipped with a pair of huge, old-fashioned Maytag washing machines with wringers. I think the only one I ever saw before was gathering dust and rust in my grandmother's basement. I didn't know there were any of those contraptions left in the world.

I forgot to mention that this place is run by nuns and lay volunteers from the Catholic Church. A nun named Sister Bernadette shows me how to use the wringer washers. "We have found," she says, "that this type of washer holds up better under heavy use."

Yeah, right. That's why my grandmother said she kept hers. But what about my hands? I have to plunge them into water that contains Clorox and strong soap and washing soda. I have to push all those dripping clothes from Castoff Hell through the wringers, shake them out, and throw them in the giant six-foot dryer.

I am convinced that they have another room somewhere with automatic washers, and that if I do my job well, I'll get promoted to it. But if that room exists, I never see it.

The cure works, though. After a month of this routine, I have lost all interest in clothes. I can't imagine why I risked everything to own things like a long princess-seamed lavender dress or a short, crinkly red one, or even a divine white suit. Sister Bernadette, whose manner is firm but sweet, works with me every day. She is not really old, though her wimple and her wire-rimmed glasses add years. She is only twenty-four, and she has become my best friend. She tells me how happy she is living a life of contemplation and serving humanity. And sometimes I think life might be a lot simpler and more beautiful if I wore a habit like hers.

Chapter 17

GENE

As I put the finishing touches on my toilette, I hear some unmistakable noises downstairs: high heels clicking, a beast yapping, a feminine voice scolding in baby talk. She has returned, breathless and all a-jiggle: my lady of property and of future impropriety, my imminent *amour*.

I put extra patchouli on my mustache and rub some on my hair. Then I lie down for a moment to plan my approach. No rushing in: that is for young fools. I need to employ wisdom, tact, and patience. I visualize her succumbing, swooning in my arms. *C'est tout accompli!* But first I need an excuse for going down there.

I feel around in my second drawer, where there is a collection of found objects I have thought might be useful. I reject a scarf and an earring, and select a frilly white glove.

My heart is pounding with unseemly nervousness for one of my maturity and experience. If only I had a corner of something in a jug to give me false courage. True courage is the best kind, of course, but false courage is better than none.

The closet! Somewhere back there, behind my shoes and manuscripts, there should be a jug I threw the last time I swore off spirits. I have to crawl and root around, but at last I emerge triumphant, cradling a dusty bottle. I smell it: Wild Irish Rose wine. It is terrible stuff—sweet, cheap, piss-colored—but it will help me to make this effort on which my life depends. I am tired of ducking and hiding from my landlady as if she were the Gorgon. To tell the truth, I am tired of almost everything. But, courage! A generous guzzle remains. I plan to take only one swig, but these days I cannot seem to stop. I drain the bottle, wipe my mouth, and feel the wonderful glow spread to my very toes.

Now to consult the tarot about the success of my enterprise. I cut the deck and hold each card to my eye. The Magician—good, good, that is myself, about to practice sorcery. The Lovers and the Wheel of Fortune—both excellent auguries. Temperance—well, there are always obstacles to the success of any project. If I had time I would shuffle and spread the cards. But I have tarried too long. Love and good fortune await the Magician.

One thing more. I have no flowers, and I have drunk my wine, but I can take some music. I have a tape of Viennese waltzes. They will do just fine.

I tiptoe down the stairs—*doucement, doucement*—and rap delicately on her precious door. Inside, I know, are two overstuffed chairs, and a sofa to which I plan to gradually lead her—unless, of course, I am invited into her bedroom first.

She answers the door, a shimmer of violet. Moving closer, I see that she is wearing a tightly belted purple satin negligee which gives unfortunate emphasis to her *embonpoint*. From a mouth that is an angry violet scar emerges a single stingy syllable.

"Yes?"

I bow. "Forgive me. I was speechless for a moment. You are so ravishing this evening, Madame, that I forgot what I came to say. May I come in?"

"Well," she says, charmingly hesitant, "I don't know—"

I produce the lacy glove. "Now I remember. I found this exquisite object in the hall, and I could not imagine where it might belong, except on that dainty hand. Is it yours?" Before she can answer, I add, "And has anyone ever told you how much you resemble Leslie Caron? Have you ever danced on the stage?"

She is melting with pleasure at my flattery, I can tell.

"Do you have a cassette player? It has been a long time since I danced a waltz. Such an elegant, romantic dance." I hold out my arms. "Or—perhaps you are in the mood for softer music."

It is so easy to make women happy. I love doing it.

"The player's on the table there." I pop in my cassette, feel for the controls, and press the button next to the end, which is always Play.

"You ain't nothin' but a hound dog," bellows Big Mama Thornton, who wrote the song before the beast Elvis was conceived. Obviously I have mistaken this for the Strauss. Often I am in the mood for the blues. But not today. I fumble and finally find the Stop/Eject button.

"Never mind, my dear. I will hum the melody."

I should be paying attention to the warning finger she raises to her mouth. But she comes into my arms and, flush with victory, I discard my cane and step out, singing "Tales of the Vienna Woods" against her hair: "Come, my dashing, temperamental Viennese . . ."

I bury my nose in her black hair. It has gray sprigs, but it is fragrant, and she is light on her feet. The stakes are high, they are literally life and death. Courage.

"You waltz charmingly. Where did you learn the waltz, my dear? Not since my youth in Vienna have I been so carried away." Well, not Vienna, exactly, but nearby. I was stationed in Frankfurt with the occupying forces.

"Shhh," she says into my ear.

"I agree. Let's not break the magic spell." I dip her deeply. Women love being dipped. I sing even louder.

Then two horrible things happen. As I whirl my land-lady closer to her sofa, her demonic beast, a pit bull, it must be, attacks my pants cuffs with vicious snarls and growls.

"Desist, nice doggy," I say, closing in on the sofa. A head like a nest of vipers rises above its back, atop a pair of naked Neanderthal shoulders. It is that lazy oaf who calls himself the janitor but who never does anything but lurk in the basement, scaring people with his mean looks and his dreadful locks.

"Who is it, Sylvia?" he asks.

"It's the second floor rear. He came to return my glove."

"Ain't that the one you told me ain't paid his rent?"

"Yes," she says, "but he didn't come about that."

"Is he drunk again?"

She wrinkles up her darling little nose and sniffs the air. "I wouldn't say he's drunk, exactly, but he's been drinking. I can smell it on him."

"Well, hand me my pants and I'll throw him out."

She flutters her hands helplessly. She does not want me to go, I can tell. She had been falling for my spell, also known as That Old Black Magic. Unfortunately another, younger black sorcerer, an evil one, was here first. I take in the situation. We are trapped, my sweet *amoureuse* and I, in a tragic triangle.

"Please don't be rough with him, Dupree," she says. "You know I can't stand violence."

"That won't be necessary," I say, "I will leave right away." I kiss my fingers to her and somehow disengage the dog from my torn trousers. It is happy growling and worrying its piece of khaki. "I will return when you are less occupied. *Au revoir*."

I close the door gently. Behind it I hear an argument begin. His voice is louder than hers, his speech liberally laced with that vile compound noun that describes the Oedipal sin.

What terrible timing. *Merde!*

But hope grows. Sylvia was obviously taken with me. I will come back later tonight, when the viper-head is sullenly tending his trash cans and his fuse boxes.

Whistling "Who is Sylvia? What is she?" I quit the neighborhood.

But when I get back from an hour or so of mellow sipping at the pub, having found Buddy in a rare generous mood, Dupree has done violence to me without ever touching my person.

All of my things are on the sidewalk, and my key no longer opens the front door.

Chapter 18

CHERRY

"Back in the sixties, we thought we were anti-Establishment," Toni Brookins is saying, "but really, we were just consumers, like all good Americans."

Patrice starts to yap something in protest, and so do I, but Toni holds up a hand on which are several fabulous rings, mostly silver, probably Southwest Indian. "Hear me out," she says. "We believed in brand names. Maybe we didn't worship them in place of God, like some Americans, but we were brand-name consumers just the same. Think about it. For dishes, glassware, cutlery, all our kitchen stuff, we went to Pottery Barn."

"That's right," Patrice agrees. "I only switched to JCPenney when their retail store closed."

"For toys, it was F.A.O. Schwarz if we could afford it, Hadassah if we couldn't."

This is bringing up memories. I groan, thinking of how many times I bought stuffed Gund animals at Hadassah and washed them so that Princess Aisha could put her own dirt on them.

"Teach," I say.

"For our blue jeans, we went to I. Goldberg."

"Still do," I say. "I get my sneaks there, too."

"For political thought, we went to Karl Marx and Chairman Mao."

I start to object, then remember all the meetings and rallies, all the folk songs, all the speakers spouting rhetoric. I didn't buy or even understand most of it. My issues were more direct, things like breakfast programs for kids, and car pools for Montgomery bus boycotters, and one person, one vote, and equal pay for hospital and sanitation workers. If I had to hold hands with strangers and sing to get them, it didn't matter whether we were singing about Jesus or somebody named Joe Hill. Though I remember wondering who Joe Hill was and what he had to do with us. I start to hum the ballad about him.

"And for genes, we went to Eugene Dessalines Green. 'Cause he had the preferred, recommended, highly advertised brand-name sperm. Can I get a witness?"

"Girl, you are too much," Patrice says, rolling on the floor in spasms of laughter. I am closer to tears, because she is telling the truth. I am almost destroyed by how stupid and gullible we were.

Eventually, all three of us more or less recover. Toni goes back to folding flyers and I bend once more over my task of stuffing envelopes. Getting busy helps me to hide my crumpled face.

Patrice hauls herself back up to her computer chair and begins printing labels. We have mailing lists of chapter officers from serious women's uplift outfits like the Negro Business and Professional Women's Clubs, the Coalition of 100 Black Women, the National Council of Negro Women, and the various black college alumnae clubs. Gene Green's women were nothing if not educated. We have voted down contacting status-conscious women's clubs like the Links, the Northeasterners, the Continentals, and the black sororities. Those groups, however serious and worthy their aims, were not our generation's style. Gene Green's ladies would not be in their ranks, because we perceived them as snobbish and frivolous. Aisha, of course, couldn't wait to pledge Alpha Kappa Alpha. She will probably be a Link someday, too. Thus swings the generational pendulum.

"That's all the labels," Patrice announces, turning off her machine. "Guess I'll start sticking them on some envelopes, unless you two need help."

Toni, who is as cool and efficient as an ice machine in white sharkskin pedal pushers and a silver tank, shakes her magnificently coiffed head. She's been working for two hours, but every hair of her glued-down finger wave is in place, and she hasn't even chipped one of her silver acrylic nails. I envy her the creative public relations job that allows her to wear stuff like this every day.

"I'm bushed, myself," I say.

"I'll make you an energy shake," Patrice offers, and disappears into her kitchen.

"Why aren't the kids helping?" Toni wants to know. "I don't mean Rome, teenagers are useless, but you two have adult kids. Why aren't they around?"

I am not about to admit the reason I am bushed, that I have been working overtime at the bank to make up for the day I spent in court waiting for the judge to set my daughter's bail. Certainly not to Toni, whose image is such cool perfection.

To my horror, that image begins to crumble before my eyes—tears melting her mascara, knuckles reddening her eyes. "Oh hell, who am I fooling? Rome got thirty days for defacing the Hall of Justice. He started serving his sentence last week. That House of Detention is a hellhole. I can't stand having my baby in there."

I nod. I know. I fumble in my purse and find a card. "Call my lawyer. If anybody can get Rome out, he can. That bottom number gets answered around the clock."

Toni, sniffling, takes the card. "Is he a good man?"

"You want a lawyer, or do you want a Sunday school teacher? He wins."

I am saved from explaining how I know this lawyer by Patrice's return with something thick and frosty in a tall glass. Lately she's been putting raw foods into juicers and blenders. She seems to have lost a little weight, too. She looks good.

"What's in this one?" I ask, inspecting it. It is a rich shade of pink.

"See if you can guess."

While Toni goes to the phone, I take a hesitant sip.

Then a bigger mouthful. Then a greedy swallow. "Watermelon," I declare.

"Yes, Missy Cherry," Patrice says, doing her Mammy imitation. "I just lubs watermelon in de summertime. All us colored do. I can't help it. I speck you can't help it, either."

"Banana," I identify after another sip.

"Dat's right!" Patrice crows. "Remember how we used to unload dem banana boats on de docks? Oh, I love to tink of dem days. Day-o, oh day-ay-ay-o . . ."

"No, I don't remember, and neither do you," I say, before she really gets rolling on a Belafonte impression. "Strawberries, too?"

"Yes, strawberries. And raspberry sherbet. Very little fat and tons of energy, so you can stuff some more envelopes."

"Yes, Missy Patrice," I say. "Work me from can't see to can't see—I won't complain. After all, it's for de chillun."

"De pickaninnies," Patrice corrects, slapping labels on envelopes as I stuff them. "Thank God for self-stick labels."

"Did you get him?" I ask Toni when she returns.

She nods. "I have an appointment at four." It is now three. She sits down and starts folding again, but her creases no longer have the precise positioning I admired two hours ago. They slant at crazy angles, and the results won't fit into our envelopes. She balls one up and trashes it, tries another, then gives up in disgust. "My kid's in the slammer," she tells Patrice.

Patrice nods and goes to her corner cabinet.

"I just got mine out," I tell her. Why hide it? I'm not as close to Toni as I am to Patrice, because she has one of those magnetic fields around her that repels dirt and most people, but we're in this thing together. "Shoplifting."

"Oh, God," Toni says. "Why did we ever think Gene Green would give us superior children? Was he ever in jail?" The only color in her face is supplied by her makeup. Underneath that she is gray.

"Only for civil disobedience, far as I know," Patrice says, and hands her a pony of something, adding, "Here, Toni. Drink this. Turn your back, Cherry."

A whiff of the brandy is enough to repel me. I hate the stinking stuff.

"I don't know why people have such quaint ideas about alcoholics," I tell Patrice. "If you think the sight of that little thimbleful of cognac is enough to make me go through all that hell again, you're crazy. Feel any better, Toni?"

She nods.

"Good. That's what medicine is for. You might as well knock off here for today," I tell her. I do not add that she has lost her magic folding touch and is therefore useless. "Go see my lawyer. He'll get Rome out, but it will cost you. You'll probably have to cash in all your assets and borrow every cent you can. Are you ready to deal with that?"

"I have to be," she says. "Thanks, girls. Sorry I haven't been more help."

"You're not off the hook," Patrice tells her. "This is

just stage one, getting our mailing out. Stage two is getting ready for our fund-raiser, finding vendors and entertainment. Stage three is ticket sales. Stage four is menu planning. Stage five is tying up all the loose ends. . . ."

"And stage six is showtime!" I finish.

"I'll be back before then, I hope," Toni says.

"If you aren't, we'll send the Mounties after your elegant ass," I promise. "Don't hang around here any longer. We don't have any money." From my vast store of recent experience, I instruct her. "Go call up anybody you know who does. Your doctor, your dentist, your drug dealer . . ."

I am joking, but the stricken look on Toni's face makes me wonder. You never know who's using what these days. I count myself very lucky, after several medical misadventures, to have found a doctor who doesn't snort.

After she leaves, Patrice turns to me and says, "Do you think Toni—"

"God, I hope not," I say. "But if she is, I have a list of good rehabs. You fold. I'll stuff."

"Right," Patrice says. "Where's Aisha tonight?"

"I don't know. She better be home when I get there, though. You think LaVonya Harris will give us a fashion show?"

"I don't see why not. You say Al Handy still has a group?"

"Uh-huh. Al Handy and his Handymen."

"Good. I've got some odd jobs around here that could use a handyman."

I want to wipe the lewd grin off her face. "They are

strictly professional musicians, Patrice, and they charge by the hour. Say, the girl who does my braids has a brother who's a stand-up comic."

"Is he funny?"

"Devastating. He kept me laughing the whole four hours the last time I had an appointment. Usually I fall asleep when she does me. I was furious. It's the best rest I get all month. . . . You know any more amateur talent? They're usually willing to work for free."

"Rome is an aspiring rapper and a portrait artist," Patrice informs me.

"Maybe we should leave Rome out of this."

"Maybe not. It might help him to get involved."

"Maybe we should wait and ask Toni," I say.

"Yeah, you're right. She's an odd person. She looks and acts like an ice princess, but today she rolled up her sleeves and got right to work."

"Ice princesses are usually scared," I said. "I know—I used to be one. The only thing that thawed me out was a drink."

Patrice gets a faraway look. "Uh—our affair will be a BYOB deal, okay? Saint says there are some good a cappella singing groups at his school. But we'd probably have to pay their travel expenses."

"That's better than paying scale," I say. "You know what, Patrice? This is fun. It's like old times, when we were raising funds for the volunteers down in Mississippi. What do we call ourselves?"

"The name on the flyer. Geneological Research."

"I caught that," I say. "Pretty clever. Too bad we're not a registered non-profit."

"We can be," she says. "All we need is three officers and a bank account."

Suddenly I am tired. "Do you really think we should be putting out all this effort just to dig up Gene Green's sorry hide?"

"It's for de chirren," she reminds me.

I sigh. "Spare me the Aunt Jemima routine and I'll work for another couple of hours. Hand me those envelopes."

Chapter 19

AISHA

AFTER I'VE HAD two weeks of hell at the Good Samaritan Gift Shop, Sister Bernadette invites me to dinner at the convent. We have roast chicken, succotash, and salad, and afterward she invites me to meet some of her friends.

Sister Mary Joseph is the chef. She's about fifty, with a face like a round rosy peach, complete with fuzz. She's talented, though. After coffee we go to the room of another nun, Sister Immaculata, and I discover that Sister Mary J. plays a mean guitar.

While Sister Mary Joseph strums and sings "My Sweet Lord," "Michael, Row the Boat Ashore," and other folk-rock spirituals, Sister Immaculata offers us drinks on a little enameled tray. I didn't know nuns were allowed to drink, but it seems that these nuns make their own peach brandy. They have a farm out in the country, and each of them spends one day a week working there.

The peach brandy tastes mild, but it has a kick like a Glock semiautomatic. Yes, I fired one once, in the days before Saint when I loved hoodlums. There's a lot my mother doesn't know about me.

I drain my little cordial glass and hold it out for more.

After a few comments about how great the beans and squash are doing out on the farm, Sister Mary Joseph excuses herself, saying she has to plan next week's menus. She's having ratatouille on Wednesday, she says, when the first eggplants will be ripe. She invites me back to try it.

Sister Bernadette excuses herself, too, saying she has to work on the shop accounts. I should offer to help her—I *was* an accounting major—but I'm feeling suddenly lazy.

"I guess I'd better be going," I say, but Sister Immaculata urges me to stay awhile. I have a buzz on by now, and the day bed I'm on is soft with lots of cozy cushions, so I don't object. I never knew nuns had so many comforts. I thought they slept on beds of nails, or something. I figured that was why the ones who were my teachers were always so mean.

Sister Immaculata is about thirty and looks like Judy Garland—a cute waif, with a pouty mouth and big dark eyes.

"This thing is killing me," she says. "It *itches*." She shocks me by removing her headdress and wimple and revealing a head of thick, curly black hair.

I gasp. "I thought all nuns were bald," I say.

She winks. "Not anymore, kiddo. It's optional these days. Even our habits are optional now." She rises. "Since it's just us girls, I think I'll get comfortable."

I had noticed a couple of women in the dining room in neat navy suits, but I thought they were lay people or visitors or something.

"Most of us wear the habit because it's less trouble,"

she says. "It protects us when we have to go out on the city streets. And if we gain weight on Sister Mary Joseph's good food, no one can tell. You know why the original habits were designed like this?"

I shake my head, spellbound as she goes behind a screen, tosses hers over it, and comes out in a jade-green satin wrap robe, more Mata Hari than Mother Superior.

"To hide pregnancies. It used to happen all the time. Still does, if you want to know. When the little buns come out of the ovens, we just pop 'em in our orphanages. The maternal nuns run them, so they don't have to be separated from their kids."

"Wow," is all I can say.

"Don't mean to shock you. Just want you to know we're human. Can I refill your glass? You don't have to keep drinking that syrup. I tire of it very quickly, myself."

She reaches back to a bookshelf behind her and pulls out a hollow book. Concealed in it is a half pint of Jim Beam.

"And let's see what else." Rummaging on her shelf, she plucks out two blue perfume bottles, a brown medicine bottle, and a couple of hollow porcelain figurines. "In case you don't like bourbon, I've got nips of gin, vodka, amaretto, scotch, and sherry. I've got vermouth in the bathroom, too, and I can shake you up a mean martini."

"Wow," I say again. Her little stashes are enchanting, like the miniature tea sets I used to play with when I was four or five.

"What's your pleasure?"

"Gin," I say. In my nights at Tequila's I developed a

taste for the stuff. "With water, and a dash of lemon if you have it."

Sister I. puts the drink in my hand, then puts on a Kenny G. album. When she turns from her player, she is smoking a cigarette. It turns me off—I despise smoking—but I never thought they were allowed to do that, either.

Sister Immaculata clinks her glass against mine.

"To the religious life," she toasts. "It's not as grim as people think it is."

The next hour is devoted to a lecture on the paths nuns may choose—social service like Sister Bernadette, helping around the convent like Sister Mary Joseph, teaching, nursing, administration, bookkeeping and clerical tasks, music, public relations. Then Immaculata goes into the experiences of the truly devout who seek bliss in cloistered prayer. She talks earnestly but lightly, throwing in a bit of humor now and then, corny jokes like: "You know why you always see two nuns out together? That's so one nun don't get none."

I break in. "I've been meaning to ask you. I don't see any black nuns around here. Where are they?"

"These days, they're all over. But we used to be segregated," she admits, making an awful face. "Out of that came a couple of black orders, the Oblate Sisters, for example, in Baltimore. Those historically black orders are still maintained, but they have a few white sisters now."

"Like the historically black colleges," I comment.

"Exactly. Free choice is what we offer. I think that's the best way, don't you? Just between us, we don't have enough black nuns. Our inner-city ministries need them."

From beneath her chair she has produced an extra pint of gin. She never lets my glass get empty. She freshens my drink now with a professional little dip and twist of the wrist that rights the bottle quickly and prevents dripping. I've seen Joe do that.

The question is out of my mouth before I think. "Excuse me, but were you ever a bartender?" I cover my mouth. "Oops. I'm so sorry I said that."

"Why be? You're pretty sharp to catch that. Yes, I was a barmaid on the South Side. A hooker, too. Sometimes I think getting named Sister Immaculata was a cosmic joke." A shadow of weariness passes over her face. "I could tell you a month of stories about the life; the other girls, the pimps, the johns. Some of the johns were pushovers.

"But some of them could get pretty rough. I'm glad it's all behind me. I'd tell any girl who might be thinking about the life, it's pretty scary. Of course, you don't entertain such thoughts."

"No, of course not."

"As a matter of fact, Sister Bernadette tells me you might be thinking about joining us."

I have told Bernadette that she is so sweet and spiritual she makes me want to be like her, and that I am tired of material things and attracted to the simple life. But this raunchy ex-hooker with her habits from the street is not exactly an advertisement for the convent, at least not to me. Her rap about the worldly privileges available to the religious is not an attraction; it's a turn-off. Why join a convent if you want to be worldly?

I rise. The floor rises, too. I have to catch the back of the day bed to steady myself.

"I haven't really thought it through," I say. "I'll let you know. Thanks for everything. I have to go now."

"Fine," she says, and pulls out a little pamphlet. I am turned off again. It is the same beginners' tract on religious instruction they handed out to us in high school.

"Thanks," I say, and put the boring little pamphlet in my purse. I start to say something else, then stop.

"Did you have a question?"

I do, but decide not to ask it. I was going to ask her—if Sister Mary Joseph is the cook, and Sister Bernadette serves the needy, what is *your* function around here?

The answer comes to me before the question reaches my lips.

She's the recruiting officer.

Chapter 20

CHERRY

I AM LATE for my meeting. I try to slip in unseen and hide in the back row. But Tuesday Night Serenity Group is about as secretive as a sound truck. We're anonymous to the outside world, maybe, but there are no secrets within the room. Several heads turn. I pretend I was there all the time, and look up front at the speaker, who is someone I've never seen before.

And, God, but he's fine. A face like an Ashanti mask I saw once, with carved cheekbones and mobile, wonderfully expressive eyebrows. A deep baritone speaking voice—cultivated, but not affected. He has silver sideburns, mixed gray hair, and a complexion that's pure butterscotch. I want to taste it. From his shoulders and his Popeye arms, which are revealed by short sleeves, I can tell that he works out.

When he moves, this big lollipop sort of glides, like a dancer. I want him to dance with me. His long, fine hands wave elegantly as he makes his points. I imagine them running over my legs.

I am scandalized by my own fantasies. I have to shut my eyes so that I can pay attention to the man's message. I want to hear it. Not just in order to glean experience, strength, and hope, but so I can have an opener for a conversation.

He mentions Chicago. I've been there.

He mentions working for a bank, something else we have in common. I'm beginning to think this is fate.

'Course, his bank kind of took exception to the way he borrowed loan funds that were meant for customers while he was in his addiction, so now he's working for lunch money while he pays them back.

Then he mentions his ex-wife and a divorce, and it's all I can do to keep from leaping out of my chair and yelling "Yayyyy!" The lower register of his voice sends its vibes right through me, like the organ in the Saint-Saëns Organ Symphony. I like to lie on the floor when I play it, to feel the vibrations better.

I'd like to lie on the floor with this man, too.

I don't even have the decency to be ashamed of myself for harboring such thoughts.

When we get to our chorus of "Thanks for sharing," I have a dozen provocative things in mind to say to him. But when I go up to shake his hand and thank him individually, I am as tongue-tied as a child reciting her first Sunday school piece. It doesn't matter. He hangs onto my hand and gives me such a long, soulful look, I suddenly need to sit down.

"Don't leave yet, okay?" he requests.

They couldn't get me out of that room if the whole group suddenly yelled "Fire!" I'd say "Fine" and stay stuck to my chair.

He's shaking hands and accepting compliments on his message. His name is Gus. I lust for Gus.

In spite of my urges and fantasies, I heard his story. No one would ever think that this fine, clean-cut, articulate brother once slept in alleys and foraged in Dumpsters. Once robbed a candy store for wine money. Once robbed a little kid who was on his way to the candy store.

That was Gus's bottom. He adores kids. He wants to inspire them and protect them from becoming the kind of scum he used to be.

Another thing I like about this brother, he is serious. To me, serious is sexy. We've been in the same room for an hour and I haven't seen him smile, just light up the room with his large eyes.

But then he does smile—at Joyce, our resident sex addict, who comes on to every new man. She's cute—café au lait, with a long tail of coarse black Indian-type hair—but she's one of those who are sicker than the rest of us.

Gus's smile is five hundred watts of pure electricity. I feel a charge arc across the room from him to me.

Encouraged, Joyce drapes an arm across his shoulder and practically climbs into his lap.

I want to maim her and do serious damage, but I restrain myself. I need to hold still and observe Gus's re-action. If he has the poor taste to want Joyce, I don't want him.

He dumps her so skillfully she never knows what happened. He takes her hand, the one that isn't around his neck, seems about to kiss it, but instead drops it, rises, and excuses himself. It's a one-two knockout combination worthy of Muhammad Ali, who had that float and sting maneuver down to perfection.

When Gus comes back, he's carrying two cups of coffee, and one of them's for me.

"How do you take yours?" he inquires, slipping into the seat beside mine.

"One cream, two sugars," I say, taking the cup of black. "But this way is okay."

"No problem," he says—my favorite phrase, especially when it's uttered by a man who's taking care of me. This thoughtful gentleman bends over and probes in his socks, which are, I notice, white athletic socks worn with brown tasseled loafers. Well, no one's perfect. In the left sock are two packets of cream; in the right, three of sugar.

I am impressed. "That may be just about the most original thing I've ever seen," I tell him.

"I've had lots of practice," he tells me. "I used to stash half a pint of gin in each sock. Came in handy when I was in the rehab."

We laugh long and hard, that hearty, hollow alcoholics' laugh of recognition. We always laugh like that when we remember how we conned everybody, ourselves most of all.

"I usually stash my wallet down there now," he continues. "Frustrates pickpockets, prevents sciatica, and leaves both my hands free to fight muggers."

"Sounds like you live in the city," I say, because I was too late to hear his introduction.

"Close enough," he says. "South Orange. How many years do you have?"

"Next month I'll celebrate my tenth anniversary," I tell him, more than a little proud of myself. It's been a grim struggle, one day at a time. Many were the nights I slept naked and refused to get dressed so I wouldn't go out and buy liquor. Once I even got in the shower and stayed wet for several hours so I wouldn't go. But I struggled no harder than anyone else; I don't deserve special praise.

"Congratulations," he says. "Maybe I'll come down and celebrate with you."

"I hope you will," I say. "How about you? How many years?"

"Eighteen this Christmas," he says. "I don't need any other presents." He adds quickly, maybe so I won't start gushing congratulations, "My car's outside. May I take you home?"

May he take me home? Would I like a medium rare filet mignon smothered with mushrooms? A week of massages? A cruise to the Canary Islands?

Let me think about it.

Yes.

I've heard all the warnings about the thirteenth step, which is what I'm taking with this man, and they make sense, but I choose to ignore them tonight. His car is an old but well-maintained Mercedes with deep leather seats that smell wonderful and swallow me up. A Modern Jazz Quartet tape is playing softly. Both of us hum along with "Django."

What I mean to say is, this man has class.

He takes my keys and opens my door for me. I put a

couple of lights on in the living room—not too many—
and a Barry White tape. My choice of his romantic ballads
is a dead giveaway, and I ought to be ashamed of myself,
but I'm not.

After I serve us some snacks and my favorite cooler,
sparkling water and peach juice, Gus gives me a back
rub. But first he tells me about himself. He has three children, all grown. He was once a musician, a pianist, but
gave it up because the nightclub atmosphere interfered
with his sobriety. He's been going to college for eight
years while he works to pay back the bank, and wants
eventually to be a secondary school teacher in a city
school. Inwardly, I cheer.

Gus swallows a healthy number of my roasted garlic
spreads on toast, my marinated chitlins on toothpicks,
and my anchovies on wheat crackers. He doesn't wolf
them, he appreciates what he's eating, but he doesn't
nibble, either. I like a man with a frank appetite. Eating
lustfully is sexy. He takes his time with the back rub,
too, working out a lot of my shoulder knots before
moving from the therapeutic to the seductive. He has
just slipped my sandals off to give me a foot rub, and
begun moving up to my ankles and calves, when we are
interrupted.

I hear a couple of heavy crashes on the stairs, followed
by a fumbling and scratching at the door, which my
daughter literally falls through. For the first time in weeks
I have forgotten all about her. It has been a blessed relief,
but a brief one.

She is drunk as a skunk, and smells just about as
pleasant.

"This is my daughter Aisha, Gus. I forgot to mention that she lives with me."

I walk over and inspect the sodden mess on my floor. "Girl, what do you mean coming home in this condition?"

"You used to do it all the time, Mother," she counters, sitting up with her arms around her knees and looking up at me cockeyed. There's nothing more pitiful than a defensive drunk—except, maybe, an apologetic one.

"That's no excuse. In fact, you're supposed to know better because of my history." I have told her repeatedly that, with two alcoholic parents, she should never touch liquor.

"Yeah, well, there are some things I have to find out for myself, Mother. I'm not surprised to see you have a man in here. Minute I turn my back, you're up to your old tricks. Whassamatter, did I interrupt something?"

"You have no right questioning me," I inform her. "I want to know where you've been and how you got into this condition."

"You won't believe me," she says, and laughs until she chokes, then collapses into a heap on the floor again.

At this point I feel a gentle hand on my arm. "Let me talk to her," Gus says.

I withdraw angrily and give the two of them space. He's right, of course. I'm her mother; I can't deal with her problem. But I resent it just the same. Am I never going to have anyone or anything for myself?

He kneels beside her. They talk softly, so softly I can't even hear. I am left, all moist and aroused and unsatisfied, to cross my legs and fold my arms and twirl my sandal on my toe—and to wish, for the first time in nine years, for a drink. That really scares me. It occurs to me that harboring a grown daughter can be unhealthy. I also wish I'd never listened to Patrice and started thinking about men again. The minute you concentrate on something, it seems, here it comes.

My gorgeous Gus finally gets my child up off the floor and into a chair by him over in the corner. In another half hour she says, "Thanks, Gus," and heads for the bathroom. I hear the shower running.

"Aisha," he says to me, "is not convinced she is an alcoholic. But she's willing to come to a meeting with me to find out."

Oh, she's willing to come with you, is she? And where does that leave me? When do I get to go somewhere with you? These and other ignoble thoughts are racing through my mind.

Intellectually I know, of course, that I can't help my daughter, and that I should be grateful for his efforts. Emotionally, I am furious.

"Her story is the damnedest one I ever heard," he adds.

"You mean about her broken engagement?"

"No, about where she was tonight."

I wait, braced for the news.

"She was at a convent, getting drunk with one of the nuns."

We have a good hearty laugh over that one. "It's just wild enough to be true," I say. "She's been working with the nuns, and—" I break off. I don't want to talk about Aisha any more tonight. Maybe, I'm thinking, she will go straight to bed and fall asleep, and . . .

He's thinking the same thing, I can tell. He moves

toward me, reaches out with both arms, then stops, drops them and shakes his head. The mood's been broken.

I see him to the door. Nothing is said about when we will resume our interrupted hour of delight. Things are back to normal around here, with all attention focused on Princess Aisha.

Who informs me, first thing in the morning, that she plans to enter the convent.

Chapter 21

SAINT

W<small>E ARE SHORTHANDED</small> at the soup kitchen. My boss and several of my helpers are away on vacation, so I am glad when Lamar shows up, even though I haven't taught him much yet.

First, I go over the stock of donated foods. There's celery, ketchup, baby pasta, evaporated milk, half a dozen expired whole chickens, some generic saltines, and three institutional cans of peaches.

I stare at this assortment meditatively, moving and arranging the containers now this way, now that.

"What are you doing, Saint?" Lamar wants to know. Since I got him a haircut and convinced him that bathing is macho ("all that dirt saps your strength, man"), he's not a bad-looking little dude. I could almost take him anywhere, if the people had bad eyesight. He still wears a greenish gold hoop in his left ear; we're working on that. He is also wearing an arresting combination of straight and cross dressing: lace-trimmed socks and moldy sneakers, low-slung khaki pants and a woman's orange U-neck T-shirt.

We'll work on his outfit later. At least he's clean, and I'm sure his well-meaning mother thinks no one can tell the difference between her blouses and boys' shirts. If I mentioned it to her, she'd probably say, "I dress my son the best I can. If you want him to look better, buy him some clothes." And she'd be right.

"Looking over these ingredients and trying to figure out what I can do with them. What do they suggest to you?"

He pulls at the air around his ear, missing, I guess, the braids that used to hang there. "Not much, man. A trip to the garbage can?"

"Lamar, this is good food," I rebuke him. "All we need is a little imagination to plan a menu with it." I snap my fingers. "I've got it. Barbecued chicken soup."

He covers his mouth with his hand and pretends to gag. "Ew. I never heard of that. Sounds nasty. I don't eat that."

"You never heard of it because I just dreamed it up. How can you say you don't eat it if you never tasted it? Find me some onions."

Crawling around the bins like the little rodent he is, Lamar digs out two large onions, old enough to be sprouting long green shoots, and a clove of garlic.

"Great. Now half fill two stock pots with water."

While he clangs away importantly, climbing the step stool to reach the faucet, I begin slicing and dicing the onions, shoots and all. I'll sauté these first to season the stock, then I'll boil the chickens till they're tender.

There is a yell and a crash. I turn to see my little helper

skating away from me on a slick puddle of water. He lands on his tail, his feet airborne.

"Lamar, I just asked you to half fill the pots, not to carry them to the stove. They're too heavy for you."

"Are not," he contradicts me.

"Are, too. Else, why did you drop it?"

"I didn't fucking drop it, I slipped. Some sloppy mother-fucker left grease on the floor."

As usual, Frank, the janitor, has left the floor hygieni-cally clean. I don't dare contradict Lamar, though—what he just said was face-saving, on the order of telling your teacher "Somebody stole my lunch money" when the noon hour arrives and you have none. You know your mom didn't have a quarter to give you that morning, but you can't let your public know that. If I leave Lamar's pride intact, maybe someday I'll be able to tone down his language. Maybe someday I'll be able to swim the English Channel, too.

"Listen, Lamar, all the great chefs began by following somebody's orders. You've got to learn to follow instruc-tions, too. Go get the mop and dry up this floor. Then half fill that pot again. *I* will put it on the stove."

That accomplished, I decided to show him how to dis-joint a chicken. I show him how the joints are marked by fat lines. "See this yellow line here? That's where you slice off a drumstick." I hand him the all-purpose knife that I bring from home every day, Mom's biggest and best from Solingen, Germany. Lamar does a raggedy job on the first drumstick.

"No, Lamar, you shouldn't have to saw back and forth

like that. Just follow the yellow line. It should slice through easily."

It does—so easily that, in his excitement and haste, Lamar slices right through the chicken and into his finger. It looks like a deep cut; the bright red blood is flowing rapidly.

I hustle him over to the sink and run cold water over the finger, then plunge it into a sugar bowl. "Keep it in there for a minute while I find some Band-Aids."

There are none. "Jesus Christ, why don't we have a first-aid kit around here?"

Mary, who has been avoiding me all week as if I were a homicidal maniac, finds a couple of Band-Aids in her purse and ministers to Lamar. She's a young, idealistic white girl, no more than sixteen. I've been rude to Mary since Aisha's news. I know it's unreasonable, but I've been feeling lately that all women are traitors, and I've been treating them accordingly.

"Don't wash the sugar off," I warn her. "It stops the bleeding."

She's convinced I'm crazy now, but she does as I say, and the sugar does its clotting work. It's a trick my mother learned from her Nana, one of her many country remedies.

"This is a pretty bad cut," Mary says. "Shouldn't he go to the hospital?"

I was grateful there were no mothers around just now when Lamar cut himself, not wanting him to be babied. I forgot that all women are potential mothers. I inspect Lamar's skinny finger. It doesn't seem to need stitches. "Nah," I say. "It's just a scrape. Right, Lamar?"

"Right," he says.

"He'll be fine. Thanks for the Band-Aids," I say as she wraps his finger in pink plastic strips. "We'd have been in trouble if you hadn't had them. Flesh color, too; isn't that what they're called?"

Lamar gets it immediatcly and laughs. "Sit me in a tub of Clorox for a week, my flesh wouldn't get that color. Would yours, Saint?"

"Well, see," I say, "that's why we're called a minority. The majority rules, even down to deciding what color flesh is."

Mary turns pink. I don't want to embarrass her, but I can't let a teaching opportunity pass. This young brother's survival is on the line. Hers isn't.

She's a good kid, though. Churchified and prissy, a stone missionary sent down here by the Presbyterians to save us savages, but decent. "I'll bring in a first-aid kit tomorrow," she promises.

"Thanks, Mary."

"But I can only get the kind of Band-Aids they sell." She is apologetic, almost teary.

" 'S all right," I say, all big and generous, and guilty as hell. I must do something nice for her soon. Let her interpret the Sermon on the Mount for me, maybe. No, I can't be that nice. I can't forget that, along with the cross, her ancestors brought the shackles.

"Okay," I tell Lamar, "we're going to sauté these onions. 'Sauté' is a French word that means to fry gently, over low heat."

"Can I do it?" Lamar is getting interested. So, of course, I let him.

And, of course, he turns the fire up too high when my back is turned, and grease splatters all over his chest and his good hand.

I repeat my lecture about following instructions while I hold his hand under cold running water, then break off two pieces of aloe vera and squeeze their contents over his burns. I forget who brought in that plant—probably Mary, who does so many thoughtful things in her quiet way—but it sure comes in handy.

"You're on your way to becoming a pro now," I tell Lamar.

"For real?"

"Sure. No serious cook gets his work done without cuts and burns."

He puffs out his little pigeon chest and forgets his injuries, so I do, too. He asks, "When do you think I can wear one of those tall white hats—what do you call them?"

"A chef's hat is called a toque. Soon. Now watch."

I don't let him do anything else. It's bad enough that I'm sending him home with both mitts wounded. I sit him down on a stool and make him watch while I shred the chicken, simmer it with the onions and garlic in improvised barbecue sauce—stock, ketchup, molasses—thicken it with cornstarch and then thin it repeatedly with evaporated milk.

I let him have the first taste out of the big ladle.

"Yeah!" he says in approbation. "This stuff is *ready*."

"And just in time," I say. "Here come our first customers."

While the hungry customers pile in, I get on the phone to wheedle some ice cream out of the Dairy Delite factory. They are reluctant to give it up. I try what I call whitemail; I say I will tell a reporter at the black newspaper that they refused to give a donation to the homeless. Grudgingly, they promise two gallons of vanilla. I send Lamar to get them.

"And come straight back," I tell him. "We have chicken soup for lunch; we don't want ice cream soup for dessert."

This job requires more juggling than a clown's gig at the circus. In addition to being chief cook and, when required, medic, I have to be the host, the housekeeper, and the social worker on shorthanded days. Most of the people are happy just to get a meal and a friendly greeting, but some of them have complicated problems.

First I run out into the dining room, swipe the tables with a rag, and help Mary set out the place mats, which are opened sheets of newspaper. We sweep all the books and toys from the after-school program into a toy box. Then I position myself behind the counter, ready to ladle out soup and smiles.

"Hi, Mrs. Griggs," I say to the first person in line. "How's your bunion today?"

"Better, thank you," says this amazing old lady of about eighty, who has raised three generations of her family. One great-grand of about four, all eyes and curls, clings to her ragged hem. "I found me these nice shoes at the Good Samaritan and I opened 'em up some." Sure enough, she has sliced a hole in her men's deck shoe for her bunion and another for the tip of her second toe.

"Good for you. Comfort is more important than fashion."

"You said it. Wish I'd known that when I was young. I wouldn't have such bad feet." She pulls the great-grand forward. "This one is Chad. Chad, say hello to Mr. Two-cent. And this is Chad's mama. She name Sharon."

I can tell from Sharon's bottomless eyes that she is high. We don't allow that around here.

"She won't be no trouble," her grandmother says quickly. "I just want to get some food in her is all. She ain't eaten in four days."

She won't eat today, either, if I know junkies, except that my Peaches Deluxe might appeal to her, if she craves sweets. Many addicts do. I bend the rules for Mrs. Griggs, who has raised all of the young ones orphaned by drugs in her family.

Next comes Monica. Monica is a regular, a skinny little wisp of a woman who never eats much, but likes to hang around. "I need a place, Two-cent," she tells me. "Landlord is putting me out Monday. You know of any places?"

I sigh. Last December, when I went to Monica's last place to put tape around her drafty windows, she had a pile of Christmas presents stacked almost to the ceiling, but hadn't paid her rent. She has a good, generous heart; that's why she's always in financial trouble. She also has AIDS.

"If I hear of any, I'll let you know," I tell her, making a mental note to call the AIDS hotline to see if they can place her.

Next in line is Raymond. His darting eyes and his jerky movements show that he is coming down. He has a smart mouth but is basically harmless. Still, anyone who gets between him and his next dose is liable to suffer.

"Yo, Two-cent, you got any ribs today?"

"No, man, the rib truck didn't pass through here today. Got some good soup, though."

"Nah, I ain't got a taste for soup. Look here, though—you got a couple of dollars you could let me hold?"

I shake my head. "No, Raymond. Sorry."

"Aw, damn, Two-cent, you just as cheap as your name. I know you got some money. You always got money. Whyn't you let me have a couple bucks?"

"Why should I?"

"Yo mama would."

I throw down my towel and my ladle and come around the counter fast. I'm mad, but I don't intend to hit him, just remove him from the premises. But the little snake starts cringing and yelling, "Ow! Help! Police! He hit me!"

This is the sort of thing that could close us down. I don't know who saw what, in case I need witnesses.

"Raymond, I haven't touched you, and you know it. But now I will." I get his arm in a hammerlock and start shoving. I shove him almost to the door, and then the wiry little snake does a little twist, slips out of my grasp and flees. When I get to the door and look out, he is a dot disappearing down the street.

I turn and see that Miss Bea Bea has taken my place and is serving the newcomers. About forty, she is mildly retarded and has never held a job except at the handicapped workshop, but she knows how to ladle soup. I have to tell her to let each person decide whether they want their crackers crumbled into their soup, but after that, she does fine. She smiles a wide, toothless, beautiful grin when I tell her so.

About this time, Lamar returns with a gallon of ice cream in each hand, still frozen. I pat him on the back.

By now, about twenty-four shabby, hungry people are seated at the long tables, spoons poised. Miss Bea Bea stands at the head of the table nearest the counter and raps smartly on it with my ladle.

"Grace!" she commands.

We all bow our heads, though I have to push Lamar's beady head down. I guess nobody ever told him about grace.

Prodded by his grandmother, Chad pipes up in a voice as clear and piercing as a church bell:

"God is great / God is good / Now we thank him for our food / We fold our hands / We bow our heads / We thank him for our daily bread. Amen."

Then all attack their rosy bowls, steam rising into smooth faces, seamed faces, fresh faces, tired faces, faces that are everything except ugly. Grace is exactly what it is.

"Wow, look at them slurp it up," Lamar says.

"Come on, Lamar, let's move this dessert out. At this rate they'll be ready for it in three seconds."

We get a little assembly line going, me scooping ice cream into bowls, Lamar plopping a peach atop each mound, Miss Bea Bea delivering the desserts as fast as she clears away leftovers from the main course. When everyone else has dessert, we take ours to a small table near the back door. Lamar is on his third helping when he remembers something.

"Oops," he says, an embarrassed hand to his mouth. "I forgot to tell you."

"What?"

"Some old guy said he wanted to talk to you."

"What old guy, Lamar? Finish swallowing so I can understand you."

"Urp. An old drunk guy who talks like a professor. He was going through the trash at the chicken place down the street, and I told him he didn't have to do that, lunch would be served here soon. He said he wasn't looking for food, he was looking for something else, but he wanted to see you."

"Why didn't you tell me right away?"

"The ice cream would have melted," he says. And of course I can't scold him—I had warned him severely not to let it melt.

I get Lamar to describe the old guy. Nice clothes, a gray mustache, a cane. He sounds like the old gent who I privately call the Professor. I'm sorry I missed him. I would like to know what his life used to be like, and what happened to bring him so far down on his luck.

"He didn't ask for you by name. He just asked for the tall young man. But I know he meant you, Saint."

I know it, too. In a weird way, I feel connected to him. I feel connected to all the poor people who come here, but I'm insulated from them, too, because I've got a home and some college and what looks like a good future. The Professor scares me, I think, because he's obviously seen better days. He's proof that it could happen to anybody.

"Show me where you saw him," I say. "Maybe he'd like some dessert."

We go up the street and check, but there is no one there.

"Guess he left," Lamar says with a shrug. "Probably still looking for a jug."

"You've got to learn to be responsible about people's messages, Lamar."

Lamar shrugs. "He'll be back."

What can a child know? I find this remark oddly reassuring, though.

Chapter 22

AISHA

I<small>T'S HUMILIATING</small> when you drop a bombshell on someone and it doesn't even ruffle her hair.

I expect an explosion of rage from my mother when I tell her my plans. I also look forward to her wallowing in a swamp of guilt for having sent me to that Catholic school.

But all she says is "Fine, if that's what you want to do."

It's like pushing hard on a heavy door and, at the same moment, having someone on the inside open it for you.

"Is that all you're going to say?" I ask her. "How can you be so cold and unfeeling?"

"I don't think I am," she says. "I just think you're old enough now to make your own decisions."

Exactly what I've been trying to tell her for years. But when she says it, it's suddenly scary. I don't recognize this woman who used to be my mother. I don't think I like her, either.

"The cloistered life is what I want, Mother. The simple life, close to God, away from the world. No tiresome material possessions. No lustful men. It's beautiful. Of course you wouldn't understand the appeal of a life like that."

"You're right, I wouldn't, at least not right now," she says coolly, smoothing her gray eye shadow with her pinky. "Check back with me in about fifteen years."

"You want to get rid of me," I say. "You want me gone so you can have men here every night."

And still she agrees with me. "I wouldn't go that far," she says, "but I think I would appreciate a little privacy now and then."

I lose it completely then. "You're driving me to this, you know, Mother. You're pushing me out of the nest before I'm ready. I have to go somewhere."

"Nobody's pushing you except yourself, Aisha," she answers. "You need to listen to yourself. When are you going to grow up?"

Then she sighs. "There have just been too many crises, too much drama, Aisha. A month ago I cried buckets over you. Now my tears are all dried up. . . . Excuse me now, please. Unless you have more to tell me, I have to go to work. I wish you luck."

Then, looking as trim and fresh in black and white checks as a health magazine illustration for an article on "Life Begins at Fifty," she trots briskly out of the apartment.

I am left without a ride to the shop. I have to dress in a whisk, grab a bite, and organize my own transportation.

No one is available to give me a lift.

I have to ride the poky, stinking bus, standing all the

way, because all of the seats are taken. I am a part of the great unwashed before I even get to my unpaid work serving them.

When I get to the Good Samaritan Gift Shop, Sister Bernadette greets me with her usual serene smile. She smiles that way through everything. She would smile through an air raid. Sometimes I think she is retarded.

But she isn't; she's just disgustingly saintly.

I head for my daily hell, the laundry room, but she puts a gentle hand on my shoulder and detains me.

She tells me I've been promoted! No more laundry. I have been such a dutiful laundress that I now get to stay in the front room and assist customers.

"Who will wash the clothes?" I wonder.

"I will," she says, and smiles as if she has just won the lottery. Sometimes these nuns are just plain unreal.

She gives me a guided tour, showing me how the things are kept: women's clothes in the front, children's in the middle, men's in back, all arranged by color and size.

"We find it best not to interrupt the people when they are browsing," she instructs me. "Some of our clients have been made to feel unwelcome in other stores, so we don't hover or ask them questions. But we do try to make ourselves available if they look like they need help."

"How do you tell?"

"It's an art," she says. "I feel sure you'll learn."

I wish I had her confidence.

"Oh, another thing. A lot of the people who come in here are proud. They will insist on paying for their items, even when they have no money. They will ask the person who waits on them to name a price."

"What do you do then?"

"I name a tiny price, and tell them they do not have to pay today—I will trust them to give us that amount when they get their next income. It's important never to assume that their poverty is permanent. I also offer the person an opportunity for service—washing clothes in the laundry room, for instance."

"Has anyone ever taken you up on it?" I wonder.

She sighs. "Not yet. But I have faith that someone will. Service is so rewarding."

Yeah, right. I snarl something that expresses my lack of enthusiasm, and Sister Bernadette puts a hand on my arm. "Do not be discouraged, Aisha," she says. "Even Saint Teresa had terrible fits of rage and depression."

"I'm no saint," I say.

"Exactly," she says. "That is why we do not expect miracles of you. You are human, my dear. By the way, did you enjoy your visit with Sister Immaculata? She spoke very highly of you."

I ignore this as best I can. There's a catch in it, and it's spelled C-O-M-M-I-T-M-E-N-T. I am not sure whether I made my great announcement this morning because I meant it, or because I wanted to produce an effect.

"She hopes that you will visit us again soon. All of us do," Sister Bernadette says, and withdraws diplomatically without waiting for my answer.

The first shoppers to arrive are a large Hispanic family. Ever notice how they take the whole family on shopping trips? It takes ten of them to buy one can of sardines. One of my girlfriends said it shows they have wonderful family togetherness. I told her it makes it easier for them to shoplift.

Of course, that's impossible here. It must be horribly frustrating to a habitual thief to come into a place where everything is free. A pro would probably boost something anyway, just to stay in practice.

My girlfriend, Beverly, said my remark about Hispanics showed that I was prejudiced. I guess Beverly was right. I never knew any Puerto Rican shoplifters. The only shoplifter I know is me.

It still hurts to call myself that. How about my other label—"incest survivor"? No—"incest participant." Does that sound any better?

Thinking about Saint still makes me nervous. I am ashamed at how intensely I lusted after my own brother. Even disgusting old Immaculata with her lurid stories can't equal the horror of that.

I am afraid to see Saint because I'm afraid I will still want him. He stirred up feelings I never knew I had. Have I been hoping that the convent will cure them?

Two of the Hispanic women see a purple glitz-trimmed dress at the same time. They each grab a sleeve and start pulling and yattering. I don't understand a word of it, but if somebody talked like that to me, I'd call the police. The dress is in imminent danger of being torn in half, which would be the only way of improving it.

Sister Bernadette seems to be busying herself with the men's ties, but I can tell she's watching to see how I handle this.

I remembered seeing a glitzy green dress on the size 14

rack. Maritza and Carmen both look like size 14's. Please, dress, be there, I pray silently as the yattering escalates in volume.

Success! I find the shiny green horror and wave it in front of them. The one I've named Maritza lets go of one purple sleeve with a yelp and reaches out for it. Both women are suddenly all brightly lipsticked smiles. It's on to baseball shirts and caps for the two boys, frilly dresses for the three girls, a romper set for the baby, and a pink cotton tent for two-hundred-pound Mamacita. I pack up their booty in brown grocery bags and hand it to them with a smile and a *"De nada"* after they thank me.

I will be helpful, gracious, and diplomatic to everyone, including Jack the Ripper, rather than go back to the steamy hell of the laundry room.

"That was quick thinking," Sister Bernadette tells me after they leave. "In situations like that, I never know what to do unless I pray."

"Do you think I didn't?" I respond, a little too sharply.

She inclines her head. "I'm glad. I think you will do very well out here."

"Thank you," I say.

And she disappears, leaving me alone to deal with the public. I have to admit that her trust makes me feel good. This is nothing but lousy court-imposed community service, something I'd never choose on my own, and she's only two years older than I am, but earning her confidence means a lot to me.

I handle my next customer, an elderly lady with a cane, with effortless ease. Fingering some batiste nightgowns, she complains that they don't make things as well as they used to. I agree with her as if I remember a time when they were made better.

She snatches up four nightgowns, and seems indignant when I tell her about our two-item-of-a-kind per person rule. We have to have some kind of rule, or greedy people would walk out with everything. So each person is allowed only two of each item—two skirts, two dresses, two pairs of socks—never three.

She has a sister, she says, who is the same size as she and is bedridden. Somehow I don't believe her—her eyes are too sharp and calculating, her rings too real. But I shrug and let her get away with it.

The next day, when she comes back pushing her sister in a wheelchair, I will be glad I did.

But today I quickly forget about her. I am kept busy by several mothers with children who chase each other up and down the aisles and tip over a hat rack. I have to tell the mother of one of them that if she can't control her child, she will have to leave. I almost overlook the old guy who is gliding through the menswear section like a ghost, melting into the wall as if he hopes no one will notice him.

But then I observe him fumbling among the trousers as if trying to examine them by feel.

For the first time that day I offer assistance. "May I help you, sir?"

"Ah, yes," he says. "Thank you." He pulls out a pair of slacks. "I was looking for a pair of khakis like these in size 38."

"You have the right size there," I tell him, "but those are gray."

He shakes his head as if bewildered. "Excuse me. A

trick of the light, perhaps. Coming in from the bright sun into the darkness . . ."

It is not dark in here, but I say nothing and move down the rack. "Here you are, sir," I tell him. "There are several pairs of khaki pants here. Short, regular, or long?"

"Regular, I believe," he mumbles, holding the pants up to his waist. Gently I take away all but the regular pair, which are the right length.

I don't know why, but I like this old guy. His curly mustache and his gray sideburns are cute. His manners are nice. He reminds me of someone, but I don't know who.

"You can have two pairs of pants, sir," I tell him. "There are some nice seersucker ones here in your size. Blue and white." He lets me take his hand and guide it to the fabric.

"Perhaps I had better take both," he says, and lifts his left foot. "A ferocious animal ruined this pair."

I can see where something has chewed holes around his cuffs and torn them to shreds. "And what about you?" I ask in alarm. "Did it bite you? Are you all right?"

Without even thinking, I find that I am on my knees, checking his leg for gashes and tooth marks.

He touches my head very gently. "I'm fine, child. Don't trouble yourself about me."

"Someone has to," I say, all angry and bothered. "Did they catch the dog and test it for rabies?"

"No," he says. "Nothing was harmed but my pride."

"If you're sure," I say.

"Oh, yes," he assures me.

For some odd reason, I want to keep this old man here as long as I can, and I want to give him things. "Can I show you some shirts? We have some lovely new short-sleeved ones for summer."

"Plain white?" he asks hopefully.

"No," I say with real regret. "Stripes and plaids, mostly."

"Then I'll pass on the shirts," he says. "I have no place to—" He hesitates, looking stricken. "What I mean is, I don't have room for more shirts. These slacks will be all I need, I think. Unless—" He is hesitant but hopeful. "Would you happen to have a straw hat?"

I think I saw a nice one come in last week. The real thing—straw, not plastic—pale beige, with a navy polka dot band.

"Wait here," I tell him.

But when I come back, he has moved. I look around the racks and finally see him at the back of the store, trying to open the door that leads to the laundry room.

I thought so before, but now I am sure. This old gentleman is blind.

And, unless I misinterpreted what I heard, he is also homeless. I feel a small sharp pain somewhere in the region of my heart.

"Please don't go in there, sir," I call out, and hurry to him.

"Isn't that the dressing room?" he asks. "I was going to change my trousers."

"We have no dressing room," I tell him. I feel bad saying it.

"Ah, well," he sighs. "One can't ask for everything."

"Here's a nice straw hat for you," I say. "Size seven and a half."

He reaches out for it, but his reach is off—about a foot to the left. I have to put the hat in his hands. They are trembling. He feels his way around the hat brim, then puts the hat on and adjusts it so that it is cocked to one side. For a moment he looks young and debonair. Then he straightens the hat.

"Very nice," I say. "It really becomes you."

He smiles. "Thank you, young lady. You've made my day." He has beautiful white teeth that look very nice against his cocoa-brown skin. He is clean, too, and clean-shaven, and wears a rich, spicy fragrance.

Suddenly I know why he fascinates me, why I don't want to let him go. He's not the typical lost soul who haunts this place. He hasn't given up.

"Forgive me for saying this, sir, but you don't seem like the usual sort of person who comes in here. If you don't mind my asking, what was your occupation?" Once this speech tumbles out of me, I am embarrassed.

But he answers gently, "Do you read much poetry, my dear?"

"I used to, when I was in college, but I haven't lately," I confess.

"It doesn't matter. I had a minor reputation once . . . but that was when I was young."

I don't know why, but a flash of lovely language comes into my mind. " 'When I was young and easy under the apple boughs,' " I quote, remembering my English teacher, Sister Mary Teresa. Dylan Thomas was her favorite poet, and "Fern Hill" was her absolutely favorite poem. It didn't take much brains to recognize that it was a good idea, if you were in her class, to memorize it.

"Dylan Thomas. Marvelous. Now you have made my day twice. I could not possibly hope for more." He takes my arm. "My dear, I would be very grateful if you would just point me in the direction of Whitecastle Street."

"I always wondered what he meant by 'the mercy of his means,' " I ask, half out of genuine curiosity, half out of my wish to keep him from leaving.

"It's obvious, isn't it? Think about it, young lady. I must go now." I lead him to the door, though his hand on my arm exerts such a subtle pressure I do not seem to be leading. I turn toward the south and touch his fingers. Instantly, they disengage. I watch him disappear into the distance with a jaunty, slew-footed walk that reminds me of Charlie Chaplin in *The Little Tramp*, and of Richard Pryor imitating Chaplin at the end of *Which Way Is Up?* That walk is heartbreaking. It says that the little tramp is still proud and hopeful, even though the world has labeled him a loser.

This old guy is probably no more of a poet than I am, but I don't care. I wish he had a home to go to, and someone waiting there to fix him a meal.

I call after him, "Sir! I forgot to ask your name!"

He doesn't respond. Probably he's too far away to hear me. I am disappointed. Then I have a surprising insight.

For the first time in ages, I haven't been thinking about myself.

Chapter 23

PATRICE

CHERRY, TONI, ROME, and I work all night, running off flyers, calling people at the last minute, and decorating the A.M.E. Banquet Hall. I sleep so late I almost miss the main event. Our Sixties Soul Extravaganza to raise money for our search—scheduled for today, Sunday, from two till eight P.M.

But I am up by noon, and have time to put a henna rinse into my new dreads. I add some peacock feather dangles in my ears. I think they set off my new tie-dyed caftan, which is mostly turquoise with streaks of yellow and green. I have cut enough off the bottom for a head wrap which, folded into a band, confines my dreads to a nest on top.

I almost leave the house without perfume, then turn back and scan my collection of fragrance oils. I love oils: they're cheap and long-lasting, and they don't dry my skin. I rub Halston oil on my palms, my earlobes, and my neck. I buy my oils from a Muslim who sells them, along with *The Final Call*, from a table in front of a wig shop.

The city chased vendors off our downtown streets, but they don't mess with the Muslims. I figure they're scared of them because they don't smile. Those other folks are so guilty they think that an unsmiling black person is hostile. Well, I got news for them: some days, there ain't a whole lot to smile about.

But everyone smiles at me today as I enter the A.M.E. Banquet Hall, which is bright with balloons, displays, and vividly dressed people. The vibes at this affair are so warm and upbeat, it's like your mama's kitchen.

I see people I haven't seen in years—people from college, people from the scattered jobs that make up my crazy-quilt résumé, people from the Movement, most of them now elegantly gray and safely professional. Briefly I envy their safety, and then reflect that it's probably an illusion. Few of our people have real security or money; most lead a paycheck-to-paycheck existence. But boy, can we dress like millionaires for an occasion! I marvel, admiring a woman in a leopard pantsuit; a couple in a matching Kente dress and necktie; leather skirts and jackets in impossible colors like lavender, white, and magenta; a red skirt that swirls like a hibiscus blossom; a white satin suit. I am encouraged by the crowd of gorgeous younger people, the children of my contemporaries. If the young people have turned out today, we must have put together the right ingredients.

I swish my way past the exhibits. More oils; lots of Afrocentric books and artifacts; enough robes and gelées and dashikis to dress an entire tribe. I make a mental note to come back and check out the jewelry table. The brother's brass necklaces and his beaded bracelets look fabulous, and some of the bracelets might be big enough to slip over my wrists, which have gotten bigger lately. Sometimes, out loud, I wonder why. But no one dares even whisper the word "arthritis" around me, so I never get an answer.

There's a reggae group on the stand, playing Bob Marley's "Three Little Birds." I glide into a merengue, the dance that works with any beat. Before I've reached the table that's set up with our flyers, I've turned a circle and a half on the floor with my secret love, Al Handy, the lean, clean bassist, who is waiting for his set; and done six or seven steps with Reg Harmon, who's exhibiting his oils. In less than two minutes I've had close encounters with two attractive men, and I'm feeling great.

I step-slide, step-slide over to the buffet table, where Lil Graves of Lip Smackers is doing her catering thing. One thing I decided way in advance was not to cook for this event. I do not plan to work at all today. I've done a month's work in the past two weeks; today, Ms. P.B. plans to have fun, thank you.

Lil charges five dollars for a platter and a dollar for seconds, but she extends me professional courtesy. I try not to be greedy with the P.C., though. I take a small yellow plastic plate, and on it I pile only one buffalo wing, one cucumber salad slice, a pinch of greens, and a tablespoonful of the beans and rice. I taste sesame in the cucumbers; it's interesting. The greens are seasoned so well I want to holler, "Mercy!" But it's the black beans and rice that are really talking. I have to have a second helping. I taste tomato and curry and cayenne pepper, but what is that other flavor?

"Licorice!" I suddenly yell. "Lil, you put licorice in this hoppin' john."

"I won't deny it," she says. "They call it anise seed at the Yellow Bird Market, though."

"I won't ask you for the recipe," I say.

"Good," she says. "If you don't ask, I won't have to say no to you."

"How about another spoonful of the rice?" I ask with a wink.

Lil smiles serenely. "Any time," she sings out, and piles a mound on my plate.

"Girl, that hat is saying something." It's brilliant yellow and about two feet across. Tall, sassy Lil is the only woman I know who could get away with wearing it.

"I hope it's saying 'Come over here and buy your supper,' " she replies.

I like Lil. She's a tall, coal-black queen with a regal carriage and unshakable confidence. For years I thought she was from the Caribbean, till I found out she was a Geechee, one of our U.S. coastal people. A lot of them were simply left on the Carolina and Georgia sea islands during the Civil War and, because of the war's outcome, were never enslaved. Since then I've met more of them and found that they all have that proper accent, that erect carriage, and that unassimilated African pride. Pure black skins and plentiful self-esteem.

"I'll talk up the rice," I promise her, and head for the bandstand, where the reggae group is raggedly closing up shop. In front of it, Cherry sits at a table with a pile of our

WANTED!!! flyers, talking to a bronze god. I mean, this guy makes Denzel Washington look like an ad for ugly, and I think Denzel is cute. He's got chiseled features and a sensual mouth and—my weakness—long, tapered, sensitive hands.

I resolutely keep my eyes down. My best friend saw him first.

"Patrice, meet Gus," Cherry says. The light in her eyes is a glad thing to see. They haven't sparkled like this since Aisha hit her teens.

"Pleasure," I say. "Excuse me for not shaking hands. My fingers are still sticky from Lil's buffalo wings." I suck them noisily to demonstrate.

"That good, huh?" this magnificent stranger asks. He's got one of those rich, deep voices that could sell me anything—even a prepaid funeral.

"Better than that," I tell him. In a generous mood, I break my no-work promise to myself, as I knew I would. "Why don't you and Cherry get yourselves some? I'll take over here."

They don't need persuading. "I also recommend the beans and rice," I call after them. I don't know if they hear me. Their arms are linked, their hips are touching as they walk, and their eyes are only for each other.

I permit myself a small sigh of envy, then get busy announcing our raffle, passing out flyers and selling raffle tickets. Toni Brookins comes along and picks up a bunch of tickets to work the crowd. Boy, can our folks pull off some wild color combinations and get away with them! Toni is wearing a peach shirt and a gold skirt under a fuchsia jacket. I was worried about her until she got Rome released. She was pale, and while she is not exactly a natural ebony, she's no Vanessa Williams, either. A smooth tan is Toni's normal, healthy complexion. But she was looking as wan and anemic as a poster child for UNICEF until today. This outfit brings her out, though, and puts some color in her cheeks.

Rome's here, too, selling his Kustom Kool-Aid Kombinations next to Lil's buffet. We have just discovered that Rome is a genius at combining Kool-Aid flavors to come up with original drinks, and, since Kool-Aid is the non-alcoholic African American beverage of choice, we have invited him to peddle them here today. From the size of the crowd around his table, his creations are a hit. The last batch I saw looked grayish-blue. I plan to try some, but I think I'll wait till he runs out of those.

An all-girl group, Vanity Fair, is up on the stand now, wiggling and singing one of those beat-me-and-mistreat-me songs that Billie Holiday made famous. We could do without them. I could also do without this new style of shrieking that is so popular among female vocalists. It's part church, part Patti LaBelle, and all hard on the ears.

I spot Jefferson Davis—yes, that's his name—who as usual is pimping our affair, handing out announcements of the next Commie Worker rally in support of political prisoners. I don't like him. I think he's an undercover FBI agent. I call him over.

"We rented this hall," I say. "If you want to pass out your shit, you have to pass out our shit, too."

He agrees, takes some of my flyers, and grins, showing some really messed-up, dirty rat teeth. The double-agent game must not pay as well as it used to. I remember, back in the day, how incredibly accustomed we became to the presence of spies everywhere. We were young then, of course, and felt invincible, and enjoyed taunting them with greetings like "Well, if it ain't J. Edgar!"

The FBI was less subtle than its informants. At our big rallies they were as easy to spot in their shapeless gray suits as moths in a swarm of butterflies. Their conversations were careless, too; they talked openly about prior assignments to kidnapping cases. I had a regular pair assigned to follow me home whom I called Nit and Dim, the Witt Brothers. I grew almost fond of those stumble-bums. When they didn't show up, I missed them. 'Course I was young, full of bravado, and too ignorant to be scared.

Today, I would be terrified. I would like to eject Jefferson Davis. But when you open your doors to the public, you can't be selective. And besides, I'm afraid he would sic some more sinister spooks on us.

The Vanity Fair girls, wiggling behinds that are much too big to be poured into straight skirts, are leaving, but not before destroying my one good nerve with their shrieks. It's what I deserve for trying to book cheap or free entertainment; they needed exposure, as did the stand-up comic who kept ringing changes on one tired joke about what he considers our only point of moral superiority: black folks are not cannibals like Jeffrey Dahmer. Well, if that's all we've got going, I say, we might as well commit mass suicide.

For an hour now, while everyone else has been partying, I have sat here adding up our receipts. Our tickets went for five dollars. We got thirty dollars a table from each vendor. The hall cost four hundred; the two paid groups of musicians, a hundred each. We are in the clear; that's all I need to know.

The stage is empty, and the Electric Slide is pouring out of four speakers mounted in each corner of the room. My son has just arrived. It's about time. I hand him our strongbox and join the others on the floor, where a hundred people are stepping, sliding, rocking, and turning in precision. This dance, while it looks difficult, is easy, and since almost anybody can do it well, it makes everybody feel good. It's the first new dance to come out in this dry decade. In our heyday it seemed there was a new one every week: as soon as you learned the Monkey, it was time to learn the Watusi; and once you got that down, the Freak had taken over. The Twist was the most popular because everybody could do it. Same way with the Electric Slide today, with the added advantage of not requiring a partner. I try not to notice by how much the single women here outnumber the men. This is one day in my life when I am determined not to get the blues. I am depressed often, though I know how to cover it up with lots of hearty bluffing and jolly noise.

By double-stepping and taking a couple of extra-long slides, I maneuver myself to the side of the room, where Al Handy and his Handymen are getting ready for their set. I wink at Al. Those Tartar cheekbones of his really knock me out. So do his widow's peak and, most of all, those graceful, capable Handy hands. He winks back, but he's getting down to business, talking about keys and chord changes, and will not take time out.

I get back at Al as soon as his group begins its romantic opening number, "Stella by Starlight," by grabbing Reg

Harmon's hand and pulling him out on the floor. Reg is an amiable, eternally boyish man who is far too nice to be sexy. His speech is peppered with sanitized expressions like "Oh, gosh," and "Aw, heck." His good looks have scarcely been touched by time. If he never opened his mouth, I could get a serious yearning for him. But he inevitably does, and what comes out, while it was cute when he was twenty, is ridiculous coming from a fifty-year-old. He's a perennial mama's boy. Old ladies love him and his oil paintings of flowers, puppies, and children. When the dance ends I feel about as romantic as a den mother who's been teaching my troop CPR. I give Reg a motherly pat on the shoulder and detach.

That depression I've been dodging all day is waiting for me when I get back to our table, along with anxiety, guilt, and dread, the Four Horsemen who lurk in the wings of most of my good times. I hear their approaching hoof-beats plainly as my son waves one of our flyers under my nose.

"Mom," he says, "I know this guy."

My denial is instantly full-blown, a rapacious monster on the order of Tyrannosaurus Rex. "No, you don't know him. You can't possibly know him." Fear of exposure is thudding in my chest more heavily than Al Handy's Fender bass.

Saint, meanwhile, is rapidly scanning the description of the Most Wanted. "That explains it," he says.

"Explains what?"

He points to the line that says: *Writer—College Teacher.* "Why he talks like a professor. He *is* a professor."

"Saint," I say sternly, "you can't possibly know this person."

"If I don't, then his twin brother has been coming to the soup kitchen every day. What's up, Ma? Who is this guy?"

"A drunken bum, probably."

"Yes," Saint confirms. "A very special bum, though. First time he came to the soup kitchen, I knew he'd seen better days."

Questions are running through my head rapidly, chasing and obliterating each other like wipes on a TV screen. What is Gene doing here? What ties does he have in this city? How can I quash Saint's curiosity? How can I get to Gene before he does?

Maybe he's wrong, I pray. Let him be mistaken.

I do not want to lose my son's trust. I do not want him to know that his mama is a liar. For twenty-one years I have told him that his father is dead.

Chapter 24

GENE

THERE IS STILL GOODNESS in the world, in spite of the harsh treatment I have received at the hands of so many. That young woman at the quaintly named shop, for instance, was generous and, unless I mistook the tone of her voice, caring.

I am bemused. How odd that someone should care about me—a man who has never been overly concerned about any human being except as an object of study or desire.

A passerby lurches into me. I hear the whine of motorcycles, the heavy sigh of air brakes, the roar of engines, and, heavily underlying all of them, the thud-thud of car radios emitting bass beats. The drivers of these wheeled jukeboxes are all young. Perhaps they find the same satisfaction in their amplifiers as infants who are soothed by their mothers' heartbeats.

I have heard that recorded heartbeats are calming to children in incubators. Still, I wonder why our society seeks to replace all human functioning with machines. Is the electronic recording of a heart superior to the sound of the human one? Is it, for instance, more reliable? No, because either can be knocked out of commission. I think that the machine is preferred because it was created by man, who wishes to dethrone God. I begin planning a new poem, to be called *Hubris*, with a monotonous beat and long, merciless lines:

Hubris
(to be read to the accompaniment of
a loud bass in 2/4 time)

Cranks crank; pistons beat; rise, fall, rise, repeat;
The heart pump, a useless lump, slides toward the
   smoking dump.
Dervishes born of a centrifuge, joylessly conceived and
   rude,
Keep coming on, violent, lewd, no gentleness perceived—

Whoosh! That was close. That cretin of a driver must have jumped the curb. My heart lump is in my throat. I should have gotten more precise directions from that charming child at the Catholic charity store. Ah, Eugene, you are a true artist. Who else would stand in the middle of threatening traffic, blind, lost, and unconcerned, composing verse?

There, I said it, if only to myself—that which I have not admitted until now. In the past I have said that I am nearsighted, vision-impaired, suffering temporarily from dim or glaring lighting conditions, needing new glasses, et cetera, et cetera. . . .

All right, Eugene, you are blind, or so near to it that

it doesn't matter. The first thing to do is get out of the line of fire.

I tap-tap away from the roar of traffic until I encounter a wall, move along that to its end, turn into what must be an alley. There is shade here, and quiet, and solitude. Here I can regroup and get my bearings. I have no special place to go, anyway.

For now, this will do.

How did my condition begin? The right eye, my Cyclopean beacon, began to dim only recently. The left eye has been useless for years. When was it destroyed?

I think it was in Mississippi, when we were in a parking lot, handing out announcements of the night's mass meeting. Martin Luther King was coming, and we were getting out the word, passing out flyers to shoppers, students, loiterers, everyone. Many of them would come to the meeting. They would get fired up and yell "Freedom now!" and "Right on!" but most of them still would not register to vote. I did not blame them. Life was too terrible down there to add more weight to blacks' oppressive burdens.

Was it then that the truckload of armed barbarians appeared?

—No, it was the day after the meeting, a day of canvassing. Things had gone rather well in town, as I remember. Everyone was still fired up from the meeting, and people were more willing to register than usual. I had my approach and my palaver pretty well worked out.

"Good evening, Mr. or Mrs. Name from Mailbox, my name is Eugene Green. I'm with the people who are down here encouraging folks to go down to the courthouse and register to vote. Are you planning on doing that soon?"

If they said no, the interview was over; but if they said yes or maybe, and told me to pull up a chair, I was encouraged. If they brought me iced tea or lemonade, I was pretty sure I had won. I'd pull out the sample registration form, and then I'd get them to tell me about themselves. If they had a family member who needed medical care, for instance, I'd express my sympathy. Then I'd point out that the man in charge of county health felt he didn't have to do anything for them because they hadn't put him in office. If enough of our people got out and voted, that attitude would change, I said.

I thought I'd done very well that day, so I agreed when someone else suggested going out and registering people on a plantation. This was dangerous because plantations were private property and posted with "No Trespassing" signs, so the owner had a right to shoot us on sight. It was damn foolishness, in fact. *Hubris*.

But we were young and full of fire. We went anyway. We didn't get very far. We got to talk to a few sharecroppers who were scared to vote; scared even to look us in the eye, because they were held in virtual slavery by the boss man. This was near the boundary of the plantation, and we had parked our car just outside. This was fortunate, because when we left the second sharecroppers' cabin, a pickup truck without license plates came swooping up and swerved to a halt in the dirt. Six men with red necks and lead pipes jumped out.

Now I remember; it was the same truck and the same

men who had menaced us on the parking lot the day before, swerving close and shouting imprecations. The others in our group got away from the plantation, but I took a pretty bad banging around the back of my head, one that, as it turned out, eventually put an end to my activism. Fortunately, I passed out. My assailants must have thought I was dead and left me there.

When I woke up, the night was pitch-black, dense and thick the way it only gets in the Deep South, and the hoot owls and locusts were singing in a loud chorus. The peace of the country is a myth. One of my problems with rural locales is that they are so noisy. All that wildlife interferes with concentration. There was no moon, or at least it was behind a cloud. And that, too, was fortunate, because my comrades, Terry and Boo, came sneaking back after dark to haul me to the car. They drove me fifty miles for treatment, because they knew the local hospital would turn me away. We waited a long time, but finally I got some stitches and bandages and a few aspirin.

The next day, I began to notice something like a torn black lace curtain coming down over my left eye. In both eyes I had black specks floating around in daylight that became flashes of light in the dark. I didn't pay much attention at the time; my horrible headache was my main concern. But I do remember wondering whether my companions had really had the benefit of a moonless night when they came for me, or if I had just been unable to see Luna's lovely orb.

—Lovely, too, was the lady who comforted me after my beating. She was named Esther. A veteran of the courthouse and the jail, a defier of rednecks and sheriffs, a silly, lovely, lanky girl from New Rochelle, New York, idealistic and dangerously brave. A descendant of servitors who should have been a queen.

After that I met more such angels, as my role in the Movement changed from participant to lecturer, traveling about to raise funds for the front line, describing my experiences, and also, incidentally, reading my poems and selling my books. In each city there was a young woman assigned to be my guide and companion. I depended on these angels for everything. I could no longer drive, so they took me to my engagements. On dim evenings they led me to the stage. Sometimes they read me my poems, to help me memorize them. Always they would spend the night, seeming to consider it their contribution to the cause. Ah, Rowena, Betty, Jean—how I need you now!

I survived Vietnam without a mark, only to be blinded by my cretinous fellow countrymen.

I thought my vision, while poor, had stabilized, but it has been deteriorating for some time. I have found ways of coping, from memorizing street signs and pacing off distances, to using magnifying glasses and then illuminated magnifiers and Visualtek machines, to feeling my way among carefully arranged objects and furniture, to this—broke, homeless, my back against a rough wall. Entropy is, after all, the law of our universe.

I will go on, of course. I can dictate my works. I will memorize my notes. I can lecture, teach, converse. I will find other guides.

But how can I arrange my life without a locus?

I want to go home. Where is my home?

The rough voice seems to come from somewhere above me. "Hey, bro, what you got in that sack?"

"Nothing. Just some clothes."

"Let's see 'em."

I pull out the trousers the young woman found for me at the store.

They are tossed back. "They don't fit me. What else you got?"

"Nothing."

"Well, if you want to stay here you better have somethin'. Money, grub, smoke, drinks, dope—somethin'."

"I truly regret that I have none of the comforts you named. I used to smoke a briar pipe, but I had to give up that luxury. I wish I did have a bottle. If I did, I would certainly share it with you, friend."

"Friend? I ain't your friend. I'm Nate. This is my alley, and if you want to stay here, you got to bring me something. 'Course, now, if you got a bottle, I'll be your friend while it lasts." Hot breath that smells like a garbage incinerator blasts my nostrils, while rough, rude hands slap around my person, checking for concealed cash or comforts.

"You don't believe me," I say with annoyance.

"I do now," says my self-styled landlord. "Why are you looking at me so funny?"

"I'm not looking at you."

"You're blind!" he says in surprise. "Hey—let's us get you a tin cup. You can stand on the corner and rattle it, and bring us some coins."

This is one indignity I will not accept. "I will do no such

thing," I inform him angrily. "I am still a man. And this is a public place. What gives you the right to say this is your alley, anyway?"

"This," he says, and grabs me by the collar, and hauls me to my feet, and propels me outward with a knee in the small of my back. My civil rights training in nonviolence comes in handy here. I land with my head nicely tucked and protected by my arms.

I fear I will not survive long out here on the street, though. Snatches of song run through my mind. "Never turn a stranger from your door" . . . "Gimme shelter" . . . "Take me home, country roads" . . . "I feel so broke up, I want to go home."

Where is my home?

Chapter 25

CHERRY

Aﬁer counting and recounting, checking and double-checking, we are able to accept the glorious truth.

We have made almost a two-thousand-dollar proﬁt after expenses. To be exact, one thousand nine hundred and ninety-three dollars.

We also have, via word of mouth, the names and approximate locations of ﬁve women: Rowena in New York; Wanda and Jean in Baltimore; Esther and Betty in D.C. Other people have promised to look up addresses and write, fax, or call us.

Today Patrice is as hyper and as psyched as someone with a major addiction to speed. Must be that new low-fat diet she's been on. I tell her so. Maybe it's nutritionally healthy, but she's taking the weight off too fast. Twenty pounds in two weeks. You can't tell me that's good for a woman of our tender age.

"I've reached a plateau now; it'll be weeks before I lose more," she reassures me, moving restlessly around my bedroom, eyes darting everywhere. "Besides, on the road I'll be forced to eat fatty things." She rummages in my closet and finds my largest duffel bag, the mud cloth one with the black snakeskin handles, and hands it to me. "There's a train out of here in two hours. Pack."

"What's your hurry?" I want to know.

"What are we waiting for?" she answers.

I calculate quickly, mentally assembling the disconnected pieces of my life. Gus and I had our hour of rapture in this very bed twelve hours ago. It was everything I'd hoped for and more. But he's gone back to North Jersey and his job for another week.

It occurs to me suddenly that if New York is one of our stops, I can snatch some time with Gus. I start packing. Shoes on the bottom, stuffed with stockings and underwear.

I have been so conscientious at my job, working long hours and Saturdays, taking no days off this year except for Aisha's day in court, that they've been bugging me about taking my vacation. I am suspicious—are they planning to sneak someone in to replace me in my absence?—but, knowing I will need to recover from our big party, I have already arranged to take the first half of this week off. I can call tomorrow and arrange to take off the rest of the week.

I add a red crepe dress with a floaty scarf that can go daytime or nighttime, and a three-piece outfit in black-and-white polka dots. All knits, of course. No wrinkles.

My daughter is on good terms with her probation officer and seems to be spending all of her spare time with a bunch of nuns. What could be safer, except that they also seem to be a bunch of drunks?

A pair of white slacks, a pair of black slacks, and a black-and-white-striped T-shirt go in next.

I've been too busy to stop and think about what Aisha's new preference for nuns might mean. Now I do. And what I come up with is a total rejection of me—or of who she thinks I am.

Packing a blue nightgown and matching robe, I tell Patrice, "Aisha is planning to join a convent."

"Bad move," Patrice says. "That set drips dry, doesn't it? Why are you packing an extra nightgown?"

"Because," I say, folding a fabulous red satin surplice-front gown that has lain in my drawer for years, "I might not have time to do laundry." I am not thinking of laundry, however. I am thinking of dazzling Gus. "Do you think all this is a reaction to us?"

"Of course," Patrice says. "She's always disapproved of us. To hear her tell it, we were wild, wayward tramps."

"Sluts," I correct her. "That's the exact word she uses. I don't mind telling you it hurts, Patrice. I know all about mother-daughter rivalry, but when will her adolescence end?" There is a dangerous break in my voice, signaling tears on the way.

"When you let it. That's why you need to go away for a long, long trip. Finished packing?"

"No!" I cry emphatically. I stuff a white shirt into the duffel. "I am so sick of my life. I work day and night and come home to nothing but problems." I add an extra pair of stockings. "I think I have problem burnout. I didn't even react when Aisha told me she planned to join the convent. Sometimes people's emotions get so bent out of shape they're like a rubber band that's been stretched too far. That's what's happened to me, I think."

"What about Gus? He's not a problem, is he?"

I pause briefly to smile at recent memories. "Oh, no. He's a joy. He makes me so happy I'm scared." He is the only man I've ever known who talks to me in bed. We share childhood memories. We both believed in the Easter Bunny, though not in Santa Claus. We both had parents who rationed our sweets. We both ate the bottoms out of our Easter eggs, hoping our mothers wouldn't catch us. These are the kind of great, dumb things we have in common.

Patrice nods. "I know the feeling," she says. "It's been a long time, but I remember."

"My child is a drunk, Patrice. I hope we do find her drunken father. Then she can have somebody else to blame besides me." Knee-highs go in next, a three-pair pack from the best source, my supermarket. Theirs are long—actually almost knee-high—and come in shades other than that ugly, pointless Off-Black. I always buy Cinnamon, which is nearest to my complexion. "Should I have sent her to some other school? Was the Catholic school a bad influence? Were we really sluts?"

"No, no, and no. We were young, idealistic women dedicated to a righteous cause. We worshiped our heroes. Some of us let them take advantage of us. Just where do you think you are going to wear that?"

I see to my surprise that I am holding a purple velvet sheath left over from the winter of, maybe, '75. This is '96, and it is certainly not winter. It is the end of June, and at ten-thirty in the morning the day is already beginning to send rivers of sweat down my face. I will donate this relic to Aisha's shop.

"You've got enough clothes in that bag for a month. Zip it up, girl. Let's hit the road," Patrice urges.

"Just let me find my sandals," I say, on my hands and knees, tunneling into the back of my closet.

"What for?"

"I might need them," I howl. "Patrice, stop pushing me. What's your hurry, anyway? You act like the Devil is chasing you."

I emerge with one patent leather sandal in each hand and inspect them. Shit. I had forgotten about the broken latch on one of the buckles. I cram them into the bag anyway, even though I know this is a nutty thing to do. I know my packing has reached its mad, manic Take Everything, You May Need It stage, but I tell myself that maybe I can get them fixed in New York.

I sit down on the edge of the bed to get my breath.

"Finished yet?" Patrice urges, hovering.

"Wait," I growl. "Let me think." I leap up and grab a couple of necklaces from my jewel box, which is a row of nails on the wall. Real crystal. Fake pearls. Now where is my silver chain? And my silver bell earrings, my dangles that dingle?

"You don't have room for anything else," this clucking mother hen, who used to be my friend, informs me.

"I told you to back off, Patrice." I see no reason to inform her that this bag has two side compartments, and that I always use one side for jewelry and reading matter and the other for cosmetics. I go into the bathroom and gather up cleanser, night cream, lotion, foundation, powder, blush, lipstick, and eye stuff.

"More?" Patrice asks when I dump it all on the bed and go back to the bathroom. "You're going to ruin your skin, piling all that junk on it."

I return with hair stuff: comb, brush, grease, gel, shampoo, spray, and moisturizer. I look at it. "Sometimes being a woman just isn't worth the trouble," I complain. "Look at all the crap it takes just to face the day. A woman's life is so goddamn complicated."

"Then uncomplicate it. Throw that junk away. Don't you understand it's part of the capitalist plot to keep us poor and distracted? Or pack it, I don't care, but *come on*."

I am unhappy. Patrice has allowed me to do my first phase of packing, which is Stuffing, but she isn't giving me enough time for the second phase, which is Thinning. I look, really look at her. There are dark circles under her eyes, as well as deep pouches from her recent weight loss. Furrows stripe her brow and run from her nose to her mouth. She looks old. I don't want to think about what this says about me. We are the same age.

"Well come on, come on, come *on*!" she cries. She is so spastic, she actually snatches the bag from my hands.

I smack her hands away. She probably needs a smack on the face as well. I wonder if she is taking diet pills. "Girl, you've been racing like a runaway train ever since you came in here. This isn't like you, Patrice. What are you running away from?"

She sighs, starts to speak, changes her mind, and mumbles something about train schedules.

"If I heard you right, we have an hour and a half before the next train. And after that, there's bound to be another train. Besides, where's *your* stuff? While you're standing here supervising me, have you packed?"

She waves a large raffia hobo bag. "Got a toothbrush and some drawers and a couple of extra caftans in here. Nothing else fits. I'm between sizes. Are you ready now?"

"Patrice, what's your hurry?" I ask for about the tenth time. "The trains run all day. Why are you tripping?"

She pants like a dog on a hot day. She struggles for breath and seems about to have an asthmatic attack. Finally she says, "I'll tell you when we're on the train. I want outta here, that's all!"

I consider. My best friend is in real distress. There's no reason to torment her by dragging my feet any more than necessary. I can shower and dress and wind up my business in half an hour. "You got it," I say.

I stop at the station to leave a message on our answering machine for Aisha. She'll get it, all right: the little electronic monster will beep and beep until she checks it. Then Patrice and I buy our rail passes, which we have calculated carefully to be cheaper than the bus, what with all the back and forth we plan. Then I push my friend, who is falling apart with nerves and hypoglycemia, into the station's cholesterol palace.

"Two big ones," I tell the girl behind the counter. "One apple juice, one strawberry milkshake, two orders of fries."

"Oh no, not fries," Patrice moans. "That's the worst kind of sabotage. I thought you were my friend. How can you do this to me?"

"I can't travel with you in this condition. I'll go insane," I tell her. "Eat."

I confiscate the carrot sticks and sunflower seeds she has pulled out of her bag and shove the burger at her.

"I can't tolerate milk," she says, taking her first bite.

"I know," I say, and nudge the juice in her direction. "The shake is for me."

I watch, slurping my shake through a straw. After three bites of her massive sandwich, Patrice improves. Her eyes grow less glassy and her hands stop shaking.

"Better?" I ask.

"Much better," she admits, and pats her stomach, and gives out a huge, hearty belch. She reaches for a french fry. I snatch the fries away and give her back her carrot sticks.

"You were right, we don't need these." Before we both get completely decadent, I take the fries to the trash bin.

Patrice is as near as I have ever seen her to tears. "You have a cruel streak, do you know that, Cheryl Hopkins? It isn't even a streak. You're cruel through and through."

"The burger was to save your life. You don't need fries, too. There's mayo on your upper lip."

Patrice wipes her mouth and sighs. "I think I almost passed out just now. I've got to do more work on the carbo-protein ratio. My energy shake this morning was obviously lacking something I needed."

"How much are you trying to lose?" I ask.

"It doesn't matter. Forty pounds wouldn't hurt, but this project isn't just personal vanity. I'm working on a weight-loss formula that will reduce world misery."

"And a cookbook, of course."

"Of course. Last night I came up with some ambrosia

that's only eighty calories. You take strawberries, diced apples, cantaloupe chunks, orange juice, two tablespoons of coconut—"

"Patrice, have you checked with your doctor?"

Her eyes bulge with anger. "Why the hell do you think I'm putting myself through this shit? I saw my doctor last week. She said my blood pressure was sky high and if I didn't take off weight I'd be in Stroke City. Satisfied? Now let me enjoy my cholesterol in peace. Ahhhh."

She has another mayo mustache, but I say nothing. I am very glad I tossed the fries.

"There is an up side to this," she tells me. "I really am doing a cookbook. Yesterday I made some divine barbecued chicken. Just two tablespoons of ketchup and two of brown sugar, plus vinegar and horseradish. No skin on the chicken. Only one gram of fat. Scrumptious."

I mumble something about virtue and necessity as the loudspeaker announces the Glub-Glub Special, bound for Booblubba, Hoo Ha, Wurfanny, and Doodaw.

"That's us," Patrice announces, and gets to her feet. "I want to get some seltzer before we board."

"Why isn't Toni with us?" I ask her once we are settled in those hard coach seats with ugly maroon upholstery that is impregnated with that special ancient railroad dust they get from the Museum of Travel Misery. Once, I would get up as soon as the conductor punched my ticket and head for the club car. I have had a lot of disasters in club cars. I am glad I don't remember them all. I stay put.

"Anxious mommy blues," she says. "She feels she has to watch Rome every minute while he's on probation. 'Course, he's only sixteen, so I can't say anything to her.

But personally, I think she can trust him. His success with the Kool-Aid did a lot for him. All he needs is another win or two and he'll be fine. I wish he knew Saint was his big brother. I think that would help. But it's up to Toni to break that news."

"You promised to give me an answer, Patrice. Why were you in such a horrible, pushing, shoving hurry today?"

My friend is silent for a long time. She sits staring out the window at a passing train, apparently not minding the sense of reversed motion that always gives me such a queasy feeling. "The same thing," she finally says. "Mommy anxiety. Cherry, what did you tell Aisha about her father?"

I think back carefully. "That he would never be any help to us, so we had better leave him out of our lives. That he was not a bad man, just a man with problems. So many problems that we would be better off without him."

"Did that satisfy her?"

I really have to think about that one. "Eventually, I think." Aisha stopped asking about Gene when she was ten. But once in a while, even now, she will start to ask me something, then break off. Or one of us will change the subject. The context of the conversation always makes me think the question would have been about her father. I also think that unasked, unanswered question may be part of the tension between us.

"Lucky you," Patrice says. I don't feel lucky at all. "I told Saint his father was dead."

The statement hits me with a dull, sick thud, like a sandbag. "Maybe he is," I finally say, but I don't believe it.

"Somehow I don't think so," Patrice says. "I'm afraid Saint will have a huge disappointment if Gene turns up. See, with his father dead, I could build up a portrait of this huge, perfect hero daddy. Genius, achiever, freedom fighter, superman, all that. I figured that, being a boy, he needed that myth."

"Uh-huh. And if the real, live, flawed dad turns up, he'll be mad at Mommy for lying to him, right?"

"You got it. He'll be worse than mad. He'll feel betrayed. He would even if his pop were perfect, and we know he isn't." Patrice is glum. The litter-strewn fields sliding by our window do not do much to cheer her up. "Saint was very interested in our flyer. He even asked me if the guy in the photos was his father."

"What did you say?"

"I said yes. I said we were just trying to find out if he has any more brothers and sisters." She lifts her several chins defiantly. "That's the truth, isn't it?"

"Sure," I say. "Part of it, anyway."

Patrice stares out the window some more. "Saint thought he recognized the guy," she finally says. "He thought he'd seen him at the soup kitchen where he volunteers. I told him he had to be mistaken."

"Of course," I say, thinking: This is the way our glorious, liberated single mommyhood turns out. Our children turn to each other, to nuns, to bums, to anybody but to us. Us, they don't trust.

"And that's why I'm running away," Patrice confesses. "I couldn't stand to answer any more of my son's questions. Not right now."

There is a long silence except for the clack-clacking

wheels taking us away from our problems and toward the unknown.

Finally Patrice says, "I've got to come clean, don't I? I've got to tell him the truth."

"Yup," I say. "But you don't have to do it today."

Chapter 26

SAINT

TUESDAY, ON THE WAY HOME, I decide to take Lamar to the free clothing store. His lace socks are messing up his image. Plus, that orange woman's top he has on hurts my eyes. I would have taken him before, but I heard Aisha was working there, and I wasn't ready to see her. Now maybe I am.

There's a big four-lane divided street, Whitecastle, between us and the store. When we reach it, Lamar suddenly decides to take off. He darts across, almost gets hit by a taxi and barely makes it to the center island.

"What's the idea?" I yell when I catch up with him. "Don't you have good sense? Thought I was going to have to sponge you up and squeeze you home. How would your mama have liked that? Huh?"

"The light was green," he says defiantly.

"It was green for that taxi, too. When he turned, he almost clipped you."

"Aw, man, taxis don't obey no rules."

"That's why you have to look all four ways. Did you?"

"No," he admits.

"All right, give me your hand."

He pulls his back. "Men don't hold hands."

"Men can cross streets by themselves."

"I was crossing streets by myself long before I met you."

"Yeah, but while you're with me, you're my responsibility. I ain't gonna give your mama an excuse to get me locked up. More likely she wouldn't bother; she'd just kill me. Put it here."

Finally he puts his grubby paw in mine. We start off after the light changes and we have checked all directions.

"See, it's always better to take your time," I lecture. "Get your butt killed or put in a wheelchair, you'll have nothing but time."

"I don't care if I get killed," he says, half under his breath. "I don't want to grow up, anyway."

Now, this is a statement that has to be dealt with seriously. I imagine this kind of thing happens fairly often to people who deal with kids—parents, teachers—but I doubt they are ever prepared for it. At least I know better than to blow it off as a joke.

"Why not, Lamar? Why don't you want to grow up?"

" 'Cause I ain't got nothing to grow up *for*."

It's wrong of me, and I know it, but I can't help lapsing into standard adult denial. "How can you say a thing like that? How do you know what your future will be like?"

"Kids around my way, they into guns, drugs, gangs, killing and getting killed. Couple more years, I'll have to join a gang, too. Plus, I got eyes, man. Just look around.

Look there." With a nod of his sober little head he indicates a couple of guys sharing a forty on a stoop. At least they are vertical, and conscious. "There, and there." He points to the pathetic heaps you see everywhere now in cities: homeless men on the street, huddled under blankets, maybe alive, maybe dead. "And there."

One is actually in the gutter, his arms covering his head. Much as I've heard the expression, I have never actually seen a person in the gutter before. It's getting on toward rush hour, and traffic is heating up.

"We better get him up from there, before that taxi comes back," I say.

As I bend to help the guy up, Lamar says, "Hey! It's him! The old guy who wanted to see you!"

It's the Professor, all right, worn out and barely conscious. I raise him and drag him into the shade. There I lift him into a sitting position. He mumbles something, but it is incoherent. He must have passed out. Not from drinking, though; there is no booze on his breath. As I study his face, his eyes open. They are the same almond-shaped eyes that were so compelling on Mom's poster. They used to be hidden behind thick horn-rimmed glasses, but now they are blank and do not see me.

He was some kind of uncrowned prince, Mom said. Serene as a Buddha, and gracious as only royalty and the very rich can be. Where he got his grandeur, coming from Jefferson Manor in North Philadelphia, she could not imagine. But he made people believe in it, she said. He rarely had two quarters to rub together, but waiters, shop clerks, taxi drivers, people everywhere respected him and treated him like a rich, important man. They fell all over themselves competing to get the best table, the best silk ties, the finest wine for Mr. Green; competing to be the first to shake his hand, or take his coat, or open the door for him.

I imagine that women competed for him, too. Mom said he had quite a few, but he respected them all and made each one feel special, like the only woman in the world. Pop, you were bad, I say, and take off my cap. You were one of the greatest. Like the song goes, you have had your fun, if you don't get well no more.

"Hey, Lamar," I yell. "You know the place where we were going—the Good Samaritan Gift Shop?"

"Yeah. I been there." He pulls at his hideous blouse. "I think Mom found this thing there."

So that was why he didn't want to go, and tried to run away. "They have cool stuff, too," I tell him. "I want you to go there now and ask for a Miss Hopkins. Ask her to come back here with you right away. Tell her—"

"Tell her what?" he asks impatiently, for it is taking me a long time to finish my sentence. There seems to be an obstruction in my throat.

Not all the heroes of the freedom struggle were famous, Mom told me. Most of them were unknown, like my father. Few knew of the injuries he had suffered for the cause. He almost died for you, she said, squeezing my hand so hard she left scratch marks. Don't you ever forget it. I'm not sure about Jesus dying for you, but I know your father almost did. He almost died fighting for your freedom before you were born. Let him be your Jesus, she said.

"Tell her I need—" I take a deep breath. I can't seem to

get enough air. It's the pollution, that's it. "Tell her I need her help with our father."

"Don't run, Lamar!" I yell after him. "Wait for the light before you cross!" But he is out of sight.

Poetry poured out of my father the way water flows down mountains, sometimes rushing and roaring, sometimes trickling softly, always natural, always right, my mother said. He spoke French like a native of Paris, she told me, though he was from Jefferson Manor in North Philadelphia. My father spoke cultivated English like someone who had gone to Oxford. He went to Penn State. He slept in someone's car all through his senior year, because he could not afford a room. When he recited his poetry he sounded like an angel, she said. He was an angel now, she told me when I was five. He was dead.

I wonder why she told me that lie. I am not angry with her about it right now, just puzzled, but maybe I will be angry later on.

I sit there on the sidewalk with my arm around the frail, bony shoulders. How did I know, the first time I saw this old guy, that we were connected? He was incredibly light when I picked him up, like a paper doll. I am so tall and solid; how could he have made me? Will I waste away to this someday?

These thoughts so occupy my mind that I am not ashamed to be sitting on the sidewalk in broad daylight, holding up an old bum. I am not even ashamed of the shine of tears on my face.

Chapter 27

CHERRY

I HAVE ALWAYS SAID I have to be up for New York. When I'm feeling low, this town can weigh me down, put me six feet under, and leave me for dead. But when I'm up, there's no place that buoys my spirits as much. Today I'm feeling good, and the crowds, the hustle, the colors, the accents all affect me like champagne.

On this warm spring day, Eighth Street in the Village, where Rowena Mitchell lives, is like a Turkish bazaar with tents and awnings hung with baubles. I buy a pretty string of beads for Aisha, a star on a silver cord for myself, and cowrie shell bracelets for both of us.

We hit the jackpot on our first try. Rowena has twins. Abdul and Aneesah Mitchell Green Ali are sixteen, lanky, and golden. Abdul is serious, reads a lot, and wears glasses. Aneesah is much too beautiful for her own good and has a sly, secretive smile. She carries herself with a degree of assurance that usually comes with more than twice her years. I feel for her mother.

Rowena Mitchell Ali is a gentle, unassuming woman from the Deep South who managed to find her way up here and go to Columbia. She, too, would be beautiful if she paid attention to things like looks. But she is too busy caring for her children and working, both in her community and as a nurse at Harlem Hospital. Most weeks, she tells us, she works double shifts to pay the bills, then puts in another day at the local free maternity and baby clinic.

She wears long, flowing skirts and, when she goes out, a white head scarf. Raised a Baptist, she says that she became a Muslim to gain protection for herself and discipline for her children. It seems to be working with Abdul, who is studious and polite. But Aneesah will need more than her long skirts and the headdresses, which I suspect she takes off as soon as she is out of her mother's sight, to make her behave. Even with her hem down to her ankles, she has a provocative walk, which she displays while going to the kitchen to bring us some juice.

Patrice asks whether Rowena has ever tried to get in touch with Gene.

No, Rowena says, because shortly after her babies were born, she married a Muslim, and though they were divorced a few years ago, by that time there didn't seem to be any point. The Muslim was good about providing for her children and helping her pay for her education, but he had harsh ideas about discipline. He had hit Abdul one time too many and was about to slap Aneesah when she told him to leave.

I believe this woman means what she says. If she asked me to leave, I'd get out, too. Her voice is soft, and her eyes are meekly lowered most of the time, but when she describes her husband's rough ways with her children, they flash green fire. To go with the green eyes she has sandy, nappy hair, liberally mixed with gray, and a honey complexion. Her wire-rimmed glasses do absolutely nothing for her, but contacts and some Clairol would turn her into a cover girl, even at fifty. She's not about to spend time and money on anything so frivolous, however.

When Patrice tells her about our fund-raiser and the resulting loot, and offers to take the whole family out to dinner, Rowena looks at us and laughs. "You got to be out of your mind," she says. "You can't get dinner for five in New York for less than two hundred and fifty dollars. You got that kind of money to throw around, I'll take it and get myself a comfortable bed to put in here in the living room. I gave Neesy my bedroom when she got her womanhood, and this old couch is plenty lumpy."

"Done!" Patrice declares, and peels off some bills from the roll she carries in her hobo bag, while Rowena goes to the kitchen to fry some meat and heat up some rice and pinto beans. She sends her daughter to the store for cucumbers and Vidalia onions, admonishing her not to loiter on the corner where the boys are.

"Those pond ganders down there have only one thing to offer you," she tells her.

"But Maaaa—" the beauty whines. "Some of them are nice boys."

"Nice nothing. You want me to slap you in front of our company?"

"No," says Aneesah, and whirls, and stomps down the stairs from their fourth-floor flat. We talk about our own children for a while, and then Rowena shakes her head. "Allah has blessed me with a good son. But that girl is 'bout to run me crazy. I only hope a good, strong man comes along to marry her."

"Is that the only future you want for her?" Patrice brays.

"Sister, I'm as much for women's liberation as you are," Rowena declares. She's been hacking up some beef chuck, and she is brandishing a cleaver that would cause anyone but Patrice to back off. "But I'm from the country, and I know the facts of life. Sometimes a girl comes into this world with red pepper in her britches, and she can't concentrate on anything until she relieves that itch. My daughter Neesy is that kind of girl. So I hope she marries early, has a couple of kids quick, and calms down. After that, I think she can do or be anything."

"Well, I guess that makes sense," Patrice concedes, "as long as she doesn't marry one of her relatives."

"Amen to that," punctuates Rowena, her Baptist upbringing showing. "It's a good thing you're looking for them." She tells her daughter, who has returned by now, "Neesy, serve the ladies juice, then come back in here."

"But Maaa," the girl whines, "there's a party tonight at Davila's."

"This is more important than any party. How often do you get to hear about new family? You have a brother besides Abdul."

"Two brothers that we know of so far," I correct.

"And a sister, isn't that right?"

"Yes. My daughter is nineteen."

For once, this restless child is silent. Her eyes are wide and solemn. "For real?"

"For real."

"What's her name?"

"Aisha."

"What's she like?"

I am searching for the right words to describe my daughter when Abdul interrupts. "I want to know about the guys."

"Romare is sixteen. He's a sophomore in high school, and he's into art, especially graffiti," Patrice says. "My son, Toussaint, is twenty-one and a junior in college. He's good at science. He likes to cook. And he can hoop."

"Cool!" Abdul exclaims. "Hey, Mom, when can we meet them?" These languid, sophisticated city teenagers are suddenly babbling as excitedly and noisily as a coopful of chickens.

"Quiet!" their mother orders. "That will happen in Allah's own time. Abdul, remove these dishes. Aneesah, go pour the tea and bring it in."

I have been hoping to spend the night here. That is, I have been hoping Patrice will stay, while I call Gus to pick me up, and go off and spend the night with him. But if Rowena is sleeping on her couch, that means she has no spare room for guests. And if I asked her to recommend a hotel, she would send for Harlem Hospital's psycho squad to intervene in our economic suicide.

Over fragrant raspberry tea Patrice and I pledge to have a get-together for all the mothers and their progeny as soon as we have located them. Rowena promises us whatever aid she can provide. She has to stifle a series of yawns. It is, after all, a weeknight, and she does have to be up at dawn.

I ask her permission to make a call—using my phone card, of course.

The phone at Gus's apartment rings and rings. I bite one nail to the quick, waiting for him to answer. He doesn't. He does not have a machine, either. Dag. I wish some people would stop refusing to enter the twentieth century. It's almost the twenty-first now.

We take our leave.

"No more trains to Baltimore till morning," Patrice says, consulting her schedule in Rowena's vestibule.

I brighten. "Know any cheap hotels around here?"

" 'Cheap' and 'hotel' do not go together in New York," she admonishes me. "In fact, 'cheap' and 'New York' do not go together, period. Do not use them in the same sentence."

There is a storm of heels and a flurry of skirts on the stairs. I turn to look. The flamencolike stamping and flourishing are only Aneesah, her crisp auburn waves shrouded in a white kerchief.

"Mother says to forgive her, she was not thinking. You are invited to spend the night with us, in my brother's room. We hope you don't mind bunk beds."

We mumble something about not wanting to put anybody out.

"It is our pleasure and our way of helping," Aneesah says. "Mother will be quite comfortable sleeping in my room with me. And Abdul likes the sofa. Don't tell our mother, but he turns on the TV and watches all night. Sometimes I get up and watch it with him, if there's a good scary movie on. Don't tell." Suddenly she is very young, and adorable.

Back upstairs, Rowena apologizes as she flings clean sheets over her son's bunks. "Almost forgot my home training. Down home in Jessup, we never let travelers go on after dark. We give them the best bed and apologize 'cause it ain't better."

"Did you say Jessup?" Patrice exclaims excitedly. "Jessup, Georgia? We might be cousins. I have people there."

They embrace briefly and start the endless exchange of names and relationships that southerners always do and which I always tune out. This is why we call the North "up South," because almost all of us have roots down there. But as far as I know, my people have been in the North for four generations.

Seems they figure out they are second cousins once removed and linked by in-laws, or something. "That makes two reasons why you're family," Rowena says. "Two reasons why I oughta to be ashamed of myself for sending you out in the dark."

"The only thing we all ought to be ashamed of is all that careless fucking we did," I say, surprising myself with my anger and frankness.

"Now you said something deep there, sister," our hostess declares. "There's no excuse for it, except we were young and all fired up with Freedom." She glances over her shoulder at her two youngsters, covers her mouth, then smiles. "I'm grateful for these two bandits, though. I guess it could have turned out worse, huh? Rest well. If we're gone in the morning, help yourself to breakfast. There's bagels and orange juice and fruit. Just lock the top lock and leave the key with the newsstand man at the corner."

Chapter 28

GENE

I AM SURROUNDED BY ANGELS. They support me, examine me, wipe my brow with soft, cool hands. A very small one crouches beside me, giving me sips of cherry Kool-Aid. It is not what I want, but it is good.

"We'll take him to my place," I hear the girl angel say decisively. "We can put him in Mom's room. She'll be gone with your mother for at least a week." She shouts, unnecessarily loud, in my ear, "Sir, do you think you can walk? It's not far." When you cannot see, I am learning, people think you are deaf as well.

The young male angel assists me to my feet, and I realize that I have not died and gone to Heaven after all. There is no pain in that blessed place. I have pain everywhere, in muscles I never even knew I possessed.

"Take it easy," I tell him as he sets off at a brisk pace. "Can we go more slowly?"

"Sure thing," he says, and then repeats, a bit hesitantly, "Sure thing, Dad. Sorry." I am puzzled by this appellation but decide, for the nonce, not to question it. When God sends angels, I believe we should not inspect them or question them too closely.

"Damp concrete is not the most comfortable couch at my age," I tell him by way of explanation.

"Not at any age, Pops," the littlest angel declares brashly. He does not mean the appellation filially, only generically. And he is not, I soon decide, an angel, but an imp. "You're educated—how come you're on the street? The Saint, here, is always telling me I got to get an education, but it don't look like it's done you any good."

"Hush, Lamar," the young man reproves him. "Show some respect."

"No, let me answer him," I say. I do not believe in much, having affected a cynical pose for so long that it has seeped into my being and become part of me, but I do truly believe that, until we draw our last breaths, it is our obligation to educate our young. "The boy deserves an answer."

We stop so that I can draw enough breath. "There are two types of education: the kind aimed at enriching the soul, and the kind aimed at enriching the purse. I chose the former.

"That is to say, I elected to become an artist, not a moneymaker. If the world were fair and just, artists would make plenty of money. But it is not, and therefore poets are poor.

"And yet, a certain kind of fairness can be seen at work here. Poets seldom have much money, but we are richly compensated by the joy of the work we do. We get to make music out of language. We get to understand meanings that are beyond the reach of the ordinary physical man and woman. We get to share these truths with others who can appreciate them. And we even get paid a few pennies for this ecstasy."

"Dag. You really answered my question. Thanks." Clearly the boy is not used to serious, honest responses. They are the main thing I believe our children need. If we can't give them anything else, we can do that.

"You're welcome. Do you understand what I said?"

"You don't have much money, but you're happy 'cause you like what you do," Lamar paraphrases.

"Exactly. Just now, before you found me, I was facing the lowest point of my life. I had no money, no home, no friends and no family, and I could not see. Yet I was not depressed, because I had just gotten an idea for a new poem."

"Saint, your poppa is crazy," the little boy says.

"Exactly," I say.

"Lamar, I told you, show respect for your elders," the young man rebukes him.

"Don't correct him. He's absolutely right. If I were sane I would have majored in Waste Management, and I would be making big bucks collecting and disposing of shit. He knows this. I hope he will be smart enough to remember it and do the opposite of what I did. Be a shit collector, Lamar, not an injustice collector. But why does he call me your papa?"

Now it is the soft-spoken young woman at my side who has stopped walking. Once again she places my fingers on her arm. "Because you are," she says. "What is your name, sir?"

I recite it with trepidation.

"I thought so. My mother told me your name," she says. "She told me about your poetry, too. Your last name is my middle name. I am your daughter, Aisha Green Hopkins."

"And I am Toussaint Dessalines Barber," the young man says. "My mother gave me your middle name."

"So you see," the young woman concludes, "you were wrong when you said you had no family. We go up four steps here."

She stops. I hear her turning keys and opening a pair of doors. Then she places my hand on a railing. "Ten steps up now."

"Where are we?"

"My house. Mine and my mother's. My mother is Cheryl Hopkins."

I think I must swoon then. I think the young man they call Saint must carry me up the stairs. I wake up with my head on a fragrant pillow. As I breathe in lily of the valley, memory stirs, and everything suddenly clicks into place. Cherry. The most ferocious, dogmatic, passionate little revolutionary of them all. Cherry of the mischievous eyes, and the proud walk, and the round, perfect, impudent ass. She was going to have a baby because Chairman Mao said she should. She would bear a revolutionary's child and raise it to wage class war.

But our little warrior is, as it turns out, a girl.

"Come here, Aisha," I say. "I need to identify you.

Please understand that I am not being fresh. Blind people require special tolerance." She meekly submits to my outrageous but respectful all-over touching.

"Yes," I sigh. "You are who you say you are. Sit down, my dear. I hope you will sit on that for the rest of your life."

My warrior, Toussaint, is not very warlike, in spite of his name. He brings me some magnificent *soupe à l'oignon,* which he has made himself. The broth is at once hearty and as delicate as a kiss. "Do you know for whom you are named, Toussaint?" I ask him.

"Yes, sir," he replies politely, and goes on to give me a perfect history of the Haitian revolution.

"Excellent," I say. "The same might be said of your soup. You are a student?"

"Yes, sir," he says.

I approach the next question cautiously. Memory is a minefield set to explode. "And your mother's name is . . . ?"

"Patrice Barber," he says, "Originally, Patricia."

Ah, yes. My memory needs no priming this time. Patricia was a revolution all by herself. Large, loud, fearless, she strode into controversy as boldly as a tank approaching a battlefield. She was all heart. And all woman.

So the two of us made this perfect young man who now waits patiently to see if I will have more of his soup. I do not need to touch him to see him. I hear him, and in his history I hear my life.

"And how is your mother?" I force myself to ask.

"She's fine," he says.

"And where is she?"

"Our mothers just left on a trip together," his sister says, "to find the rest of your children."

It is all too much for my poor exhausted heart. I am overcome. I hand him back the empty bowl and fall instantly asleep.

Chapter 29

PATRICE

WE DRAW A BLANK IN BALTIMORE. The woman we are looking for, Wanda Henderson, has moved and left no forwarding address. We trudge wearily back to the station to await the next local to D.C. Taxis here seem to be as scarce as Bengal tigers, but then, we are in a black neighborhood, where they seldom venture. I am sure that they are as thick as bumblebees around a rosebush down by the harbor. But we are forty blocks from the harbor and its posh development, which also does not come near our folks. My feet hurt.

I am having doubts about the value of our mission. Strike that. I am having doubts about our ability to carry it out. My knees hurt, and one of my hips crunches with each step. A glance in the mirror this morning informed me that I am of an age to be sitting in a rocking chair, knitting afghans for my grandchildren.

Cherry must be reading my mind. "We can't have grandchildren till we find their aunts and uncles," she says. "Nobody is getting married until we find out who is who." Her emphasis on that "nobody" has the thump of a judge's gavel.

She is right, of course. One thing the black community does not play about is blood relatives. And we don't do things halfway, either. Among us there is no such thing as a "half" brother, a "step" sister, or an "adopted" or "once removed" cousin. Relatives are relatives, and when it comes to lust between relatives, the rule is, hands off.

Of course there are those who break that rule, but the punishment for them is expulsion from the very large families our interpretations of relatedness tend to create.

So this excursion is necessary. And it is fair. It is payback for our youthful playtime.

But how does Gene fit into all of this? Is he still getting off scot-free, without paying any dues? I imagine him somewhere in one of those velvet smoking jackets he used to affect at home, brandishing that briar pipe and fascinating a whole new generation of women. If he is still enjoying the carefree life of a lazy lion, nothing in this life is fair.

"Gene didn't ask us to have his children," Cherry pipes up in the coach seat across from me.

"Will you stop that?" I scream. Her sudden psychic ability is really getting on my nerves.

"Stop what?"

"Reading my mind."

"I wasn't. I was just thinking. We chose him because he seemed to be so wonderful."

"And we chose single motherhood because we wanted to be liberated."

"Different from our parents, who were slaves of the system."

"Boojy tools of capitalist oppression."

Talk about precognition *and déjà vu*! The same conversation will be repeated tonight in the living room of Esther Easton, social worker and mother of Levi, eighteen; and tomorrow while munching sandwiches in Rock Creek Park with Jeanie Burrell, whose Assata is seventeen; and Betty Burns, whose Burghardt is twenty.

Together we agree on many things. Our thinking was sound. The system was and is rigged against us. Revolution against it was an honorable choice. Only our conclusions were false.

Our parents, poor dears, were no better and no worse than anybody else's. From the vantage point we have now reached—putting it kindly, the far side of forty—they now seem to be heroes, in a quaint sort of way. They achieved home ownership, solvency, and educations for their children in a time when Pullman porters and waiters were an elite and teachers had to begin their careers in one-room schoolhouses in the South, where they often roomed with the village hens.

Gene and I used to laugh about Jean Toomer's comments about hostile poultry. But living with egg-layers was once a necessity for educated black folk.

Our longest-standing and most bitter arguments with our parents concerned our hair. We agree that we could probably have been bomb-throwing terrorists or axe murderers and been deemed acceptable by our families if we had straightened our hair to make it look like white women's. Our parents could take anything—bombs, prison records, streetwalking, bastard grandbabies—anything except those kinks and braids that crowned our arrogant, confused young heads. And that, I think now, was what I despised most about the middle-class status that I was handed and that I repudiated—its valuing of appearances over character, and surfaces over substance.

My father was a postal clerk, a Mason, and the owner of a Lincoln Continental. A deacon in his Baptist church; a solid citizen. Of all my time with him, I remember most his insistence that I cover my nappy natural head when he took me somewhere—and my naive query about whether it was raining, and his shocking, profane reply.

Esther recalls a day when her mother came after her with a knife and announced, "Your braids or your throat. Choose."

Worse, Esther believed her. Black parents have always said, and meant, "I gave you life, and I can take it away."

Quaint.

Our natural hairs, graying now, are still there. We congratulate ourselves. While perms and wigs have retaken the rest of the world, we have remained true to our revolutionary principles.

But having babies without marriage was not revolutionary.

And trying to raise them alone was not wise. Often all we had to fall back on was each other. Cherry freely admits that she could not have held her job if I had not kept little Aisha. Saint and I would not have survived if it had not been for the small amounts she paid me, plus freelance writing—term papers, ad copy, and political speeches—plus welfare.

All things considered, though, we did a pretty good job. None of our offspring are in prison, though three have records.

To us, this does not mean that our children are criminals. Betty, a lawyer and a D.C. public defender, says, "The American justice system revolves around us. As Richard Pryor says, it should be spelled, 'Just Us.' "

Jeanie, who teaches English at UDC, agrees. "When I teach James Baldwin's *Go Tell It on the Mountain*, and we get to Richard's story, I always elicit empathy by asking those who do *not* have a close friend or a family member who has been incarcerated to raise their hands. When hands go up, they are always white."

As Rock Creek roars music from its pagan throat across large boulders, our census continues. Two of our children are in college; two are headed there. One is a concert violinist. Another is a published poet. None are on drugs. None, except for Cherry's and my narrow escape, have married each other.

With more cause for congratulation, we clink plastic cups of Chablis and Perrier. We pass the Brie. We also pass the stuffed chitlins that are known as Jeanie's Mean Tortellinis. We have come through handsomely. We are entitled to a little attitude.

The mothers of Gene Green's children are bright, capable, educated women. Our numbers include a lawyer, a professor, a banker, a nurse, a public relations expert, a social worker, and a writer. We have all been on welfare, but to look at us, you'd never know it. We have little money, but we dress well. We also talk well and conduct our lives without undue chaos. We pay our bills and our taxes, though not always on time. We uniformly want college for our children. We have come from sleeping with romantic but penniless revolutionary heroes to freely asking the men in our lives, when there are any, to help us with our expenses.

"I don't need a man to buy me perfume," Esther Easton declares, "I tell 'em in a minute, bring me some groceries. Especially if they want to eat at my house. Yes, indeed. You think I'm gonna thaw out some steaks I bought with my hard-earned money, to feed myself and my child, and cook 'em up for some one-night man? Oh no, babee. See me do that, you know this fool's gone and fallen in love."

"Now see, you girls are lacking in sophistication. I don't ask for anything as crude as all that," Jean declares. She waves a slim hand on which a blue stone gleams prettily. "I talk about how much more appreciated I'd feel if I owned a sapphire, which happens to be my birthstone."

"It happens to be your name, too," says Esther drolly, "Sapphire" being, after the old Amos and Andy character, community code for all the B words—bossy, ballsy, brassy, and so forth.

Jean ignores her. "Or," she goes on, "I talk about this little investment club I've joined, and how sad I am that I can't afford to keep up with its recommendations, when all I need is just a few tiny shares to update my portfolio."

"They fall for that?" Esther wants to know.

"Girl, they love it!" Jean declares. "Makes them feel all worldly and sophisticated to be advising me on the market and helping me buy my cute little shares."

I like Jean, and she is buying into capitalism. Perhaps we are not so revolutionary after all. We have to admit that, in spite of ourselves, we have become what we despised: members of the group we come from, the black middle class.

The only thing we cannot agree on is the character and personality of our children's father. He is, depending upon which of us you talk to, a dirty dog or a fine fellow. He was a genius, a fake, a revolutionary hero, or a spy for the FBI. He was a great lover or a disappointment in bed. He was brilliant or dumb, handsome or homely, worldly wise or an idiot, lazy or energetic.

"Just stop it, girl," Betty tells Jeanie, who has just finished saying that Gene was good about helping her around the house. "Stop it right there. That man never picked up anything but a winter cold. Unless it was a summer cold."

"But he could write," Jeanie declares, as if that makes up for all of Gene's other deficiencies. "I still teach his *Drumfires* in some of my courses."

"Where did he steal it from?" Esther queries. "I have a letter he sent me that was full of mistakes. I mean peppered with them. I think he even said 'mens' and 'peoples.' " She looks at me for confirmation. "Didn't he?"

"I don't know," I say. "I was so dazzled by his French, I never paid any attention to his English."

"Hmph," she says, still steaming. "Bet it wasn't real French. He gave me a diamond, and that sure wasn't real."

"Me, too!" Betty screams. "One time when things were tight for me and Burghardt, I took that thing to the pawnbroker. He gave it back to me and laughed. It wasn't worth a can of beans, which was what I needed to feed us."

"How did you make it through that time?" Cherry wonders.

"Oh, you know," Betty says, sipping her Chablis, real silver and diamonds now flashing on her hands. Her deceptively plain denim dress is from a designer I recognize. "I wrote a bad check," she finally admits. "I loaded my cart up with all it could carry—I mean, that thing was so top-heavy I had to l-e-a-an on the shit while I was pushing it, to keep it from falling out—and I wrote a bad check for enough food to feed us for four weeks."

We are all serious now, remembering hard times. I am glad to get away from the Gene-bashing. In my heart there will always be a soft, warm place for the romantic old phony. Besides, nobody made any of us crawl into his sleeping bag.

"I stole a turkey once," Esther admits. "Tucked it up under the front of my skirt and buttoned my coat over it to look pregnant. That sucker was cold, Jim! And heavy and slippery! When I got in line with my little quart of milk and my little dollar bill, it started slipping. I thought I was going to have to pretend to faint. But I made it. I clasped my hands under Tom Turkey like he was my belly, and we waddled on out of there. People were holding doors open for me and everything."

"Kind of a dumb thing to do, wasn't it?" Cherry comments primly when the rest of us have finished laughing. She is hard on shoplifters since Aisha's little episode.

"No," Esther says. "You and your kid must not ever have been hungry. When they look at you with those big eyes and say 'Mommy, I'm hungry,' you'll do anything.

'Sides, ever count how many meals you can get off a big ol' turkey?"

The rest of us all nod and say "Uh huh" knowingly. Many's the time I've made a turkey last through the entire holidays, making turkey sandwiches, turkey hash, turkey à la king, barbecued turkey, and finally, when things got real bad, dressing and turkey gravy. But I've never had the nerve to steal one. Came close, though.

"The worst," Jeanie says, "is having no money to buy Pampers. You know how it is, when you get down to the last one in the box, and you go to shake change out of your purse, and all you hear is two lonesome pennies clinking? Panic time!"

Everyone sympathizes except me. I hope no one notices.

Esther had a solution. "Bottom of the cart. I mean *under* the bottom of the cart, below the food. If they catch you, you can always say you put them there and forgot them. Right, Patrice?"

"I always used cloth diapers, myself," I say, knowing that this will not win me any popularity. "I have the same ones my mother used for me. It's sort of a family tradition."

"Dag!" Esther says. "Next she'll tell us she bakes all her cakes from scratch."

"She does," Cherry informs her.

"Damn! Does she grind her own flour, too?"

"Practically," Cherry says. "She's a really good cook. She writes cookbooks."

I appreciate my friend standing up for me, but I am uncomfortable. The other women look at me like I am a museum exhibit. An unattractive one, like sadirons or a ragged mummy with protruding bones.

"Well, I don't have time," Betty says.

"Me, neither. Anything that says 'convenience' on it is for me. I couldn't live without my microwave," Esther declares.

Jean, who I think is the nicest of the D.C. three, says, "Maybe Patrice will let us taste her cooking sometime."

"You know it," I say. "All of you are invited to be our guests for a holiday weekend. July Fourth if we get lucky and find everybody by then, Labor Day if we don't. I'll do the cooking, and we'll try to hold onto enough of the money we raised to pay for your fares and hotels."

"And if we don't have enough?" Cherry wonders. She has that little vertical double ditch between her eyebrows that shows she is worried. She can't help it; she's a banker. A bean counter. "I mean, it seems like we raised a lot of money, Patrice, but you and I will have more expenses before we get home, and you're talking about four moms and six kids already. That's ten people. I don't mean to sound cheap, I'm just being practical. Maybe you all need to start saving just a little for the trip."

"If we can't pay for the hotels, they'll stay with us," I tell her, looking around at these women with enough love to embrace the whole world. "You're forgetting something. They're *family*."

Chapter 30

AISHA

Ever had a day that was just one hassle after another? That was my day Wednesday. First I get bawled out by my probation officer for leaving the store Tuesday and not coming back. Never mind that I have done exemplary community service for twenty straight days. Never mind that I took off to see about my ailing, long-lost father. My probation officer is one hard, cold alligator. She said she wouldn't make an exception if I'd gone to see Jesus Christ.

I have to have perfect attendance, perfect promptness, and my hours and performance checked off as flawless by the nun in charge, Sister Bernadette. No lapses and no excuses. If I mess up again, I will have more hours added to my sentence—or, worse, spend more time in jail.

What's more, my probation officer—whose name, I swear, is Zenobia Battle—wants to see my mother. She looks like Zenobia Battle, too. When I tell her my mother is out of town, she scribbles furious lines on a note pad, tears it off and hands it to me. "I need her signature on this as soon as she gets back. Tell her to call me immediately." I do not tell her that my mother is off playing detective with Patrice Barber, the two of them probably acting like horny teenagers, mugging newsboys and high school freshmen. I say that she has been called away on a family emergency.

"You are her primary family emergency," Zenobia declares, lighting a Camel and breathing out twin funnels of smoke like the dragon she is. "When the judge released you into your mother's custody, she promised constant supervision. That meant that she was always to be present in the home."

"I guess she thought I was doing all right, and since it was only for a couple of days, she thought she could . . ." I go on like that lamely for a couple of minutes, mumbling excuses for my delinquent mother. No wonder she has a delinquent daughter.

Then I have a bright idea.

"My father is at our house. Can he sign this for me?"

Zenobia Battle looks puzzled. She never heard my father mentioned before. She looks as though she doesn't even know people have fathers. But she is, grudgingly, glad to know I have at least some parental supervision. I do not tell her, of course, that mine is the supervisory position in our household. She smiles as if she has just been given two snapping turtles to eat. "I guess so, yes. I still need to hear from your mother, though."

Poor Daddy. He is so tired, he still sleeps most of the time. I will have to awaken him to tell him that the daughter he thinks is the Virgin Mary is a felon and has a criminal record. Otherwise, why would all those numbers appear after my name?

He was kind of cute when he woke up yesterday. He seems to have taken a liking to that dirty little boy, Lamar, who follows Saint around. When I looked in on them, he was sitting up in bed, reciting some Langston Hughes poems to him. Lamar liked "Mother to Son" so much he almost had it memorized. Said the part about "no crystal stair" reminded him of what his own mother often said. Said he hoped to make big money someday to make life easier for her.

"Then don't be a poet or a teacher, Lamar," my father warns him. "If you want to make big bucks, choose something else to do."

"Yeah, but sometimes maybe knowing some good poems be helpin' you be that something else. Maybe poems be helpin' you get through a tough day of shovelin' shit or whatever you be doin' to make big money. You think so, Mr. Green?"

"I definitely do think so," my father says. "I think poems do be helping when you be having a hard time shoveling shit. Did I say that right?"

"Naaahh!" Lamar is furious. "You supposed to be talkin' proper, Mr. Green, so I can learn how. You ain't supposed to be talkin' ignorant like me! And you ain't never supposed to say 'shit,' neither. No way."

"Sorry," my father says gravely. "I meant to say, 'waste management.' Yes, I do think that some inspiring verse can help you get through a hard job of waste management. Now, this one is by Langston Hughes, too. It's called 'Here to Stay.' "

I can see that my dad is a natural-born teacher. I think that's what I want to be, too, in spite of his advice to Lamar—whether as a nun or as a civilian, I haven't decided. I have been sneaking looks at the teachers' college brochures in the library.

Carefully, Lamar repeats each line after him. The two of them are so cute, I wish I had a camera. My father still looks like he's been yanked through a keyhole or some other small opening, with sagging cheeks and dark circles under his eyes, and he could use a shave and a haircut, and he's an alcoholic bum, I guess, but I'm proud of him. I'm glad he ate everything on the tray I fixed—soup, sandwich, Jell-O, juice. I hope we can get Dad well enough to return for his fall term at that awful graveyard-sounding place where he teaches. He's still very weak.

Maybe Saint will give him a shave when he comes in from his job. He is selling men's clothes in the mall now, saving up for school, and only doing soup kitchen duty once a week.

I am hoping that Sister Bernadette will fix her records to make it appear that I only took an hour off on Tuesday, not all afternoon.

But when I ask her, she is adamant. "You are asking me to commit a sin," she tells me.

I say that I would never want to do that, not at all. The only thing is, taking the day off has gotten me in trouble with my probation officer, and a change in my work record is the only thing that will pacify my P.O., who has the power to put me back in jail.

"You could say that you made a mistake," I coax her. "Say I came back, and you forgot to make a note of it. Come on, Bernadette. You're my friend."

Behind her ugly convent-issue wire-rimmed glasses, her eyes are stainless steel.

"The only thing I can suggest," she says, "is that you go to the convent and see Mother Mary Benedict."

I can sense what is coming. They want me to take my vows. But hey, vows can be unvowed, or at least that's what I've heard. Anything to get Zenobia off my back. "What about Sister Immaculata?"

"She can't help you."

"Why not?" Immaculata is weird, but at least she is fun.

"She's not with us anymore."

This sounds grim. "You mean she died?"

"No." And that is the only answer Bernadette will give me.

I wait on customers. I also arrange the racks, putting the clothes in order. I even do a couple of loads of laundry when the store is quiet, hoping to impress her. My strategy doesn't work.

At the end of the day I take the long bus ride to the convent. Mother Mary Benedict, a plump, middle-aged woman, is pleasant, but as firm and no-nonsense as an Army officer. She hears my request but does not respond.

"I understand," she says instead, "that you were thinking about joining our order."

"I'm still thinking about it, Sister," I say.

"I see," says this mistress of noncommunication. Nothing more.

"I was wondering," I say next, "about a nun I met here called Sister Immaculata. I would like to see her, but I understand she has left the convent."

The Mother Superior hesitates, then reaches into her desk and pulls out a card. "You may go to see her here," she says. "Visiting hours are noon until eight."

The card says:

Serenity House
A Franciscan Facility
Fr. Joseph Martino, Director

I am in Serenity House for half an hour, waiting for Sister Immaculata to come out into the waiting room, before I realize that it is a rehab. You know how you can see something obvious, but it doesn't register? That's the way the large scripted sign, *Think, Don't Drink*, catches my eye without making an imprint on my brain.

Soft, soothing music has lulled me into a pleasant stupor. Now I wake up and pay attention. I riffle through a pile of pamphlets and recognize some of the AA slogans in them from the meeting I went to with Gus.

That Gus. Mom really lucked out there. He's clean, he's decent, he's straight, and he's honest. Plus, he's cute. I hope she snags him.

Won't it be a trip if my mom gets married before I do?

I try that one on for size and decide that it's an uncomfortable fit, but that I'll deal with it if it comes up. I think that maybe I might be growing up.

I look up, and there's Immaculata, standing before me

and smiling. She's wearing a navy headdress and one of those standard navy convent-issue suits. She's gained a little weight. She looks healthier. Her handshake is firm and quick.

"I am glad you came, Aisha," she tells me. "I have amends to make to you."

I start demurring, and she says, "Please. I am sorry I gave you a false picture of convent life. It is not fun and games and glamour, not at all. I said that to ensnare you."

"You did the opposite," I tell her, because, hey, we're being honest here, aren't we?

"Good. When I led you to believe that you could join us and still have the pleasures of the world, that was my liquor talking. I am sorry I misled you. You should never take a big step like that under false assumptions."

"Hey, it's okay. I wondered how you got away with some of the things you did."

"Our Mother Superior is a wise woman. She let me have the freedom to get overconfident and hit my bottom. Once I realized that I was a mess, not clever at all as I thought, I was ready to come here."

"Was that true, your story about being a hooker once?"

"Oh, yes," she says. "I am one sick sister."

"What about the convent babies?"

Sister Immaculata shrugs instead of answering. These nuns are really good at taking the Fifth.

"If you are still thinking about joining us, you should talk to Mother Mary Benedict," she says. "She will tell you the truth. And the truth is, the religious life is very hard."

"Are you staying?"

"If they let me."

We take a little walk around the establishment. It is pretty classy. Posh Persian carpets, antiques, that spooky narcotic music piped everywhere. "This place—is it just for holy drunks, or does it take civilians?"

"It takes everybody, I believe. But for the laity, it can be pretty expensive."

We say good-bye then, and I take the long bus ride home in a somber, thoughtful mood. Rum must really be a demon if it can sneak over the walls of a convent and grab a nun. The thought gives me the shudders. I hope I never have to go through all that. I hope I can just leave the stuff alone.

When I finally get home, I am handed more reasons for abstinence.

The place reeks of gas, alcohol, and sour vomit. A lunch tray has been overturned in the living room. I follow a trail of spilled food into the kitchen, where I find all four burners, unlit, turned on full blast and Daddy slumped over the table. First I turn off the gas burners. Then I struggle to open the stuck kitchen window. It finally gives on the third shove, and fresh air rushes in. I run back to the living room to open more windows, and almost trip over a small bundle of rags with a foot sticking out.

I drag Lamar back to the kitchen and slap him awake. I don't know how I accomplish it, but soon I have both him and Daddy out on the fire escape, and we are gasping great lungfuls of air. Thank God it is one of our rare clean air days.

"Where did he get booze?" I wonder aloud.

"I got it for him," Lamar confesses. "He asked me to. Please don't be mad."

"They sold you liquor?"

"Not exactly. There's always guys out in front of the store who will cop for you if you let them keep the change. Please don't hit me again, Miss Aisha."

I lose it then. I blame Lamar the way I used to blame my mother's friends for getting her drunk.

"Why, you little snot-nosed bastard, you made my father sick! I should have known better than to trust you with him. You couldn't be trusted with a sick goldfish! Get out of here. Don't ever let me see your face around here again!"

But Lamar doesn't leave. He has nowhere to go but the shelter. It is indicative of its horrors that he stays. He cringes, with a terrified expression that stops me in the middle of my crazy tirade. This kid has probably been abused, and besides, he didn't know any better. It's wrong to blame him the way I used to blame Mommy's friends.

"Don't ever do that again, Lamar, okay?" I say in a normal tone of voice.

"No, ma'am."

The place has aired out, and my father is beginning to make noises that sound like normal snoring. If he really is my father, that is. Saint showed me the picture, and it's him, but I'm beginning to have my doubts. Three days after I've found him, I want to disown him.

"Come on, help me get him back to bed." The runty kid is surprisingly strong; together, we accomplish this with relative ease. There is nothing to do but let the old man sleep it off. I survey the mess that my mother's usually immaculate apartment has become, and groan.

"Why were the burners on?" I ask Lamar.

"I don't know. I was watching TV when I fell asleep. But it looks like he was trying to cook some eggs." He points to a yucky yellow waterfall down the front of the stove.

"Oh, my God," I say out loud. My four extra hours after work, fooling around with the nuns, almost cost my father's life. Two lives.

I fall into an armchair, flattened. This man cannot be left alone. But I have to do my community service. Saint has to work. And Lamar is only a child.

By the time Saint shows up, I am a blithering, gibbering idiot. I hold onto him, gasping, sobbing, explaining what happened. He comforts me with awkward pats, pats. He agrees with me that we have taken on more than we can handle. He doesn't have any more ideas than I do about what we should do next. Still, I am suddenly glad to have a brother. I am not in this alone. I never have to be in anything alone again. I feel an immense gratitude for that.

The trouble is, we are still both kids—three kids, counting Lamar—and we have no experience handling situations like this. Saint picks up the empty liquor bottle, lobs it into the trash can and shakes his head. We sit in opposite chairs, staring at each other. The silence begins to get heavy, so I get up and put a Lionel Ritchie tape on. The music helps. Gaining energy from its rhythm, we go about picking up the rest of the trash, scrubbing the kitchen walls and vacuuming the floors, until the place is clean and tidy again. We exchange no words.

This does not mean that I am quiet inside. I am screaming the same two words over and over in my head.

Mommy! Help!

Chapter 31

CHERRY

MAYBE PATRICE DOESN'T REMEMBER her hard times the way I remember mine: kerosene heaters, thrift shops, and all those Crock-Pots full of pinto beans that fed me and Aisha. When Jeanie confides that she is not doing as well as she pretends, and that she has had to cut out Assata's piano lessons, Patrice peels off a couple hundred dollars. I want to kick her, and later, verbally, I do.

"We'll have to walk home if you keep this up," I chide her. We are staying at a cute little hotel in Northwest Washington, the Lombardy, and I have been enjoying every one of its comforts, especially the Continental breakfast in bed, but I am mindful of the expense.

"You act like it's your money."

"If it were my money I wouldn't mind," I lie. "It's money we raised for a mission."

"Since the money worries you so much, you keep it," she says, and throws the shrunken bankroll in my lap. "God! You sound like we've been married for thirty years."

"You're hardly my type," I say, counting. We are down to twelve hundred dollars. I am relieved. I expected worse. What she said has a kernel of truth in it, though. In every successful pair, there is one Scrooge and one spendthrift. Guess which of us is which.

"I know I'm not your type, and I know who is," she says, licking the crumbs of a lemon Danish off her fingertips. "A gorgeous, penniless reformed drunk. You and Gus will have a lovely old age together, clipping and redeeming cents-off coupons. I wish you much happiness."

"What happened to your diet?" I ask her, to get us onto a different subject. She is starting on my Danish, having already finished hers.

She begins a juicy dish session as if she hasn't heard me. "That Esther, what a sleazebag, stealing Pampers," she says. "I wonder if she teaches that to her welfare clients when she visits them."

"I hope not."

She takes another bite of the Danish. "And Betty. Did you see that paper-thin suede thing she had on? She can't be saving any money, the way she dresses. How can she send her kid to college?"

"The same way you do. Gene Green kids are smart, they win scholarships, remember? How can you eat that greasy thing?"

"I can't cook on the road, you know that."

"No, but you don't have to eat all that pastry. You know what your doctor said. Have my bagel."

"Okay," Patrice says, in that surprisingly sweet, submissive tone she adopts on those rare occasions when someone makes her see reason—i.e., sits on her and pounds her into submission. I pass her my whole wheat bagel and pour myself some more coffee, wishing I were not required by my program to be honest and could steal the dear little silver pot it comes in.

I decide to call home for my messages.

Zenobia Battle, my daughter's aptly named probation officer, wants to see me as soon as possible.

So does Gus. "Hi, lovely," says the rich voice on my machine. "I'm lying here thinking of you and getting all warm inside. I had to spend a weekend in Boston and almost died of loneliness up there. Call me, sweetness, before I expire."

Who could resist? I almost call him then and there, but there are two more messages. Aisha wants me to call her before I come home. My mommy antennae go up, sensing mischief, but Gus is too urgently on my mind. I ignore them.

The last message is a woman with a slow, halting, careful voice. "Hello. My name is Alberta Brown. A friend of mine showed me one of your flyers and explained what it was all about. I knew Gene Green a long time ago. We have twins, Bertram and Bertice. They are in their first year of high school." She goes on to give a Long Island address, a phone number, and the best times to call.

I repeat the message and write everything down. Then I turn to Patrice. "Bingo! Aren't you glad I put my phone number on our flyer, too?"

"Yeah. I never did learn how to remote-access my machine." And this from a woman who practically invented computers. She is licking the last of her second

Danish off her fingers, but I choose to ignore that. Instead, I try positive reinforcement.

"You've lost a little weight. Congratulations."

She beams. One of the nicest things about Patrice is how easy she is to please—and how radiantly she shows her pleasure. "Do you really think so?"

"Yes. Why don't you celebrate by getting yourself a decent outfit?" We noticed a snazzy little boutique around the corner last night. "You didn't bring a single nice thing to wear. That little shop around the corner ought to be open. You can go grab something while I pack."

"I must be dreaming. You, the Queen Skinflint, want me to spend some of our mission money on myself?"

"Looking decent is a legitimate expense." I give her a little shove. "Go."

"I better hurry, before you change your mind."

"That's a good idea." Getting rid of Patrice gives me a chance to call Gus in private, exchange phone kisses and other endearments, and plan an exact time to call him again from New York, where we will almost certainly rendezvous.

I begin to hum the Shirelles' "Will You Love Me Tomorrow?" as I pack. I sing, "Tonight you're mine completely," while dancing my red satin hussy gown around the room.

Patrice is back all too soon, with a mournful, hang-dog look.

"What'd you buy? Let me see," I ask.

"Nothing. Cherry, I need your help."

Oops, I think, I forgot to give her back the money. How

embarrassing for her. But it isn't that. On the way downstairs, where we pause to check out, my friend explains
that she hasn't bought anything but caftans for ten years,
and has no idea how to choose anything else. "I don't
even know my size," she practically sobs.

This is a major crisis. I go into the shop with her and
steer her away from the patterned items, the hot pink and
orange horizontal stripes, the zigzag yellow and black
lightning bolts, the huge red coin dots on an ivory ground.
The bored salesgirl, buffing talons an inch and a half long,
lets us explore in peace. Over in the corner, behind a mannequin, are some navy-blue pieces in size 18—a wrap
skirt, a tunic, a pair of pants. They are so plain they
scream "Expensive!" But what the hell?

I toss them at Patrice. "Try these on," I command.

And, wonder of wonders, they fit. The wrap waistline
arrangements help, but my friend really has gone down a
size, and in these clothes, she doesn't look fat. What's
more, a line has been drawn through the tags—each piece,
once eighty dollars, is now half price.

"Grab them. You look sensational," I tell her, and for
once I am not lying. Miss Nails comes to life and suggests
a gold scarf splashed with navy stars. "My treat," I say,
and haul out one of my own twenty-dollar bills.

Then I have another inspiration. "Listen, Patrice," I
say. "Didn't you have a lead to someone in Atlanta?"

"Yee-ss," she admits suspiciously. "Gene lived there for
several years. Toni is pretty sure he was tight with at least
one woman down there. Why?"

From what we have uncovered so far, it is impossible to
imagine Gene Green being anywhere for even a day

without getting involved with a woman. Atlanta has to turn up something—probably an entire high school graduating class. 'Course, he was older by the time he got to Atlanta, forty or more, possibly burning out, at least winding down.

"Why don't you go check Atlanta out while I run up to New York and see this sister named Alberta? I only have two more days off, but that's all I need. You can mosey on down to Gaw-gia and take your time. Your folks are from down there. You know how to talk to those people."

"Don't say it like that," she reproves me. We have been through the North-South dichotomy thing before. I happen to think black folks have better things to do than refight the Civil War.

"I don't mean it like that, whatever 'like that' means."

" 'Those people,' " she repeats. "It sounds like 'you people.' "

"You people" is the most offensive phrase well-meaning white folks use when they talk to us. I am appalled at my rudeness. I try to wiggle out of it.

"I just mean you're used to the language and the customs. When somebody offers you hush puppies, you won't look around for a leash. Besides," I say, "in those new things, you'll look fabulous. Ready to have a whole new town drop dead at your feet."

We split the money and embrace at the station. Miss B. promises to be frugal, not take cabs, stay with friends or relatives, et cetera. I promise to get all the dope on this Alberta person, be home by Saturday, and also to check on Saint for her first thing.

My train is announced. The way we cling and weep as

we say good-bye, you'd think one of us was going off to the gulag. Actually, I think Patrice is. Even D.C. is too far south to be comfortable for me, but I don't tell her that.

Then, with a knowing wink, she says something that brings laughter through the tears. "Don't forget to say hi to Gus for me." No one ever said Patrice Barber was deficient in the smarts department.

ALBERTA BROWN LIVES in a low-slung brick rancher in a working-class neighborhood, the kind where every house has a Ford Escort out front and a Lincoln or Chrysler up on blocks in the driveway. Scattered statues of the Virgin Mary indicate that not all the European Catholics have moved away. Or maybe the Hispanic ones have already begun to move in, although the neighborhood seems hopelessly drab and lacks the careless color I associate with Latinos.

The minute I meet Alberta, I regret not bringing Patrice with me. She would love this woman.

In the first place, she is southern. Her voice is thick with sweet honey in the rock, and she is probably the person I sent Patrice tearing off to Atlanta to find. Alberta met Gene while he was teaching at Morehouse. She was working in the campus cafeteria.

She still works in a school cafeteria—at the local elementary school this time. She has taken the afternoon off today to spend it with me. She is short, very dark, and would be considered homely by those who accept only European standards of beauty. Both her figure and her features are full—especially her lips, which are naturally wine-colored and have that large, luscious Naomi Camp-bell pout.

She has come to perfect terms with how she looks and who she is. "An-to-ni-a," she says, meaning Toni Brook-ins, "explained what this was about and described you-all to me. I know I ain't pretty or educated as the rest of you-all."

"You aren't as old as the rest of us, either," I remind her. It's hard to tell with smooth black skins, but I would put her at not much more than thirty—thirty-five, tops. When she met Gene, she was probably still a teenager.

She clears her throat, embarrassed. "Well. When I met that man, he was on his way down. He needed me. I'm from the country, and I was all by myself in that big city, so I needed somebody, too. I went up there planning to stay with my auntie, but she died soon after I got there, so I moved in with him. For a while, we helped each other."

I think she is beautiful—from the inside out. Her humility and her simplicity make tears rise almost to the surface of my eyes.

"Why'd you break up with him?" I ask her.

She wrinkles her nose in distaste. "His drinkin'. It was gettin' so he was drunk all the time. He didn't seem to want to do nothin' about it," she says, "so I didn't even bother to tell him when I found out I was pregnant. I left him before I got to lookin' like a big ol' basketball." She laughs, showing ivory teeth with a big gap in the center. "All a man got to do is point that thing in my direction and I get pregnant. That's why I mostly stays to myself now. Anyway, I figured he couldn't help me, and being a professor and all, he probably wouldn't stay with me anyway, so I guessed I'd better move on and start making a home for myself and my babies. 'Course I didn't know I'd have two of them." She laughs again. Fifteen years have passed, and she still sounds about fourteen years old.

Memory is stirring. I met Gene in a rehab, the first, I have heard, of many he has tried. I didn't have any better sense than to take up with someone who was as shaky as I was. We had three weeks of rehab apiece, all our insurance would pay for. When we got out, he slipped backward almost immediately. I felt myself on the verge of drowning along with him and broke it off, but not before I conceived Aisha.

Of course, I have had my own lapses since. The last one was at her tenth birthday party. Ten little girls, mixing a giant batch of what they thought were mint juleps in the bathtub, while the hostess's mommy passed out in the kitchen. Then all of us vomiting at once while the tub ran over and the landlord pounded on the door.

I have been sober since.

"I 'speck you want to meet my kids."

I nod slowly, coming out of the past.

"Rest yourself. Bertram and Bertice be home directly," she says. "I tell them, come straight home from school. They mind me."

"How do you manage to make them do that?" I ask her.

She looks at me in shock, as if no other possibility has occurred to her. "I tell them the Lord is watching everything they do, and will strike them dead and send them straight to Hell if they disrespect their mother."

It is my turn to be shocked. Now I recognize the soft

music in the background. It is a gospel station. They are playing "The Rough Side of the Mountain." Alberta hums along.

"Now and then, when I need a man to take a hand in raising them, I call on our pastor," she adds. "You a Baptist?"

"Methodist," I say.

"Oh, well," she says, with a hint of pity. "We all worship the same God, is what I say. You saved, ain't you?"

I really don't know how to answer this. Then I think, I have my daughter, I have Gus, I haven't had a drink in nine years. "Yes," I say.

"Good. They's a lot of good things for the young people to do at our church," she goes on. "Choir, and Youth Fellowship, and—" She breaks off this discussion as if thinking, why tell all this to a heathen Methodist? "Around this time, I generally makes myself a cup of tea. Will you have one?"

I assent gladly. I am wondering how I'm going to manage to call Gus without feeling like a scarlet woman in this holy household, when the children come home, clean, neat, sweet, and respectful. Dark angels, short, compact, almost jet-black, they resemble their mother as if she had cloned them, except that they have Gene's poor vision. Both wear thick glasses.

There is no time for any but the scantiest conversation with them. Alberta is an old-fashioned mother of the seen-but-not-heard school. After introductions and "Where are your manners? Shake hands with the lady," she assigns chores. "Bertram, rake up the yard. Bertice, fold the laundry and set the table. Then both of you get busy on your homework. And I better not hear no TV running."

The daughter lingers.

"What did I tell you?" Alberta scolds, her face in a fierce contortion that scares even me.

"I just wanted to tell the lady she has on pretty clothes," Bertice says softly.

"Thank you," I say, glad she likes my four-year-old black-and-white polka dot ensemble and my new red scarf.

"No time to be thinkin 'bout clothes. Got to get busy on your homework," Alberta says. The child disappears. "Kids look as ordinary as mine got to be twice as ready as the rest," Alberta tells me. "Nobody gonna hire them or promote them for cuteness."

I don't dispute her. I know she's right. "How did you get up here from Atlanta?" I ask.

"Well . . ." She sets her cup down; this is going to be a long story. "This was my brother's house. His wife left him while he was sick. He asked me to come up here to take care of him. My children were six at the time, just ready to start school, so I said yes."

"What was his trouble?" I ask.

"Liver trouble," she says, adding unnecessarily, "He was a heavy drinker, too, like my kids' father. When he died and left me the house, I just settled on in."

I am caught up in realizing how many of us who have been involved with drunks also have them in our families. Alberta's brother. Patrice's grandfather. Toni's aunt, forever sipping out of tiny flasks and nodding off. My father, me, and now my daughter. Maybe the Gene pool was flawed, after all.

I am stricken, remembering the little catch of desperation in the poised message Aisha left for me.

I ask to use the phone. Alberta points. "Help yourself," and continues to sip her tea and rock in her rocker.

So I have to talk to my lover, this man I desire intensely, as if he were my insurance salesman. Worse than that is what I must say to him, right after I hear that melted-caramel voice.

"Gus, I have to go straight home."

Chapter 32

SAINT

I DON'T KNOW what Romare Brookins's mother has told him about his father, and I don't care. I have been baby-sitting the Professor around the clock, and somebody has got to give me a little relief. Rome doesn't sound particularly thrilled on the phone, but he agrees to come over.

I have spent two days seeing the old man through the worst of his withdrawal. Two days seeing him shake and have chills, and piling on blankets. Feeding him broth, juice, and tea. Cleaning it up when he can't keep it down. Watching him get the D.T.'s and see rats coming through the walls. Talking him out of the rats, only to have him see snakes. When he asks me for a drink to help him over the worst of it, believe me, if I had it, I would give it to him.

And when, in a moment when he thinks I'm still out of the room, I see him kneel beside the bed to pray, it is hard to be mad at him.

But I have to get back to work. Patricia says I have to have a thousand dollars saved for school, and in matters like that, Patricia does not play. Besides, she doesn't know it, but I have another little expense in the making. Long tall Tanya and I have been playing house on the weekends, and she just told me she is pregnant. Tanya turned out to be a sweet girl once she shed her wild attitude along with her excess hair and makeup. She hates my mother, of course, which complicates our future. But the future is rushing at us with all deliberate speed anyway. Its name is either Josephine Bonaparte Barber or Henri Christophe Barber, depending.

Because of Josephine or Henri, I will not be returning to Morehouse, at least not right away. It will be community college by day and work at night, if I can get it, or vice versa if I can't. My boss, when I last saw him, was impressed enough with me to make me night manager, but it's been two days since I've been able to go to work.

So I am very glad to see my little brother. I lay it on him straight. "There's a man in the bed in the next room, Rome," I tell him, "and he's your father. Mine, too, as it happens."

Rome seems unfazed. His body continues in constant motion, dancing to rhythms only he can hear through his Walkman. "Cool," he says.

"I need you to help me look after him while I'm at work. Don't leave him alone. And whatever you do, don't give him a drink."

Rome rips out his earphones. "Why I gotta do that?" he demands. "I never saw that man in my life. Why'd he wait till he was old and sick to come back to us?"

"I guess he didn't need us before now," I tell him. "People are like that a lot of the time."

He nods. "Well, okay. I need something to do, though. You got any art materials around here?"

I explain that this is Aisha's apartment and her mom's, and I don't think they keep things like that around.

"That's okay. I just remembered. I saw an old chair in the trash down the block. I can carve it." He runs down to the street and returns in a few minutes with four amputated chair legs, one of which he immediately attacks with a wicked-looking knife. It's magic. In ten minutes the piece of wood comes to life as a small person.

Rome is not as tall as I am, but already, at sixteen, he is filling out, with a broad chest and shoulders. His voice rumbles, now, more than it squeaks. He wears paint-stained, baggy pants that hang so low they seem about to fall off his butt, but that's the style. He has large, dark, intense eyes and his mama's wavy hair, which he refuses to cut. His version of dreadlocks, I guess.

Once I asked Rome why he seemed to have a compulsion to cover every wall he sees with demented writing in angry colors—orange, black, red. "Kids are hurting, man," he told me. "This is how we scream. Plus, it's how I make my mark, gain respect."

The court psychiatrist has referred Rome to a day hospital to keep him busy until school opens. But the corny projects there, making ashtrays out of tiny tiles, just don't cut it for an artist of Rome's scope.

Oddly enough, carving little wooden people does. Every night I bring him more trashed lumber and more paint from the hobby shop at the mall. In two days he has a regular army of figurines: heroes and historical figures, athletes and singers, and enough tiny children to fill a kindergarten. When he pulls out the checkerboard, I get the point: it's an African American chess set. He and the Professor put it to use right away. Listening to them while they play is a real trip.

"My Muhammad Ali has your Martin Luther King in check," Rome says after he moves.

"I believe," the Professor says, "that your move has put your B.B. King in check from my Queen of Soul."

Rome studies the board, his long hair flopping into his eyes. The old man is right. Rome replaces his knight and instead moves his bishop, who resembles Louis Farrakhan. "Preacher to Preacher Four," he announces.

"My Jesse Jackson takes your Minister Farrakhan," Pop crows.

"Dag. How come you saw that, when I didn't?" Rome demands, banging his fist into his palm.

"Because you merely use your eyes. I use my mind," he is told. "Besides, you just can't beat a winner. Checkmate."

"If you're a winner, how come you don't have a job?" Rome wants to know.

"But I do have a job. I'm a college teacher. This is summer recess."

Rome absorbs this silently as he sets up the pieces again. In the process he moves the board slightly. Pop hesitates, his hand hovering over the board. "Where have you put the pawns?" he asks.

"You can't see!" Rome exclaims.

"I thought I just told you that. I said, 'You use your eyes, I use my mind.' "

"Yeah, but I thought that was just—"

"A figure of speech? A metaphor? No."

"But blindness, that's awful. I couldn't stand that."

"That's because you are a visual artist. I am not. You would get used to it, though. People can get used to anything."

Rome is a funny kid. He's an artist with the soul of a stubborn scientist; he likes to investigate everything he's told. He ties a scarf over his eyes and tries to play the next game blindfolded. He does pretty well, probably because the pieces he's carved are so distinct, but halfway through, he tears the bandanna off his face and stamps on it. "No way, man, I could never get used to that. No way."

After that he is reverent toward the Professor, as we mostly call him—doing whatever he asks, calling him "sir."

Lamar is still hanging around. He won't go home at night until we chase him. If I lived in a shelter, I wouldn't want to go home, either. He has been so contrite about buying the old man that pint, he even let me cut the new snakes off his head when I gave Pop a haircut. Aisha really chewed him out about that. I don't blame her; she thought it was safe to bring the Professor here because there's never any booze in this apartment, and then Lamar blew it. With the new jeans and the phat striped shirt Aisha brought him from the free store, Lamar looks quite decent these days. Sometimes looking good is all a guy needs to give him confidence.

Sometimes being needed does it. That's what works for me at the soup kitchen.

It seems to be working for Rome, too. He seems quite

content to spend his days carving figures, listening to music, playing chess and reading to the old man, and going straight home at night.

When Aisha and I come in, we take turns fixing supper. Whoever doesn't cook helps Lamar clean up. We usually feed Lamar before we chase him home. Then we relax, play some sounds, watch TV, and talk. Aisha tells me about the nuns and how she's turning over the idea of joining them. I disapprove. I tell her about Tanya and the baby and how I'm thinking about marriage. She disapproves. But it's a friendly, comfortable kind of disagreement. It's relaxing, playing house with Aisha instead of with Tanya, who doesn't mind as long as I call her every day. Things are getting quite cozy. But of course they can't last.

On Saturday, Aisha's mom walks into the living room and plops her duffel bag down in the center of the floor. She seems surprised to see us, but not upset. "Hi, kids," she says. "Rome, I'm beat. Move out of my chair." He gets up quickly. Aisha moves just as quickly to get behind the chair and give her mother a neck rub.

Mrs. Hopkins swats her daughter's fingers away. "Later for that. Just get this necklace off me before it chokes me."

Aisha removes the little silver chain, and offers aspirin, tea, and a drink of water in rapid succession. "No thank you, no, and no," her mother says, and kicks off her shoes. "I just need to put my feet up. No, I need some sleep." She's right. She's yawning. Her face is so tired, it's gray.

Mrs. Hopkins swings her legs down from a footstool—

and, old as she is, I can't help noticing that they are nice legs—and gets up. "You kids be quiet in here, and Rome, keep that TV noise down. I have to get a nap."

"You haven't told me about your trip, Mother," Aisha says, blocking the doorway to her mother's bedroom.

"I will later. Aisha, get outta my way. What's going on?"

"Umm, Mother, I was wondering if you would want to rest in my room instead. See, I've been using your room while you've been away, and it's not as neat or as clean as it ought to be."

It's a brilliant stroke. Muttering, "Clean it up, then," Mrs. Hopkins changes direction and heads like a zombie toward Aisha's room.

Brilliant, like I said. It almost works.

Then the doorbell rings, and Aisha runs downstairs to see who it is. I keep telling her that's not a smart thing to do in the city; but she won't use the intercom, she only trusts her eyes. I tell her, at least use the peephole before she opens the door, but she rarely bothers. This time she's lucky, as usual. She knows the visitor. I hear her greet him with a lot of delighted squeals and the name Gus.

Mrs. Hopkins immediately darts into the bathroom. Women are a trip. I don't know what she does in there, but she comes out in a minute looking rested and twenty years younger—fresh lipstick, bright eyes, dew on her face. A cloud of perfume surrounds her.

Then this guy walks into the room, and the rest of us might as well not be there. She lights up like a jack-o'-lantern with a candle inside as he takes both of her hands.

"Cheryl," he says, lingering over her name, giving it

three hoarse syllables. "I rushed down here to see if I could help with your family crisis."

"I don't even know if I have one, Gus," she tells him. "I just got here. So far, everything seems to be under control."

They only have eyes for each other. It's embarrassing seeing people their age so plainly in love, but it's nice. I cough.

Mrs. Hopkins finally remembers that they are not alone, steps back and lets her hands drop. "Gus, these are my daughter's friends, Toussaint Barber and Romare Brookins."

The three of us shake hands.

"Actually," Rome says, "we're her brothers."

I like this guy Gus. Except for an eyebrow that leaps up for a moment, this news doesn't seem to faze him. His handshake is just right, dry and firm. He seems solid, steady, and real. I'm a guy, so I know how selfish guys are, but I believe he's really here to help Mrs. Hopkins and her kid if they need him.

Then an awful hacking cough starts up in the bedroom and goes on for several minutes. We all start coughing, too, to cover it up, but Mrs. Hopkins, though she has been too sleepy or too distracted until now to notice things, is not fooled.

To make it worse, the moment he stops coughing, the Professor decides he needs a drink of water or something.

"Toussaint!" he calls in his rich, rumbling voice. "Lamar! Romare! One of you scoundrels come here!"

Chapter 33

CHERRY

THERE IS A MAN IN MY BED. First, I scream. Then I pull the shades down and snap them so that they fly to the tops of the windows with a series of loud reports, and light pours in. The man flinches at the noise, but he doesn't blink.

At first I am not sure who he is. He is familiar, but I don't know him. Then I see past the gray hair, the sunken cheeks, and the claws clutching at the blankets to the strong, handsome features I remember. The chin has caved in, but the nose and eyes are the same.

I think—yes, I am sure. I turn to Gus. "Gus, this is embarrassing. Please believe me—I didn't know this man was here. I haven't seen him in twenty years, but I think he's my daughter's father."

Gus is an angel. Totally understanding. "Do you want to be alone with him?"

"I think so, yes."

After Gus leaves us, I pull a chair up to the edge of the bed. "How have you been, Gene?"

His voice, at least, is unchanged. Rich and mellow as ever. "Who is this? May I touch your face, please?"

Reluctantly, I assent. It is not unpleasant. His fingers are as light and soft as birds' wings feathering over my face. He completes his examination and falls back on my pillows. "Cherry. My sweet little Cherry. No. You were never sweet. My tart little Cherry tart."

I don't like either designation, but I let them pass. "Gene. Are you blind?"

"Yes. It's been coming on for years, but I only realized it recently."

"How can you not realize a thing like that is happening to you?" I wonder.

"Denial, my dear, denial. Surely you understand that."

Indeed I do. I ask, next, what is always a perilous question at our age. "How is your health in general?"

"Oh, quite good, considering. There are a few aches here, a few pains there, but you know—they go with the territory."

This man is occupying my bed, he is trespassing on my turf, he has become a burden to my child and to my friends' children. I am not in a mood to make it easy for him. "No, I don't know. What territory is that?"

"My time of life. My pecuniary embarrassment. My regrettable habits."

"I see. Have you been sober, Gene?"

He drops his head. His receding chin touches his chest. "There was a disturbance here a few days ago, I'm afraid. My old enemy got the better of me again."

He is far too old to try his shamed bad-boy look on me, but he does it anyway, rolling his blank eyes, then dropping his face into his hands. I wait to see if he will peer at me between his fingers for my reaction. He doesn't. Still, I don't trust him.

"Gene, do you want to get sober?"

"Of course," he says. "That last bout almost killed me. If it hadn't been for those angels out there—"

"They aren't angels, they are children, and they have better things to do with their young lives than take care of you."

"Ah," he says, "but they tell me they are *my* children."

"Where would they get such an idea? And even if they were, would they owe you anything?"

"No, of course not. But, Cherry, life is not a ledger book of debits and credits such as the ones you use in your work. God's grace and mercy are not bestowed according to your system of accounting."

I don't need sermons on grace and mercy from this tres-passing bum. I don't need snide comments about my work, either. Once he says he wants to get sober, it's my responsibility to help him, but he makes me so angry, I can't.

Still, when his hand gropes for mine, I help him find it. He grips it hard and hangs on. He is still strong.

"Cherry. Do you remember the time Stokely came to Chicago?"

Tears come to my eyes. "Of course." We were in love then. Gene was still my hero. And the poem he wrote for the occasion made hairs prickle on the back of my neck. Something about "Brave as a blade, our young black knight cuts the confining bars . . ." And then something about opening a window on the stars.

"I've been trying to remember that poem I wrote for the last couple of days, but I draw a blank around the third verse. Do you think you could help me get it down?"

And all of a sudden it comes back overwhelmingly. The romance, the reasons why I fell for him in the first place; why all of us did, probably. The power of talent. "Sure," I say, hoping he can't hear my snuffling. Darn my watery eyes. Darn him for getting them going. "I'll be glad to help if I can. But first we've got to get you sober."

"Oh, that," he says with a wave of his hand. "You know, I think I just might have a chance at sobriety now. I think I always knew I had children, deep down. I heard hints and rumors, but I never checked them out. I think I drank to run from paternity. Maybe I don't need to drink anymore. I don't know, though, Cherry. If you only knew how many times I've tried—"

"They don't matter," I tell him. "They're in the past. All you have to do is stay away from booze today."

"Will you help me, Cherry?" he asks. But he doesn't mean it. His hand moves up my arm to my shoulder and from there down to my breast. I draw back. This man is hopeless. No—no one is hopeless. My trying to help him is hopeless, that's all.

"I can't help you that way, Gene. That sort of thing is definitely over between us."

Thank God for Gus, I say, a phrase that will probably become my mantra for life. I go out to the living room and whisper in Gus's ear. He goes in immediately. I stay out there to cross-examine the children.

"All right," I say. "Who wants to speak first?"

There is a chorus that rivals the tower of Babel, but

finally I sort it out. Saint takes most of the blame; he's the oldest, and it was he who recognized Gene from Patrice's poster.

"He'd been coming to the soup kitchen, and I took an interest in him because he was so different from the others."

"I'll bet. Now, whose idea was it to bring him here?"

Aisha owns up to that one. "Mother, he was sick. He was on the street. He had to go somewhere."

"Well, he has to go somewhere else now. You know that, don't you?"

She nods. "Yes, Mother, and I have an idea. I know a fabulous place." She goes on to tell us about this gilded rehab where they've stashed her favorite drunk nun, a sort of resort for addicted holy folk. Persian rugs. Antiques. Piped-in music. Jacuzzis and billiard rooms and masseuses, probably.

"Sounds expensive," I say.

"What about the money you raised at the benefit, Mother? Can't we use that to pay for Daddy's rehab? I mean, really, what better use could you find for it?"

Already it is "Daddy," I notice. And already nothing is too good for this man who has contributed nothing, absolutely nothing, to her raising. I feel anger rising in me. I feel my blood pumping much too hard. I take several deep breaths to keep from being overwhelmed by rage. Then, patiently, I explain, "It wasn't that much, Aisha, only a couple of thousand, and half of it's spent. As far as a better use is concerned, we've been thinking about scholarships for some of you. Besides, I know your father. He would never fit in at that Catholic place. He would insult their pious beliefs the first day, spit in their holy water or something, and get thrown out."

"You don't know that, Mother. Couldn't we at least try to get him in?"

It takes all my self-control not to pop her one. "No, I don't think so."

"Hey! I can put Pop up at our place for a few days," Saint offers. "Mother isn't back yet, and he'd feel right at home in her room, with all the tropical decor and everything. He's been telling me all about Haiti and how much he misses it."

"He won't be able to see the decor, Saint," Aisha reminds him.

"Oops, that's right. I can play him our merengue records, though."

I can just picture Patrice coming home and finding her bower occupied by a blind ghost. I stop short of imagining what she would do. Her anger can get pretty creative.

One thing I will say in Gene's favor. He may be half Haitian, but he has never used his background to set himself apart from and above the rest of us. Unlike too many people from the islands, he has never laid claim to "special exotic black" status. He knows we are all part of the same dreadful diaspora.

"We have a spare bedroom," Romare volunteers. "It's my mom's office, but she doesn't really need it."

I think I would feel much better about that declaration if I heard it from Toni. I have to shout to shut them all up and get myself heard. "Hey! All of you. Stop it! Stop trying to fix this situation. You've done a wonderful job, all of you."

"Do you really think so, Mrs. Hopkins?" Romare asks, his eyes wide with wonder.

"Yes. I was upset at first, but now I am really proud of the way you coped. Now, though, it's time to let us grown-ups take over."

"Well, what are you going to do, Mother?" Aisha demands.

I don't know. I am about to say so when Gus emerges from the bedroom.

Like I said, thank God for Gus.

Chapter 34

PATRICE

Aᴛʟᴀɴᴛᴀ ᴡᴀs ᴀ ʙᴜᴍᴍᴇʀ. All of my old friends had moved and left no forwarding addresses, and everyone I met seemed to be from somewhere else, down there hustling their way to the pot of gold they thought was buried somewhere under Peachtree.

Finally I became desperate enough to read an announcement on Sunday at Ebenezer Baptist. I got lots of kind invitations and fellowship from those good church people, but no leads. Nobody even seemed to have heard of my quarry or any of his women.

Turns out, Gene must have been slowing down by the time he got to Atlanta. He had only one woman there—Alberta, who moved and is the one Cherry went to see on Long Island. Cherry hit the jackpot again there. Twins. She has a surprise for me, she says on the phone. Not concerning Aisha, who has sensibly decided to enter teachers' college and not the convent, but involving someone else.

Maybe she and Gus are getting married. It's Cherry's lucky year.

The Atlanta cuisine did not agree with me. After my low-fat regimen, Georgia grease gave me so much indigestion I started carrying a whole box of baking soda around with me. But there was no escaping southern cooking. I ate fried chicken, chicken-fried steak, gravy, corn bread, and so many biscuits I began to look like one—round, thick, and oven-browned—and soon gained back all the weight I'd lost.

When I decided that Gene Green's trail was hopelessly cold, I took a side trip home to Wayne County to get healthy on okra, corn, field peas, butter beans, collard greens, and tomatoes. I forgot that Aunt Mary wouldn't let me stop at her homegrown, home-canned vegetables. She and all of the cousins insisted that I had to eat with a different one of them every day—fried fish, fried chicken, fried pork chops, fricasseed rabbit—and that I had to eat everything. After a week of that, Toussaint's mother was even rounder and ready to be rolled home. I headed for the station with a box full of home-cooked food my relatives had fixed for me, just in case I started to starve on the way home. A whole fried chicken. A dozen biscuits. A whole pound cake, which I planned to save for Saint.

"You come back soon, you hear?" the cousins called to me as I left.

"The next time you see me, I will be in a box," I muttered, though they really are a bunch of dears, and their country church services made me cry, the testifying was so sincere. I knew the portable provisions dated from the day when no meals were available to our folk traveling anywhere below the Mason-Dixon line. So I resolved, as my choo-choo pulled out, to treasure that food, maybe even varnish it and display it on my mantel. But on no account would I eat any more of that rich, greasy, calorie-laden—

An hour out of the station and I am gnawing on a drumstick, and my lap is covered with cake and biscuit crumbs. My belch is so loud the entire car jerks to attention. When I get home, I am feeling fat, gross, and futile.

Arriving at my house, I am forced to step over my son to reach my room. He is lying on the floor in the posture I have come to expect over the past seven years: stretched across our hallway, intimately entangled with the telephone cord. He does not offer to take my bag, nor does he interrupt his conversation to greet me; he does not even retract his endless legs to let me pass unobstructed. Instead, the only acknowledgment I get from him is a nod.

Strange, I think. Rude. I thought I brought him up better than that. True, a mother's everyday arrival home does not rate any special attention. But when she comes home from a long distance after a week's absence, she should receive, if not red carpets and brass bands, a hand with the luggage, concern for her fatigue and an eager ear for her news. Whoever is on the line can be politely dispatched or told to wait until that minimal courtesy is shown.

But Saint talks on and on, in hushed tones, into a receiver shielded by a cupped hand.

And I head for my room unassisted, there to flop and steam.

I doze off briefly and wake up sensing a presence in the room. I roll over to find Saint's figure looming over me. His face is so strained, his jaw so tight, I am momentarily afraid of my son.

"You killed my father off," he accuses.

"What?"

"Why did you kill my father off? Why did you tell me he was dead?"

Here it is, the moment I have dreaded. Now that it's here, I am oddly calm. "I thought it was best," I say. "That way, you wouldn't get to know about his faults. You would always think your dad was a great guy."

"I should have had the chance to make up my own mind," he declares.

"I think you're right," I say. "Now. But back then, I was afraid to take chances. I wanted you to have a father you could look up to."

He continues to stand there, staring down at me, studying me like he's never seen me before. His fists are working, clenching and unclenching. "You lied to me. How am I ever going to trust you again?" His voice breaks on "trust," and he runs from the room.

I feel curiously calm and empty after that. My worst nightmare has come to pass; what else can happen? I dial Cherry's number. "So, what's your big surprise?"

I can hardly hear Cherry's response. I know what that means. She's scared to speak up, doesn't want to be understood.

"Patrice, I don't know how to tell you this, but—"

"Just tell me. Straight up. Without preambles or fanfare."

The louder my voice gets, the more hers fades. "Er, uh, the person we were looking for, is, well—there are things you don't have to spell out for Saint. He, uh, he knows some of them already. So you can stop worrying. And—"

At this rate, we'll be on the phone all night. I bang it down and go over there. I figure maybe the four-block walk will burn off some calories and lower my blood pressure. Instead, by the time I climb her stairs, it has climbed to something like 300 over 250. I hate secrets, that's why, and I don't understand evasiveness. It just makes me mad.

I confront her, panting and heaving. "All right. I'm here. It's just me, your old friend Patrice. I don't breathe fire and I haven't grown fangs or anything, so you don't have to be afraid of me. Whatever it is, just whip it on me."

It is about ninety degrees, but Cherry is looking maddeningly tiny and cool in an ice-blue satin tank. "I'm not afraid of you, Patrice, just of how you might react," she says. "You know you told me you were close to having a stroke not too long ago. Maybe you'd better sit down. Let me get you a glass of water."

"Don't handle me," I growl at her. "I hate being handled."

"All right. Here are the facts. Gene's in town. Saint found him."

It feels like an elevator left my heart on the fortieth floor and rapidly dropped the rest of me to the first. I take the offered chair. "Go on."

"When I got back last week, Gene was right here in this apartment, sick, in my bed. Our kids were taking care of him."

"Must have been a shock for you," I mumble, though I am mainly busy sorting out my own feelings. Underneath the numbness I find fear and a new, unspecified pain. "Where is Gene now?"

"Drying out, in a facility Gus found for him. Saint found him on the street, homeless. The booze had almost killed him."

"What did Saint have to say for himself?"

"Oh, he took all the responsibility. He was the one who recognized Gene from your poster, though it was Aisha's idea to bring him here. Patrice, I think Gene was in town all along, or at least all spring. Saint said he had been coming to the soup kitchen for some time."

"I know," I say.

"You knew?" she echoes.

"Saint told me he'd seen him, but I told him he had to be mistaken. Because I wanted him to be, you see." I think I recognize the pain now. I can name it. Grief—for the loss of the innocent, trusting relationship I had with my son.

"Aisha gave him some clothes at the shop, too."

"Wonderful," I say, "considering how much he did to feed and clothe them."

"It's not fair, is it?" For a fleeting moment Cherry's mouth gets a bitter little twist that matches the tone of my voice. "Patrice, what's hard to take is, our kids are all crazy about him. The way they dote on him, we might as well not have existed."

"Maybe it's temporary," I say. I hope the same is true of my son's anger, and of this new pain under my heart, right in the spot where I once carried him.

"I doubt it," she says. "Gene even won Rome over, and you know how indifferent Rome is."

"So much for glorious single motherhood, and the nobility of our solitary struggle, and the undivided loyalty it was supposed to win us from our offspring, and all those other grand illusions," I say.

"Yeah," Cherry says. "Saint will forgive you, you know."

"No, I don't know that. It is not guaranteed."

"By the way, Aisha says he has a girlfriend. It's serious, she says. They're talking about marriage."

"Fine. From now on I will come to you whenever I want news of my son." I am overdue for a bath and a change, so, though I am in no hurry to reenter the frigid atmosphere at home, I make an effort to heave myself up from my chair.

"Wait, Patrice," Cherry says. "We have to plan. How much money do we have left?"

I find my share of the bankroll and toss it over to her as if it were trash. As it is to me, now. With that big, sweet old spoiler back in town to ruin my good relationship with Saint, nothing else matters much to me. "Why did he have to come back and ruin everything?" bursts from me like a child's wail.

Cheryl will be a banker till she draws her last breath. She does not look up from her counting. "He didn't tell you to lie to Saint about him," she says.

I want to kick her. I want to call her disloyal. But she is merely honest. So I do not disturb her while she smacks currency down on her coffee table like a veteran pinochle player dealing hands.

"Wonderful," she says when she has counted and recounted the bills. "We still have a thousand dollars. Enough for a really solid scholarship."

"What about our party?" I want to know. I never felt less in the mood for a party, but a promise is a promise. "We said we would throw one for all the moms and their kids."

We argue it back and forth a bit. Finally, Cherry calls Toni to break the tie. She suggests a workable compromise. A get-acquainted party and a five-hundred-dollar scholarship, both to become annual institutions kept going by contributions.

IT'S BACK TO caftans for me, at least for a while, so I have a fabulous new white one made to wear for our Fourth of July party. It's crystal-pleated, and has a band of crocheted cotton at the neckline. I feel that I look just as good as any of the other women, even Cherry, who arouses much envy by pulling a snug yellow T-shirt over her perfect little boobs and showing off her waist with a white cinch belt.

While the others do an elegant Electric Slide, stepping pretty high for a bunch of old ladies, I look them over and take stock. If I were wearing buttons, I'd be busting them with pride, but I gave up button fronts years ago, when my 42 D's went to 44 double D's. We have plenty of reasons to be proud. All of us appear hale and fit, though I happen to know Jeanie is recovering from a tiny stroke, and Rowena just had a scary breast biopsy. We are, after all, reaching the age where a lot of excrement happens, but we are a brave and hearty band. Comparing notes, I find that all of us have had The Operation, which makes me even more suspicious than before of the medical establishment. I plan to look up the stats on the rate of hysterectomies performed on white females by age fifty. Surely it is less than a hundred percent.

We've all recovered, though, and the surgical scars don't show, except in certain styles of bathing suits that none of us, not even Cherry, has any business wearing. All of us have been on welfare, but we've recovered from that, too, and are going on ahead with our bad selves. Hey!

I take a turn kickin' it, and tell our D.J., Rome Brookins, to repeat the record, "My Beautiful Electric Slide." It *is* beautiful today. Only my son's absence mars the day's perfection. He promised to spend this holiday with his lady. She bears a grudge over the way I threw her out of my house, and didn't want to be with me.

Well. For a picnic, we're pretty well turned out—the gold bangles jangle, the perfume wafts, the designer labels might as well be on the outside. I count nine college degrees among us, and enough income to run a small Third World nation. My soul looks back in wonder at how we made it over. If we could each hold back just twenty bucks from Macy's and Bloomingdale's, we could start a small empire. But we sisters love to dress. The habits on our backs keep us from rising. What can be done?

Cherry has a plan. Uniforms for the next family reunion. Green, to remind us of our purpose: saving and investing. It is also, perhaps, an unwelcome reminder of our common bond, but I don't tell her that, she is so excited about her plans for our investment club.

Our venue for this picnic, a public park, is already saving us money. The city provides free barbecue grills, tables, benches, shade, breezes, and grass. Each green T-shirt we sell will put ten dollars into our investment fund, which will provide scholarships and emergency loans. Fine, we all agree, as long as we don't have to wear the ugly things.

Gus has grilled the first batch of hamburgers, and now I take over at the grill to do my roasted potato slices and my special herb-marinated chicken breasts. I have also brought corn bread, cranberry relish, and sweet and sour slaw. Toni has contributed an entire roast turkey, and her son has made seven rainbow-flavored jugs of Kool-Aid. Toni has also brought a gallon of white wine nicely concealed in a thermos jug. The teetotalers and the masochists among us can drink Cherry's lime seltzer and eat her frozen imitation cheesecake dessert. It's pretty good, but I argue with her that imitation cheesecake is an obscene idea, the whole point of cheesecake being to pile richness on richness. She has also brought the standard grill fare—burgers, franks, and buns—and her righteous man to prepare it for us.

Spurred on by fresh air and exertion, we fall to with gusto and pile it in. I am waiting for the right moment to share Cherry's news. Maybe after lunch, when the women are relaxed and sleepy from eating. They will be slower and easier to catch, too, if murder is on anybody's mind. We don't have enough money in our kitty yet for serious bail.

Alberta and I have the same politics, we discover in the

course of a hot discussion. All of us have benefited from affirmative action, but her comments on the subject are the shortest and the most to the point. "Shoot. Now you gone and made me cuss, talkin' 'bout affirmative action. These damn white folks done had affirmative action all their damn life. They was born with it, just like they granddaddies was born with it. They got it from our great-granddaddies and -grandmamas pickin' they cotton." I applaud.

While we digest our lunch contentedly, "Shotgun" by Junior Walker and the All Stars blares its impudence. After years of boring disco and tragic ballads, the lively rhythm and blues oldies are enjoying a revival. The children shiver like leaves in a breeze, doing a current version of the boogaloo combined with the fast shuffle. I notice that all of them can dance, including Rowena's little Muslims. Even Abdul has some nasty little moves, and the way Aneesah shakes her booty is a wicked disgrace. It can't be helped. It's in them.

I also notice that the children are coming back for seconds on everything, then disappearing, alone or in pairs. As one or two return, one or two vanish, as swiftly and silently as ghosts. Just now Assata slips unobtrusively into the dance, and Bertice, her overall pockets stuffed with enough croissants to give her a bust, starts to make her exit.

But Alberta is an observant mother. "Hold it right there," she yells. "Where do you think you're going?"

"Nowhere" is the soft answer, delivered with downcast eyes.

"Don't tell me that, I know better," says the rough voice of maternal experience. "What have you got in your pockets?"

"Bread," says Bertice. She pulls out and displays a bun, then improvises brilliantly. "Me and Levi were just going to feed the birds."

I say nothing, though I know that the local avian species do not go for chicken salad, which the croissants contain. I also know that Gene's rehab is a ten-block walk from here, which would be like crossing the Gobi Desert for me, but is no effort at all for teenage legs.

"Oh. Okay," says Alberta, deceived. "You can feed the birds right here, can't you?"

I move to more shade and overhear a conversation between her Bert and Romare.

"Our father is smart, man," Rome brags. "He writes books. We're smart, too."

"I don't know, man." Bert hangs his head. "My mom says kids like us will always have to work extra hard."

"What's she mean? Kids like you and me? With our brains, we got it made."

Cherry starts to interrupt them, but I put a hand on her arm. "Shhh. Don't you see? They don't need us."

"She talkin' about our looks, I think, man." Bert tucks his large head into his shoulder, as if to hide it. "We ain't good-lookin' like you. We look like her."

"You look fine, man. You one handsome dude. Come on, I'm gonna paint your portrait on this wall I know. Paint it for all the world to see."

I only hope Toni doesn't know her son is decorating walls again. As for me, I won't tell.

"Know something, Ro-mare?" Bert says. "You got a talent people would pay for. It don't make sense, wasting it on walls, giving it away free. You got to learn to get paid for it."

Nope, I am thinking, with mixed joy and sadness, they don't need us anymore.

In the meantime, Bertice and Levi have disappeared.

"Bertram!" Alberta yells. "I thought I told you to watch your sister. Where'd she and Levi go?"

To give Bert credit, he is cool. Cool as a thirty-year-old who owns his own mind, and maybe his own company. "To see our father, probably," he says as he and Rome vault over a low wall on their way to a high one. They really, truly, don't need us anymore. Maybe that was the point of all this effort. To learn that.

Pressed for details, I give them. I keep stressing that Eugene Green is a sick man. I even embellish that a little, saying he may not recover. "He won't if I can get my hands on him," Esther promises.

This woman's eyes are bulging, and her hands jerk convulsively, fists opening and closing. Cherry and I coax her and soothe her and reason with her until she calms down. The rest make a lot of hostile noises, but they don't mean it. They are not about to get somebody's blood all over their fine outfits.

When quiet is restored, I clap my hands for attention and make a little speech. "Lissen up, ladies. This cry for revenge is most unbecoming. This man did not talk us into having his children. It was all our own idea, right?"

They mumble and hiss like a nest of adders, but I detect a note of agreement.

"As far as I know, he never even knew the children existed. So how can we blame him for not helping us raise them? We saw something in him once, and maybe it was there, because he did give us fabulous children. I think we should take a cue from them, and forgive him, and wish him well."

The forgiveness and goodwill I call for are not forthcoming. The mamas' mood is not one of reconciliation. One woman shouts, "Is she for real?" Another says, "I'll forgive that turkey when I see him in his coffin."

But at least no one is getting killed today.

Saint and I attempt to settle our little misunderstanding a few days later.

"I'm sorry I lied to you," I tell him.

"I know, Mom," he tells me. But the pain is there in his eyes.

"If I had my choice about when you'd learn the truth, I couldn't have picked a better time. You're grown now, twenty-one. You can handle it. Do you hate me?"

He hesitates just a fraction of a second before saying, "Of course not."

That tiny pause is enough to make me want to impale myself on a bamboo stake. I don't, though. I choose the next most painful punishment. I go back on my diet.

Saint and I are conversing normally now instead of avoiding one another. We are still wounded and hurting, but reconciliation and healing have begun. I suggest the next step: going with him to visit his father.

It is enough to inspire thoughts of homicide, to see Gene sitting like a pasha in a paisley robe from Aisha's thrift shop, while Rome reads to him and Aisha combs his hair.

At least he isn't in that papal palace that Aisha recommended, with room service and chamber music and happy hookers. He's in a place Gus chose, one the drunks have nicknamed Hardcore House for its grim austerity. Its regimentation is like boot camp. This place not only has Up stairs and Down stairs, it has Sunday stairs and weekday stairs. Ditto doors, and woe unto anybody who uses the wrong ones. Everybody has to do chores like scrubbing the toilets with toothbrushes, but Gene's blindness exempts him.

Everyone has to pay as much here as they would at any other facility, too, but again, because Gene is legally blind, his treatment is free, coming out of some federal funds for the disabled, or something. I wish I understood these things more. Maybe there's a fund somewhere for fiscally challenged ladies with eating disorders.

Anyway, while the others are scrubbing toilets and picking up trash, Gene is getting bussed to blind school, where he learns to navigate in a world without light. I wish some of those angry women would think about the challenge he faces, and could see how calmly he is dealing with it.

'Course, living here, he is almost lucky to be blind. The place is painted battleship-gray, with institutional brown floors and woodwork. There are no rugs, no pictures, and no curtains. There's no recreation to speak of at Hardcore House, either, and no visitors are allowed for the first two weeks. After that, only family can visit. This gets the children in and leaves me out, until my son decides to lie and says that I am Gene's sister, his aunt Patricia.

All of this is very hard for me to take. Hardest of all to

take, of course, is the children's universal and total adoration of their hitherto absent father. Mothers, who have always been there for them, get taken for granted, but Dad, simply by showing up, is an instant celebrity. Do I begrudge him all this unearned affection?

Of course I do.

Am I jealous?

Certainly. I remind myself that this man is blind and addicted, but it doesn't make my sighted eyes any less green.

Seated in his favorite chair on the sunny side of the rehab, Gene looks positively regal, as if posing for his next jacket photo. I snap him, just in case I am right. The chair, one of those wicker peacock jobs, resembles a throne. I expect him to clap his hands and summon servants, but he doesn't need to. His children are all around him, eager to perform whatever services he might require. Aisha has brought him a bowl of banana pudding ringed with vanilla wafers; Rome, a personal hand-carved chess set for him to keep and share with the other patients. It is truly beautiful, with ancient African figures like Queen Nefertiti and Ramses II.

"Gene," I say, "you know what amazes me? How gifted all of your children are."

"Of course," he says smugly. "They are mine."

The urge to kill arises.

"Well, of course, that's why we chose you," I admit.

"You chose well," he says.

Does this man deserve to live?

I know that all of the mothers' thumbs would turn down in response to this question.

But Rome's design for a mural on our new train station has won a contest, and he has an after-school job pin-striping sports cars. Aisha works at a day care center and has been accepted into a nearby state teachers' college. Both of them are off probation.

What's more, Alberta writes, Bertram has a scholarship at a camp for computer geniuses. Bertice has had her first poem published, news which really excites Gene. Burghardt has also published several poems. Aneesah, whose mother has reluctantly put her on the Pill, is a candy-striper at Harlem Hospital.

My son, however, informs me that he is not returning to Morehouse. Instead he is about to make me the first grandmother in our group. I am not thrilled by this news, but I am acquiring a life of my own. I am going to school to become an herbalist like my grandmother. I have found one amino acid, L-glutamine, which I bring with me to help cure Gene's craving for alcohol, and another, L-carnitine, which is helping me to burn off pounds.

Rowena is studying herbs, too, in the hope of curing her cancer. Abdul is taking freshman science courses at NYU while still a sophomore in high school. Levi is first chair with the D.C. Youth Orchestra. The back and forth exchange of this news keeps me happy and excited.

I have to admit that Gene is right.

He reminds me that I was his first *amoureuse*, or very nearly, and that my son is his oldest child—a very special child, because he was conceived in the freedom of the Black Republic.

I tell him about the grandchild on the way. We talk of

taking Saint and his offspring to Haiti someday to soak up history and ambience.

Gene's tobacco pouch and his old briar pipe rest on a table beside him. I fill the pipe, tamp it, and hold the match for him while he draws and gets his light. The odor is rich and rapturous.

At least he can't see how fat I am. I am *une grosse mambo,* as they would call me in Haiti, but he doesn't know it. He whispers to me in Creole and calls me something else, something scandalous. I squeeze his hand. He is putting on flesh, too, but he needs it. He no longer looks like the ghost Cherry described. He looks like my old friend, like someone I am not ashamed to be seen with. And he still has the arrogance that was always part of his appeal. He shouldn't be the one to say we chose well, but can I dispute him?

"Damn right we did," I say.

Kinfolks

Kristin Hunter Lattany

A Reader's Guide

A Conversation
with Kristin Hunter Lattany

Q: Where did the idea for *Kinfolks* come from?

A: I knew a number of women in the sixties who had been involved in the movement, the revolution, and who went to the extreme of having children without a husband. It was a trend going on around the country at the time. Back then people were doing anything they could to not be part of "the system"—and marriage was definitely part of the system. It seems strange now, but that's what was going on. They didn't have to take that path—these women had full lives and were very successful—but that's the choice they made. I then began to wonder about the results of those past decisions in the present day. What would happen if the children they had were actually siblings? And in fact, I knew a number of kids from those single mothers who were siblings. I didn't personally know their father, although I had heard about him, and I began to wonder what his appeal could be.

Q: Why did you write such an amusing book at such a grim period in our history? Considering the seriousness of the race problems in this country, did you ever consider addressing them and the other grave problems African Americans face in a more solemn fashion?

A: It is my considered opinion that the race crisis in America is so dreadful and persistent that it has driven many people mad—particularly those who contemplate it seriously and intently all the time in search of solutions. Taking time out to laugh at and with ourselves may be a way of staying sane. It's my way, anyway. I think it's also the way in which the blues foster mental health.

I do what I can, in whatever ways I can, to address serious problems. I have written some angry articles and stories that deal with the cruelty of racism. Now I have written a humorous, but not, I hope, frivolous book.

Q: **You've written a book narrated by black women. Does it advance the cause of feminism by bashing black men, like other recently popular works?**

A: God, I hope not. That was not my intention; in fact, I tried to take great care to make Gene oblivious to the situations he had left behind and to make the women fully responsible for their choices. I love black men and do not think a people already under siege and desperate are helped when one half of them is set against the other half.

Q: **What do you think the feminist movement has to offer black women?**

A: Not much. Mainly it sets us up to front the causes of others who tend to reap the benefits and then desert us. I have noticed that a lot of creative sisters tend to bow to white feminism as if they feel they must in order to get their work out there. I don't like that tendency. If we need a movement to celebrate our already strong sense of sisterhood and self, let's get one of our own. We don't need to hitch a ride on someone else's train. It may not be headed for a destination that is good for us.

Q: **What, in your opinion, is the most important book published by an African American in this century?**

A: *Roots* by Alex Haley. Not because it was an engrossing or easily readable book (it wasn't), but because its wide popularity made people go out and find their scattered relatives and start having regular family reunions. And from those reunions we are slowly developing other important things: a sense of who we are, our history, including where we came from, pride and unity, but also new relationships with kin, support networks, business networks, family projects (like history books and restored homesteads), and, hopefully, family institutions (like scholarships and credit unions).

Q: **What, in your opinion, is the single most destructive force in America as far as black folks are concerned?**

A: Television. It made us riot and loot in the sixties by showing us the casual wealth of most American households and making us realize for the first time that we were poor. (Rioting, of course, was not all bad, though looting was and is something to be concerned about because it says that we have caught the national lust for stuff.) We watch more TV than other groups because it's free and we have less money. It has made too many of us crave possessions at the cost of our humanity, and given our youngsters role models of ruthless violence as a means of acquiring them.

Q: **What is your next literary project?**

A: My next project will be a serious memoir in collaboration with my husband, John Lattany. By describing a successful way of life black people once had in the rural South, we hope to suggest some strategies for the present and the future. I also have a comic screenplay under way that contains a serious message, and am thinking about another novel.

Q: **Aren't you planning to write about the inner city anymore?**

A: No, because the news from the ghetto these days is all bad, and I like to give my readers hope. I do not believe the despair, degradation, and danger that have overtaken our cities is the fault of the people who are trapped there. It is the fault of the employers and successful people who have fled, and of cynical profiteers, including dope importers and distributors, and the media who keep beaming our children messages of violence and greed.

Q: **Is there a theme that predominates in your fiction? What is it, and where does it come from?**

A: Yes. The theme is the search for family. *The Landlord* trying to find a family with his tenants; Miss Lean adopting a son in *The Survivors*; the orphaned Bella in *The Lakestown Rebellion* calling the residents of her small town family and informally adopting her husband's child; Lou in *Lou in the Limelight* finding not one but three surrogate mothers—Jerutha Jackson, her Georgia cousin, and the nurse who looks after her. And in *Kinfolks* the circle of mothers who consider themselves kin because their children are kin.

All of this, of course, reflects my personal lack of close blood family and my lifelong search for family substitutes. It is probably, also, reflective of a search for affectionate mothering, because my mother's love was rather tough. I may also have expressed a fairly idealistic view of how families relate because I haven't really known much about that and have been guilty of a lot of wishful thinking. I am becoming realistic, though, and learning that family life isn't all hugs, kisses, acceptance, and support; that it often is not a picnic in a meadow, but a minefield. The love and support are often there, of course, along with a sense of responsibility for one another, but families also harbor a lot of anger, guilty secrets, resentment, hatred, and just plain craziness. Learning to accept this is, for me, part of growing up.

Q: **You mean you aren't grown up? How old do you feel?**

A: My new motto is "Forever Forty." Sometimes I feel about three hundred years old because I lived through decades that felt like speeded-up eras: the fifties, with their witch hunts and their conservatism; the sixties, in which my people suffered for the right to live with human dignity while the majority only wanted the right to get high; the seventies, which brought a renaissance in the arts for black folks and opened doors for us in academia and the professions; the eighties, in which this country resumed business as usual, raping and pillaging the rest of us. And now the nineties, which have shut most of the doors the civil rights struggle opened, and resemble, in their meanness and violence, the reaction to Reconstruction a hundred years ago. Looking back on it all can make one tired. And depressed.

Q: **To which black women authors would you like to be compared?**

A: The late Zora Neale Hurston and the late Toni Cade Bambara, for their healthy self-esteem and their humor. If I ever approach either woman's metaphysical growth I will consider myself fully successful.

Q: **What about Terry McMillan?**

A: I am grateful to her for building a wide readership for the work of black women writers, but I think we are about different things.

Q: **Your books have been widely translated and well received and have earned numerous awards and honors, including a National Book Award nomination. What sort of pressure comes from that kind of recognition and success?**

A: The pressure comes when publicity turns you into a public figure. I think that's bad for a writer; at least it was for me. It puts a false patina on our relationships with others. I'd much rather people focus their attention on what I write rather than on me as a "personality." I love being with people and having relationships with them, but being a "celebrity" sets up an artificial relationship. I used to be able to slip in and out of scenes unnoticed. I would get a chance to observe people instead of having to talk about myself all the time as you and I are doing right now. When *The Landlord* was made into a movie I was invited everywhere. Everyone introduced me as if my name was "Landlord," because they were mesmerized by the Hollywood connection. People become interested in you when what you really want is for people to tell you about themselves because that's where your material comes from.

Q: **One reviewer wrote, "The voices and movements of these characters are so distinctive that you don't even have to look at the top of the page for clarification as to whom you are listening or watching." How do you find and latch onto these distinctive voices?**

A: I don't really know. I try to have a feeling for the people and from that I get the way they would express themselves. Cherry, for example, is kind of neurotic and serious because she's a recovering drunk. Aisha is spoiled. Saint is just a good boy—everyone's ideal son—until he starts to mess up. The father, Gene, is pretentious and blind even before he actually loses his eyesight. He would have to be blind to his surroundings to leave this trail of children and not even know about them.

Q: **What do you see as the main difference between the generation of Gene, Patrice, Cherry, and the other mothers, and the generation of their children?**

A: The older generation is concerned about causes, about reform, and about the group as a whole. The children, for the most part, are more self-absorbed. They're not involved in any political movement, never were, and probably never will be. They're involved in their coming careers and each other and that's about it. Unfortunately there's no big movement for them to latch onto, so they've become more concerned about simply surviving or making it.

Q: **What do you want readers to get out of this book?**

A: I'd like them to get a good feeling. I'd like them to try to emulate the caring that's in this story and to realize that that's one of the strengths of a good community. When caring is missing, everything else falls apart. Caring is the glue that holds things together.

Reading Group Questions and Topics for Discussion

1. There's a saying, "It's a wise child that knows its own father." What might be some of the meanings in that saying?

2. Why might it be important to know your father—who he is, what he is like, some facts about him? Why was it important for the young people in this novel?

3. What about health? If you found out, for instance, that your father had diabetes, would you get checked? Would you cut down on sweets in your diet? If he had high blood pressure, would you cut down on salt? Would you want your children to know about their father's conditions and do these things?

4. Are family reunions a good idea? Have you ever been to one? Did it live up to your expectations or did it disappoint you? What do you think people should try to accomplish at family reunions? Why is family so important?

5. If you were a mother, would you be hurt if your children made a big fuss over their father and took you for granted, as the young people did in this book? Why do you think that happened?

6. Saint and Aisha seem to adjust rather quickly to the fact that they are brother and sister. Do you think this easy adjustment is realistic? How would you feel if the same thing happened to you?

7. Has this book influenced your ideas about being a parent in any way? How? Has it, at least, made you think about it a little more? In what ways?

8. After reading this book, would you prefer to be married to your children's other parent and stay with him? If not, and even if you were angry with him or her, would you make sure your children knew that person?

9. What do you see as the main difference between the two generations represented in this story? The mothers made some radical decisions for political reasons. Do their kids have the same kind of social conscience that their mothers had? Why was the older generation more concerned about causes, reform, and the black community as a whole than their kids are today?

10. What do you think kept Patrice and Cherry—best friends for twenty years—from revealing to each other the identity of their children's father?

11. Do you think Patrice did the right thing in lying to Saint? Is there any justification for this action on her part? How would you feel if your mother had kept something like that from you? What would you do if you were her?

12. Why do you think Aisha turns to shoplifting?

13. Twenty years ago, premeditated single motherhood was a political statement. Is that still the case today? How has this changed? Why do you think all these women were attracted to Gene Green?

14. What does this story have to say about the resilience of African American women and, by extension, the African American community as a whole?

15. Have you ever known anyone like Gene? Do you believe there are people like him? Is he a sympathetic or unsympathetic character?

ABOUT THE AUTHOR

KRISTIN HUNTER LATTANY received the Moonstone Black Writing Celebration Lifetime Achievement Award in 1996. She is the author of nine published works of fiction, four for children and five for adults. All of her novels have been widely translated and well received. *God Bless the Child* (1964) won the Philadelphia Athenaeum Literary Award; *The Landlord* (1966) was made into a film in 1970; and her popular novel for teens, *The Soul Brothers and Sister Lou* (1968), received the Council on Interracial Books for Children Award, the National Conference of Christians and Jews Award, and many other awards.

Kristin Hunter Lattany has been a writer for the *Pittsburgh Courier*, an advertising copywriter, an information officer for the city of Philadelphia, and, until her retirement in 1995, an instructor in English at the University of Pennsylvania. A Delaware Valley native, she lives with her husband, John Lattany, in southern New Jersey.

Excerpts from reviews
of Kristin Hunter Lattany's *Kinfolks*

"While exploring all of the comic possibilities of her story, Kristin Hunter Lattany also raises some serious questions about family, parenting, sexual freedom and responsibility, and African American values and priorities. She reminds us that a family—mother and father, brothers and sisters—has many sides, many hearts, and the brilliant capacity to persevere through any storm."

—*Carolina Times*

"Heartwarming, with vivid characters (especially among the children)."

—*Kirkus Reviews*

"Lattany succeeds in enticing the reader into the miasma and holds us there in an often mesmerizing vise."

—*Rapport*

". . . she juggles several characters in chapters named exclusively for them, chapters through which each can stretch their thoughts. The voices and movements of these characters are so distinctive that you don't even have to look at the top of the page for clarification as to whom you are listening or watching."

—*Savannah Herald*

Experience the richness and diversity of African American Women's Fiction from **One World / Ballantine**

The New York Times Bestseller

Big Girls Don't Cry
by Connie Briscoe
ISBN 345-41362-8 / $12.00

"An empathetic portrait of a modern woman wrestling with issues of love, work, and family obligations."
--*Publisher's Weekly*

"Brims with warmth, energy, and a positive message."
--*San Francisco Chronicle*

"Contains an infectious hope and optimism."
--*Los Angeles Times*

The New York Times Bestseller

Your Blues Ain't Like Mine
by Bebe Moore Campbell
ISBN 345-38395-8 / $12.00

A *New York Times* Notable Book of the Year

"Compelling. . . Campbell is a master storyteller."
--*The Atlanta Journal*

"Powerful."
--*The New York Times Book Review*

Daughters of Africa

An International Anthology of Words and Writings by Women of African Descent from the Ancient Egyptian to the Present

by
Margaret Busby, editor
ISBN 345-38268-4 / $19.95

"A Stunning Wealth of Writing."
--The Washington Post Book World

The River Where Blood is Born

by
Sandra Jackson Opoku
ISBN 345-39514-X / $23.00

stunning feat. Sandra Jackson Opoku manages to weave the physical
ld with the spirit world and numerous generations of African and
ican American women into a tapestry that I found simply brilliant."
–Gloria Naylor, author of *Mama Day*